I0587783

Once Upon a Farm

Tales of Discovery

Ellis Worth

Edited by
Dean O. Smith

Annandale Press

Published by Annandale Press

Spokane, WA 99224

Copyright © 2021 Dean O. Smith

All rights reserved

The characters and events portrayed in this book are fictitious. Any similarity to real persons, living or dead, is coincidental and not intended by the author.

No part of this book may be reproduced, or stored in a retrieval system, or transmitted in any form or by any means, electronic, mechanical photocopying, recording, or otherwise, without express written permission of the publisher.

ISBN-13: 978-1-7364534-2-1

Printed in the United States of America

For inquiries, contact Annandale Press at annandalepress@gmail.com

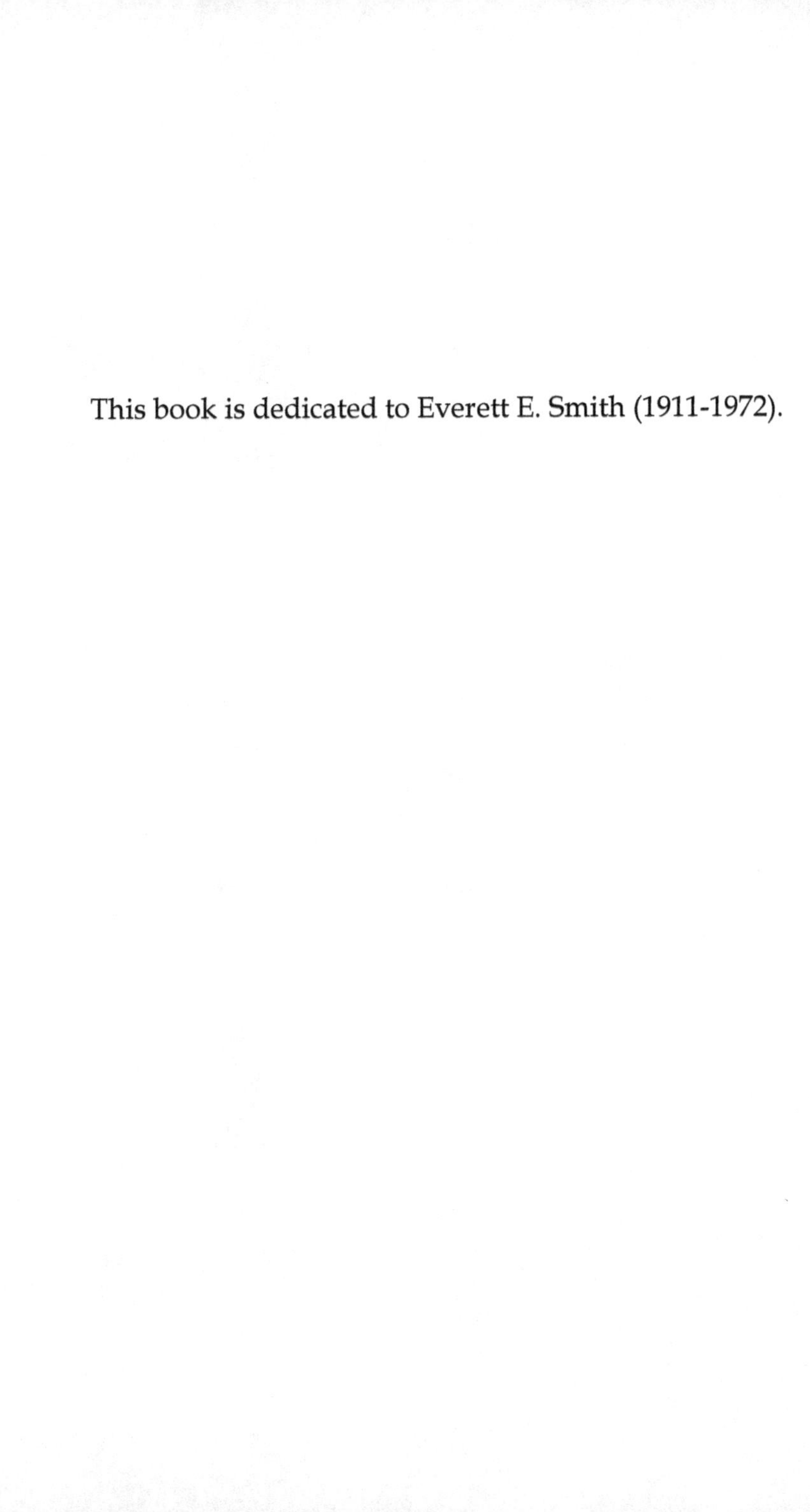

This book is dedicated to Everett E. Smith (1911-1972).

Contents

Acknowledgments

I thank Curtis F. Smith for his role in the preservation of these stories. I also thank Karlene A. Hoo for her invaluable encouragement, critique, and support during the preparation of this collection of stories. And, I acknowledge Barney, my beagle, who lay faithfully at my side as I worked on this project.

The cover art derives from a commercial reproduction of an original oil painting by J. Aulaire.

Two of these Ellis Worth stories have been published previously in small literary magazines that are no longer in business. "Once Upon a Farm," *The Kinsman* (1962) and "New Maps for Old," *The Enterprise* Centennial Issue (1967). I wish to acknowledge their contributions to the literary arts.

Foreword

"Somewhere along the road, I went astray. If ever a boy was destined to be an inspector of sunsets and cloud formations, it was I. Abundant evidences of my manifest destiny were strewn all over the place, but I ignored them all until it was too late to do anything about it—except to reminisce as I am doing. I became, instead, a well-fed, portly peddler of legal quibbles and quiddities: an earnest, respected, dignified, learned Sonora Springs lawyer."

So begins Ellis Worth's signature tale *Once upon a Farm.* In this and other tales in this collection, he reminisces about not only his childhood on a Minnesota farm but also many other episodes in his life. These are not sentimental recollections; nor is this an anthology of first-person memoirs. The reminiscences are embedded within enjoyable stories about fictitious characters in equally fictitious settings. But, in accordance with Mark Twain's assertion "Write what you know," Ellis Worth wrote what he knew. In this fictitious context, he relates his own experiences, personal discoveries, and outlook on social mores of the time, the mid-twentieth century.

Ellis Worth tales are unique. They are usually quite short and compact, offering an amusing and occasionally ribald narrative of some incident in its characters' lives—that is, presumably in his life. Worth seeks to entertain through his use of colloquial, everyday vernacular, bringing his principal characters' personality traits humorously to the forefront. He also seeks to provoke thought, sometimes leaving it up to the reader to join him in imagining the end of the story or to ascertain the symbolic meaning of some passage. In that way, these stories deliver subtle alternatives to prevailing wisdom.

Worth noted in his diary: "As a writer, I have been a maverick. My stories, too, are different. In effect, I have sought to establish new standards for story telling as well as a new vision of existing reality and a new glimpse of what ought to be. I have sought acceptance for myself, yes—and to that extent have been selfish—but I have sought first to establish a basis on which acceptability would be available to all." Indeed, by design, Worth seeks to entice the reader into personal introspection: "I can relate to that; I know what he means."

The collection begins with a thinly disguised autobiography, *The Eldon Jones Sextet*. In these six stories, Worth chronicles a youth's (Eldon Jones') early years on a farm in Minnesota, punctuated by the sudden death of his father. It continues through his years as a young lawyer in Washington, D.C., as a member of the Judge Advocate's Corps during World War II, as a patient in a mental institution following an acute nervous breakdown, and as a father with two young sons as he slowly recovers his mental health. This autobiographical beginning establishes the context for the subsequent stories in which Worth examines his own past through the lives of others: their foibles, their interactions with each other, their discovery of fundamental truths about themselves. Hence the subtitle: *Tales of Discovery*.

As a lawyer, Worth featured the legal profession in one way or another in many of his stories: a practicing lawyer, a judge, a courtroom trial. Usually satirical, they narrate Worth's disenchantment with the law and his failed private practice. After closing his law office, he was unemployed for two years. During that time, Worth often wrote about characters he met, recounting their tales, while sitting on a park bench enjoying the sun or in a tavern. Out of financial necessity, he returned to the law but from a different angle, taking a routine editorial job at a company that produced law reference books. That menial workplace became the setting for several other amusing stories, rife with satire.

Throughout, Worth extols his sense of place, the Minnesota farmland of his youth and the Colorado Rocky Mountains of his middle-aged adult life when he wrote most of these stories. Indeed, the Midwestern fields of grain, the lakes, the mountains, the sunsets, the cool high-altitude breezes are as much protagonists as the characters themselves.

Equally noticeable is the historical timeframe of these stories. Worth wrote them in the mid-twentieth century. Accordingly, they refer to people and events of that era. In that regard, these stories chronicle interesting tidbits of the history of that time period. Likewise, Worth used terminology of that era, terminology perhaps deemed culturally insensitive in the twenty-first century. I have chosen not to edit his use of words, leaving it as part of the historical record.

At the time of his sudden death at age 61, Worth had published over thirty-five short stories and had about fifteen or so under consideration by editors of various literary journals around the country. He was proud of these achievements. In words taken from his diary: "Of all the achievements of my lifetime so far (aside from what I have been able to do for my children, which is paramount), I am proudest of my published short stories. But few—only one or two—of my friends know how I spend my spare time. I don't broadcast what I'm doing. My social life is minimal. My hermitage is on an old-time ranch. Are these strange quirks? Ah, but I'm proud of my military record in World War II also, but I don't go around bragging about that either." In other words, Worth had discovered happiness as a writer: a wonderful discovery for anybody.

Other books by or about Ellis Worth include another collection of short stories, *The Sonora Springs Tales: A Collection of Ellis Worth Short Stories* (Annandale Press).

Dean O. Smith
April, 2021

The Eldon Jones Sextet

I. The Legend of Drowsy Hollow

There are times in any hero's life when he is pretty unheroic—for example, when he's being born. So it was with Eldon Jones. Though in later years Eldon claimed to have dim intimations of life before birth, he never had the nerve to pretend he recalled his first breath or the doctor's slap on the buttocks that started it. His birth was in the hands of others, as was much else afterward.

A neighbor who visited Drowsy Hollow Farm early that August morning observed to Farmer Jones, the father, that the sun had risen early. "Yes," Farmer Jones agreed, "but my newest son rose even earlier." No other proclamation was made of the event. The attending doctor was derelict in the matter of a birth certificate so that years later, Eldon had to take steps to have the omission corrected. That wasn't difficult. His birth was an undeniable fact. Only the record was faulty.

Dr. Randy had delivered two other children at Drowsy Hollow Farm and was to deliver two more for Farmer Jones and his wife, Anna. The first, Amy, had come five years before. Willie, a premature baby, preceded Eldon by nearly three years. Abbott and Hester were to follow at three-year intervals.

Willie, who weighed only three pounds at birth, had required a good deal of care on the part of Mother Jones. Thank goodness, she thought, this new baby, an eight-pounder, will have more vitality. Amy and Eldon Jones, Senior, were of the same opinion. If Eldon himself was glad that he didn't need so much care as Willie had and did, he was too young to say so. He just nursed and grew.

He loved his nurse, Junie. For a number of years he was predisposed in favor of any girl or woman named Junie. As for this particular Junie, she was pretty pleased with her charge. Whenever the baby would chuckle or show a faint smile, she would call attention to it and declare, "You can see he isn't nursed on a dill pickle." The nurse may have been overly optimistic about the baby's temper and disposition, but if so, the remark at least spoke well of her own sweetness of character.

Junie left the Jones family when Eldon was about two years of age. His next Junie came two years later—Junie Glessman, who was twenty years older than Eldon and not a nurse but a traveling companion. She drove Eldon and his parents to Excalibur to visit Uncle Fred (the Joneses didn't have a car). A good job of driving she did, too, for Excalibur was fifty miles away—quite a distance in those days at the beginning of World War I.

To show his gratitude and his love for Junie and just to show off, Eldon did a surprising thing. He read the Sunday funny papers to an eight-year old boy who also happened to be visiting childless Uncle Fred's and Aunt Sadie's house. Vern had been exposed to reading and writing for several years but still couldn't tell the Little Red Hen from Chicken Little. Father and Mother didn't know Eldon could read, but they weren't surprised. Nothing of that kind astonished them anymore. Had they known Eldon was reading for Junie and not simply to Vern, they would have been amazed.

In the first grade at school, Eldon met Junie Starnes. Her sister, Irma, was skinny and pale, but Junie was plump and sturdy and cute, with pretty blue eyes like Mother's. Alas, Junie was yanked out of school and taken to Chicago when tragedy struck the Starnes family. After that, there were no more Junies for Eldon.

But wait, he did see Junie Starnes again—many years later when they both had returned on a visit to Warm Spring, the home-town of their childhood. They met on the street. Junie recognized Eldon who said, falsely, that he remembered her. He didn't then, and he didn't later when Willie supplied details about the Starnes farm, about Irma and about Herb, the brother. Then, slowly, on his own, Eldon recalled his cute little first-grade classmate. What a trick of memory to bury her.

Drowsy Hollow Farm consisted of a house, a barn, various outbuildings, and 100 acres of land. The buildings were situated in a gentle, rounded hollow. The two-story, four bedroom, white clapboard house faced south and was close to the dirt road with two rural mailboxes at its side. The road led west to another dirt road which connected the town of Warm Spring to the south with the village of Cold Spring to the north.

The buildings were well-protected from the north winds of winter by a woods. The south winds were not feared, and from the house one could see meadows, pastures, fields, and as far beyond as the school building in Warm Spring. The orchard on the east absorbed the infrequent winds and snows from that direction. The west flank was exposed, and though much was said about the sad situation, nothing was done about it for years. That was something to talk about, a conversation piece, something Father would fix one day, when time permitted.

Farmer Jones had plenty to do. The fields on Drowsy Hollow were few, and they were small. They needed to be expanded in size, increased in number and merged together. Trees were chopped down and pulled over;

stumps were dynamited sky-high; brush was cleared away with scythe and axe and grubhoe. This process of clearing the land and breaking the sod was extremely hard work. Simply following on foot a plow drawn by a team of two or three horses was hard enough for most farmers.

Farmer Jones was a stockily-built man of average height. His face, with its frank, light-brown eyes, was rather handsome. He looked the countryman, the farmer, although certain of his numerous idiosyncrasies belied that status. One of his eccentricities was that he would not wear overalls—couldn't stand the bib on his chest. Nor would he wear blue jeans. He preferred a pair of pants of yellow twill similar to a soldier's suntans or dark whipcord such as western cattlemen wear. Though living where fishing was easy, he wouldn't eat fresh-water fish. Also, he took a delight in hard work—in doing things the hard way—that was unusual even for those days.

Mother Jones, too, seemed to have regarded strenuous activity as part of the Divine Order of things. She was busy from morning to night in the house: sweeping, scrubbing, making beds, churning butter, baking bread, cooking, washing dishes, washing clothes, knitting socks and sweaters, making shirts and dresses, darning and mending, etc., etc. One time, a tramp stopped for a handout. Mother Jones knitted him a pair of socks while he waited, and the poor fellow didn't have long to wait.

Mother Jones was black-haired, blue-eyed, and of medium height and build. People told her she was as pretty as a French girl, and she accepted that as a fact, as did the two Eldons. Everyone knew, of course, that she was not French, but that did not detract from the compliment. Though born abroad, she was of this country in which she lived as much as a native. She spoke its idiom, was wholly satisfied to be so, and let the rest of the world go hang.

Sometimes Eldon was taken out to the field with his father and Willie. He watched them rather than vice versa, for baby-sitters hadn't yet been invented. If Eldon was left home, it meant he was left to his own devices, for Mother and Sister were much too busy for anything but an occasional glance.

In a sense, the Jones dwelling was a temple to the Gospel of Hard Work. Eldon wasn't considered an especially devout adherent of the faith. "Did you water the chickens?" Although that particular chore, among others, was Eldon's very own, he invariably had to answer in the negative. "Well, then, go and do it. Right now!"

To the amusement and satisfaction of Amy and Willie, Uncle Fred and Aunt Sadie (on their rare visits to Drowsy Hollow) defended Eldon. "Pshaw," they'd say, "Eldon's not lazy, Anna; he's just indolent."

Eldon at least found the world's work interesting to watch. Draining swamp land, either by ditching or tiling, was all the rage around Drowsy Hollow at the end of the Great War. The ditching was done by a huge plow pulled by a caterpillar tractor which, sometimes, floundered in the soft, earthen gumbo and had to be rescued. Tiling was back-breaking work done by a tiler who dug a narrow ditch a foot or so deep with a spade and then, as Eldon saw, fitted the tubular, baked-clay or cement tile together, end-to-end, ever so carefully. Then the tile was covered with the loose earth which had been dug up by the tiler's spade.

Once, Eldon was "invited" to go with Farmer Jones, Willie, Abbott, and a tiler on a purchasing trip to the tile factory fifteen miles away. It was great sport, with a lumber wagon and a steel-wheeled wagon, and, of course, two teams of horses. Ring, the dog, trotted under one or the other of the wagons all the way. There were sandwiches for lunch and a liberated watermelon for dessert. The high point of the trip was crossing the Mississippi near Chugwater. Father drove the wagon in which Eldon was riding right onto the ferry, which was shoved out into the river with a loud rattling of chains and carried by the current to the other side.

Ah, there was one type of work which Eldon definitely did not care to see. That was butchering. The squeal of a pig selected as a victim (when it was a pig selected for slaughter and not a calf or beef-animal) drove him to distraction. He would retreat into a clothes closet, close the door, and cover his ears.

The friends and neighbors who called at Drowsy Hollow were of various sorts, though mostly farmers and mostly of German descent. At that time the countryside around Cold Spring was mainly populated by folks of the German Lutheran persuasion. South of Warm Spring was a so-called Swedish settlement and beyond that a Finnish neighborhood. The French, Irish, and Polish each had their little strongholds.

The German Lutherans, usually regular church-goers, seemed to merge their Christian faith quite easily with the Gospel of Hard Work. Some even worked harder than the Eldon Jones family. Sunday was a blessing. Work by no means ceased—there were always the farm chores—but it let up. The Joneses, or at least Eldon and others, could sit on the front porch in the mornings and watch the stern-faced worshippers driving by in their

Sunday best on their way to church. The horses were well-brushed and curried—their coats cleaned of all sweat and loose hair and their fetlocks freed of cockle-burrs and sticktights—and the black buggies shone.

The calls or visits of the Scandinavians gave Willie the greatest pleasure. He could imitate their accents for a week afterward. He liked such German sentences as "Throw the cows over the fence some hay," but his enjoyment of topsy-turvy diction was mild compared with that induced by the Swedish sing-song pronunciation. Abbott, for his part, took careful note of the German he heard spoken and in time had a fairly good understanding of the spoken tongue. He was the only Jones child to take any interest in the foreign languages heard spoken around the farm and in the villages.

A foreign language might be of special value to a housewife with a penchant for gossiping over the telephone. The number of those listening in—rubbernecks they were called—could be drastically reduced by conducting the conversation in German or Swedish or French. Once, Mother Jones, who had her hands covered with flour and dough from kneading bread, said to Eldon, "Oh, there's two longs and a short, the Kunz ring. Get the phone, Eldon; maybe Minnie's home." Eldon pushed a chair to the brown-varnished, wooden-box instrument affixed high on the wall, got on the chair, removed the black, bell-shaped, hard-rubber receiver, listened a minute or two, and hung up.

"What was it, Eldon?"

"*Dis bin ich.*"

"Oh, that means Minnie is back from the old country and wants Herman to come and get her at the railroad station."

"Mother, what does *ein heldenleben* mean?"

"Did you hear that on the phone?"

"Yes."

"You did? That's Dutch [*sic*]. Forget it."

Another time, Eldon asked, "Mother?"

"Yes."

"What's *enfant du siecle*?"

"Did you hear that on the phone?"

"Yes."

"I don't know. That's not Dutch. Forget it."

Drowsy Hollow extended back to a lake and river. The lake was named for a little girl who had drowned in it years ago, Clementine. In the winter, some Finnish farmers would stay, with permission, in a fishing shack on the shore of Lake Clementine. Undoubtedly they drank plenty of whiskey during their sojourns (Prohibition notwithstanding), but they also got many fish, which they shared with the Joneses. Later on when Eldon heard the expression "All the Finns do is fish and f---, and in the winter it's too cold to fish," he knew it wasn't true about the winter being too cold for fishing. The temperature might drop to thirty below zero now and then, but it seldom stayed that way for more than a day or two. The Finns, like everyone else, had those long sheepskin coats with the fleece inside and the skin backed by a cloth much the same color as the skin. Caps varied, but all had fur flaps for covering the ears. Children, fishing or not, defied cold weather by wrapping up in everything except cellophane, which wasn't used then, even for cigarettes.

In his pre-school days, Eldon especially enjoyed the calls of the neighbors who shared with the Joneses the south shore of Lake Clementine. They were the Sowerbys. These friends had no accent, no stern religion.

Walt Sowerby embraced the Gospel of Gab. It was his wont, when he came for the mail delivered in a box beside that of the Joneses, to come into the house and wait for the mailman to go by. As he sat comfortably in the kitchen, he would tell tales. Ostensibly, he talked to Mother Jones, but she surely was too busy to listen. Eldon was Walt's audience; and a more rapt and attentive one the old man could not have wanted. The white beard lent authority to the oracle's voice, and the moist brown tobacco juice which oozed into the whiskers added a certain glamor to the storyteller's appearance.

A horse stepped on Mr. Sowerby's foot. An infection developed that could not be controlled, and soon Mr. Sowerby was gone. Mrs. Sowerby, a mannish woman who looked a bit like one of the plain folks, relayed gossip but told no stories. Leslie, the grown son, was a dashing figure in the evenings as he raced down the wind-swept private roadway just to the west of the Joneses in the Sowerby's black sleigh or buggy (all buggies were black) behind a spanking chestnut mare, gone gallivanting, courting. But he had no stories either, and besides, for all his energy and momentum, the son lacked the mystique which his father had derived from his actual, obvious link with the legends he recounted.

Eldon seldom visited the Sowerby's, but he had done so. He had seen, more than once, the cane press in operation after dark in the fall, with Old Tom, the horse, plodding around and around and around. The scene was dimly lit by the moon and the fires under the cooking juice. The old man fed the flames from time to time and kept moving the thickening sorghum from one compartment of the flat, yards-long kettle to another. Eldon knew this process, this after-dark ritual, had gone on for years on the Sowerby farm. Now it was done for.

The son might handle the business. He couldn't carry on the black magic of sorghum-making for the community.

In his lifetime, at least, Walt Sowerby had found salvation in the Gospel of Gab; and for more than that he hadn't asked.

To the east of Drowsy Hollow was a set of farm buildings which the owner rented to others. For a while, Bennie Dahl occupied the house and carried on a bootlegging operation there. The Dahls didn't associate with their neighbors, but Eldon walked to school with their boys. When misfortune befell the Dahls and they moved out, Eldon and Abbott played ball with the Resnick boys. Afterward, the childless Burrs, an elderly couple, arrived from God knows where, stayed a few years, and left for parts unknown. Their means of livelihood were not clear to the neighbors, and the couple chose to leave that matter in doubt. They came at rare intervals to see the Joneses and were cordially received, but, for the most part, they kept to themselves—to themselves, their four dogs, aged cat, pet crow, and parrot.

Their experiences in life may have given the Burrs a wealth of material for tales, but Eldon realized that the romantic treasure would be buried with them. They were not storytellers. Anyway, the boy distrusted the Burrs—never felt at ease with them. Had they ever chosen to speak, Eldon would have listened with one ear for entry and the other for exit.

Once a year, a Swedish-born old widow woman whom everyone called Grandma Jones would spend a week or two at the Joneses. She brought a spinning wheel with her. (The Joneses would get a supply of wool from a nearby farmer who raised sheep.) She had an accent that pleased Willie and plenty of gossip which interested no one. It was all old stuff about her children and her cousins and her sisters. Eldon looked upon the wheel as quite remarkable and liked the feel of the white wool and the yarn, but he was allergic to the spinner of yarn.

The neighbors everyone in the Jones family loved were the Millers. He was taciturn and she mildly acidulous of speech, but both were kind-hearted and well-intentioned. In brief, they were good neighbors. From them, Eldon never heard a pious word or saw a mean action.

Though both the Millers were too simple and too good to be interesting, some intriguing things went on at the Miller farm. There was the sawmill patronized by everyone for miles around, and there was the smokehouse which used certain kinds of the sawdust to produce hams, bacon, and smoked fish. Another nice thing about the Miller farm was its pasture, which was across the road from the Jones house. In winter, it was a nice place to hunt rabbits and trap weasel. In August, when the fields smelled of grain and straw and the heat caused the corn leaves to curl up to save moisture, the thick hazel brush gave off its characteristic aroma, similar to that of oak trees at the same season. The odor, not especially good in itself, signified the climax and fruition of summer and foretold, as well, how delicious those hazel nuts would be that fall and winter in candy and cookies (for the Joneses were at perfect liberty to pick all the nuts they wanted).

Many of these neighbors, together with distant ones from Grand Prairie, Kendall Prairie and roundabout, would assemble on a few occasions during the year. The Fourth of July featured baseball and horseraces by day and fireworks after dark. Mother Jones was particularly fond of the fireworks display and would exclaim, "Oh look! See the reflections in Pageant Lake!" The Old Settlers Picnic, held every June on the grounds of the historic but definitely operational water-driven mill near Cold Spring, was a wonderful time for gossip and noticing how the old folks were growing older and the youngsters were growing up. The ring-hunt dinners in the fall with their menus of stewed oysters and game were as long on talk of crops and family news as they were on food. Once the dinner in the village hall was over, children were hustled home, and the clean-up crew took over.

While Eldon had learned to read on his own, he had to be taught to write. His father showed him in an evening or two how to write numbers. All came quickly to Eldon except the number 2. Farmer Jones explained "2 is like a duck sitting on water. See?" It was a happy reference, for Eldon had often observed the Sowerby ducks fly downhill and splash onto the Jones pasture-pond, and he saw clearly, by the light of imagination and the kerosene lamp, how those ducks sat on the water like so many twos.

At school the teacher taught Eldon how to form letters, pointing out, naturally, how the letter *h* had a tail like a horse and how the letter *o* was as round as the eyes of an owl.

Eldon's school career had a most unpromising start in a two-room schoolhouse at Cold Spring. Miss Singleton was no novice, but she followed the methods of that time and place. When she said "Sit in position," that meant the pupils were to sit straight, looking forward, with their hands clasped just so on their desks. When she said, "Class rise," that had a definite meaning too. "Class march," got them all over to the recitation bench by the window as the teacher had explained. Then, on one occasion, Eldon jumped onto the bench, hoisted himself swiftly through the window, ran, and hid in an old stove in a burned-down store across the road from the school ground.

There was a great hue and cry, but Eldon was not to be found. The search was given up so classes could be held for the other pupils. At noon, the hungry boy stuck his head out of the stove to look around, and he was spied. He had to be dragged and carried back to the schoolhouse by the big eighth-graders. After that, Eldon was a model prisoner. At the end of the year, he was promoted to the fifth grade and out of Miss Singleton's room. For years afterward, though, the teacher remembered and asked his parents about Eldon.

Eldon's memory of Miss Singleton dimmed with the passage of time, but he never forgot certain things his first teacher had stressed.

Oats, peas, beans and barley grow
Oats, peas, beans and barley grow
Nor you nor I nor anyone knows
What makes oats, peas, beans and barley grow

First the farmer sows the seed
Then he stands and takes his ease
He stamps his foot and claps his hand
And turns around to view the land.

Equally memorable was the tune and the way in which the second verse was to be acted out.

At home the day began with Father or Mother chanting the formula, "Wake up and hear the birds sing." At school, the matinal (not called that) was:

Hark, hark, the lark at Heaven's gate sings
And Phoebus hide us rise.

Miss Singleton, God bless her, also taught other unforgettable verses, including Eldon's favorite:

Little drops of water, little grains of sand
Make the mighty ocean and the pleasant land.

It was a rule that no pupil could take a book from the school library to read unless his lessons were prepared, but that rule didn't apply to Eldon. When knowing Elders asked him what he studied at school, they expected him to say "The three r's" or the equivalent. He confounded them by replying "Library books."

The children had the usual rustic games: One Old Cat, Two Old Cat, Prisoner's Base, Fox and Goose, Pum-Pum Pull-away, etc. Besides that, they sometimes made rubber-ice, a sport which usually ended with wet feet for somebody or everybody. In warm weather, they would take the waste pail from under a water-fountain, fill it with water from a nearby pump, and pour it down a gopher hole. This was called "drowning out gophers." When the victim emerged, he was trampled to death by scampering, screaming youngsters. These were the good old days before juvenile delinquency.

During World War I, some ill-feeling existed between the pupils of the German School, run by Cold Spring's Lutheran church, and the children of the public school Eldon attended. The students at the German School were taunted in various ways. One of the favorite epithets was "Pro-German." Now and then a juvenile brawl would break out. No one ever got hurt much.

School was over a mile from Drowsy Hollow Farm. It was fun to drink from the spring at the river's edge by the bridge. In the spring, bloodroots and mayflowers blanketed the roadsides. In winter, it might be possible to walk over the crusted snowdrifts. It was worth a try and the next best thing to walking on water. Also, it was great sport to hook a ride on the runner of a passing sled or sleigh. There might be, if one were fortunate, a vociferous dog to silence with stones or snowballs.

One day a bunch of school kids going home were passed by an old man in a buggy. He had whipped his horse into a furious spurt of speed. The children didn't recognize the rider at first, and when they did they cried out, "It's Old Man Brown." He shouted back, "Don't worry your ass about Old Man Brown."

One time an airplane landed on the school ground, and the children were dismissed to see the strange mechanical bird with two flapless, cream-colored wings on each side and a propeller in the place of a beak. The pilot was a barnstormer, and his business was to sell rides. A gasoline truck stood by in readiness—and perhaps to assure doubters there were no risks from a shortage of that indispensable element. Like all the pupils, Eldon took note of the daring and curious as they came forth with a tremulous smile and a ten-dollar bill and asked to be shown the marvels of the sky. He listened carefully, too, to what the riders reported on their return to earth.

On Armistice Day two years after the end of World War I, the sad, sad news came to Eldon and Willie and Abbott at school: Your father's dead! He died suddenly of a heart attack. Amy received the sad news at Warm Spring School.

Eldon was numb. The earth's foundation had given way, sunk. The world was no longer the same and never would be. Walt Sowerby's death, the demise of an admired friend, was one thing. It was possible to understand that as natural. Father's death was different, totally inacceptable. Life went on, of course, for Eldon and Mother Jones and Willie and Amy and Abbott and Hester but not as before. It went on dully and only slowly gained a semblance of reality and cheer.

Eldon was a bright boy, but if anyone had asked him the day before Armistice, 1920, if he and his father were close kin, he would have answered "Not especially." The day after, he wouldn't have been able to answer at all. While he lived, Eldon's father had been fallible. Even Eldon had doubted his father's judgment that automobiles were a passing fad because flat tires were too hard to take off, patch, and replace (all then done at the roadside). In death, the father was Father, faultless.

Amy was going to high school at Warm Spring at the time of Farmer Jones's death. After two years there, she went to Avondale to finish the course. Willie went to Warm Spring to graduate from the eighth grade, and that was the end of his schooling as he was to do his best to replace his father in the fields and at the farm chores. Eldon also went to Warm Spring for his last year of grade school.

The school at Cold Spring had only two rooms, whereas Warm Spring had a slightly bigger establishment. None of the pupils, however, pretended to dress in fancy clothes. Like the rest, Eldon wore overalls and a matching blue denim jacket, the same clothes in which he had milked his quota of cows in the morning. One time, the beautiful brown-eyed teacher, Miss Beauvais, politely suggested to Eldon that he remove his jacket for the rest of the school day. Quick as a flash he guessed what must be the reason for the request. The back of the jacket had been widely, if thinly, splashed by the droppings of a cow.

Eldon won first in a county spelling contest that year, sixth in a statewide contest, and graduated at the top of his class. He was as nonchalant about these trivial honors as were those who hadn't won them. It was a matter of course, such as being in demand as a baseball catcher. However, he had no intention of quitting school after the eighth grade, as so many farm boys of that era did, as Willie did.

To go to school at Avondale, seven miles away from Drowsy Hollow Farm, was not easy. In the winter he had to board and room at Avondale. In milder weather he managed one way or another—walking, walking part way, arranging for rides with others—to get to the town and back daily. The winter he boarded with the Porters, he was introduced to the fact that radio could be a mystery and an obsession, for the Porter boy, a year or two ahead of Eldon in school, was forever building, rebuilding, and experimenting with the family set and his own crystal set. He tuned in such fabulous, distant cities as Cincinnati, Chicago, Detroit. Distance was something much desired and was called dx.

While staying at Avondale, Eldon would go home week-ends. As a rule, he returned to his lodgings Sunday evenings, thanks to Willie and his Ford runabout, but a few times he took the train Monday that left Warm Spring at four-twenty a.m. The five-fifty train would have been early enough, but it didn't stop at Avondale, which was not a watering and coaling station as Warm Spring was.

Eldon and others would push open the door of the coach, letting in great gusts of cold air. If the door were pushed too far open, it fastened open on a catch and had to be carefully released. Those already ensconced in seats, their clothes rumpled, hair tousled, faces dirty, eyes bleary, weariness in the lines of their bodies, would stare at the newcomers resentfully. The trainmen would have to help the intruders get seats. Most of the passengers were going on to Minneapolis, more than fifty miles away. The red-plush upholstery looked clean, but, at the end of his seven-mile trip, Eldon's hands would be dirtier than if he had been shocking corn bundles.

There was a tale about train rides that Eldon relished. A passenger getting on with a lot of baggage one cold night blundered so as to fix open the door of the coach. Another passenger who had got on some distance back, cried out, "Close the door! Where were you born—in a barn?" The new arrival leaned forward, put his face in his hands, and began to weep, whereupon the other got up and closed the door and said, "There, there, don't take it so hard. I meant no harm."

"Well, the truth is I was born in a barn, and every time I hear the bray of an ass it makes me homesick."

During the three years Eldon spent at Avondale High School, it became the fashion for boys to wear long slacks instead of knee-length knickerbockers or knickers. This change in style, however, came in Eldon's senior year, and he made no concession to the new but durable fad. He was only fourteen years old that year, of average size for his age, and he still tended to think of long slacks as the prerogative of men.

At that time, Latin enjoyed a certain vogue. Even so, much of the time Eldon was the only boy in the class.

Because, or partly because, of embarrassment at being in the midst of so many girls, Eldon's report card showed an *F* in that class for one six-week period. He rectified that lapse so thoroughly that the teacher once inadvertently called him "Caesar." A number of girls seized upon the name and tried to make it stick as a nickname in widespread use. In that they had little success. Eldon was Eldon, not Ell, not Don, not Caesar.

One time in history class, Miss Gray said, "Eldon, what did Charles the Hammer do for history?"

He replied hesitatingly, "Well, er, Pippin was his son." There was a roar of laughter from his classmates.

"Oh, you're one of those who believe history is made at night."

Usually, Eldon had a better answer, although he studied little compared to his colleagues. They couldn't believe he really knew his lessons. How could he, with practically no homework? Their explanation was "he bluffs."

During his high-school years, Eldon got acquainted with *The Three Musketeers*. It was his favorite book. He read it and re-read it. "One for all and all for one," seemed to him the noblest motto ever devised. He went on to read some of Dumas' other books, but none impressed him. It was no fault of his English teachers, surely, for he had some good ones, but the novels of the English writers (W.H. Hudson excepted) seldom appealed to Eldon, then or later.

On the farm, Eldon continued to help with the work, but not on such a scale as to win applause. In the summer when he went to round up the cows for the evening milking—the pasture was a long, narrow strip which extended to the east end of Lake Clementine—he would tarry on the way to eat wild strawberries, gooseberries, raspberries, black currants. He certainly was not Speedy Gonzales. What was worse, the cows would jump over the fence now and then during the day, and the chances were good that Eldon would be fishing on Lake Clementine whenever that occurred. The chances were good because few boys did more fishing than Eldon and his brother Abbott.

Daydreaming was not at all beyond him as he hoed the family garden, a patch of potatoes or his own melon patch. He would stray to peep into bird nests on the way to the meadow of hay ready for the barn. Oftentimes, he would sing or whistle as he worked, although this was before Walt Disney's *Snow White and the Seven Dwarves*. Hymns were on his repertory as well as such popular tunes as "It Ain't Gonna Rain No More," "Barney Google," and "Yes, We Got No Bananas." Indeed, he was quite as likely to go into an agonizing rendition of older songs, for example, "How Ya Gonna Keep Him Down on the Farm" or "Parlez-Vous."

Those who sang less did more. So Mother Jones thought. She herself sang not at all, although she had many old phonograph records (some of them grooved on only one side) of Caruso, Galli-Curci, and Schumann-Heink. She was a good listener when she found time to stop for breath. So was Abbott, who would crank up the tall record player and let it play "The Missouri Waltz" over and over. Only, he called it "the misery waltz." Amy preferred the hymns of the Evangelical Church at Warm Spring. Willie and Hettie left vocalizing and records to others.

Eldon had gone, often enough, with Amy to the Evangelical Church. When, at harvest time, the congregation sang "Bringing in the Sheaves," they put their heart into it. It all had meaning. So, also, the hymn,

"We Shall Gather at the River," fitted easily, plainly, beautifully, sadly, into the context of the farm life everyone knew. No wonder Amy thrilled to those old-time hymns. So did Eldon.

The countryside around Drowsy Hollow Farm was liberally dotted with lakes. All were deep, but some had sandy shorelines with gradually sloping bottoms. Summer resorts with cottages for rent to vacationers were numerous. As most vacationers were fishermen, there was a demand for frogs for bait, and Eldon, with scarcely a competitor, endeavored to supply the demand. Every day or two in June and July, he would catch dozens of frogs on the banks of the creeks and ponds of Drowsy Hollow and then peddle them to the various resorts by bicycle. As he put it, he "pedaled to peddle." Whenever he sold a dozen or two frogs (and often enough when he had sold nothing), he'd volunteer the information that fresh eggs, country butter, and spring chickens also were available at Drowsy Hollow Farm. Customers often became durable friends of the Joneses (while remaining customers).

When he peddled frogs, Eldon cut about the same figure as when he caught them or performed his other tasks around the farm. He had curly black hair (combed, but seldom well-combed) and eyes which were basically blue but seemed to be light blue, dark blue, gray, green and even hazel depending on his mood and the color of his clothing. He wore overalls, the invariable work uniform of farm boys at that time. Usually the pants legs were rolled up as if he expected to encounter a puddle or a creek to be waded. The sleeves of his shirt were rolled up above the elbow, too, as short sleeves were unknown—unknown to Eldon and virtually everyone. To protect his head from the summer sun, he wore a broad-brimmed straw hat. The chances were he would go barefoot, without embarrassment, even when he was making a sales pitch to the city folks at one of the neighborhood's summer resorts. The chances were, too, the city folks enjoyed seeing a barefoot boy.

One of the strange things about these strangers from the city was that they expected this unprepossessing country boy to have exceptional talents of all kinds (almost insisted that he did have). This will to believe, on their part, sometimes made a difficult task easy for Eldon. Unlike his brothers (both of whom were excellent marksmen), Eldon had little experience with and no taste at all for firearms. One time, as Eldon made his way, with his frog basket, toward the end of a cottage-lined beach, a group called peremptorily to Eldon to take a shot at the target they had set up. He did so, and by sheer luck hit squarely in the bull's eye the first shot. "Oh-h-h," went up from the group, but they did not press him to remain. They took it for granted he could do as well with a rifle as Robin Hood with a longbow.

It was vaguely understood by the Joneses and their neighbors that high school was not the end of the scholastic road for Eldon, but he spent the summer following graduation undecided about the next move. Meantime, he threw himself into the various activities of the local 4-H Club for farm youth. His project, a small flock of big black chickens, was to rate a blue ribbon at the county fair, but he scarcely took note of that. It wasn't that which he wanted to do before he left the farm. What was it? He was like an editor who never knows what he wants till he sees it.

Scattered around in various places on the farm, in the midst of the leafy trees, were some evergreens. They clearly were not pines but were variously called cedars, fire, junipers. They weren't of the type ordinarily sold in nurseries, whatever the variety. Eldon dug up a dozen or so of these small cedars and hauled them, root balls and all, up to the house. Then he dug evenly-spaced holes for them west of the house, on the near side of the private roadway leading to the Sowerby place. He planted the little trees in those holes. That done, he could think of the future. Drowsy Hollow Farm would have a windbreak on the west. He had done what Father never had found time to do. He was ready, finally, to accept the challenge of the Big City—nay, two cities, the Twin Cities.

II. Eldon Loved Twins

In the fall of 1926, a fifteen-year-old boy left Drowsy Hollow Farm near Avondale and went to Minneapolis. Mr. Oberg of Benson Business College had arranged things in advance. In fact, he had arranged things well, for Eldon had a part-time job working for his meals in a cafeteria and a room, complete with roommate, in a home for young men which was run by a group of Protestant churches working in unison.

Eldon had just turned fifteen, but he had decided to change his age to seventeen and to keep it two years ahead of his actual age indefinitely. He could easily pass for at least seventeen. He looked older than he was, and, if anything, acted older than seventeen—at least superficially. For Eldon's teachers, schoolmates, and roommate, superficial appearances were equivalent to truth: and so Eldon's *ipse dixit* changed his age as effectually as an official decree.

Benson Business College was one of a number of such schools in downtown Minneapolis. There was another on Marquette Avenue, even one on Nicollet and one on Hennepin—all fairly close together. The other schools were bigger than Benson, but Benson was big enough. The student body fluctuated in number, but in the heart of the school year approximated fifty students, about half male, half female and all predominantly young.

For the most part, everyone studied the same subjects. Typing, shorthand, and bookkeeping were the meat-and-potato courses. For frills there were Business English, Comptometry, Rapid Calculation. To his surprise, Eldon was barely average in typing and below average in bookkeeping, which, before long, he dropped. His roommate, Chuck Larson, discontinued everything but bookkeeping. He was more patient with figures than Eldon and less averse to homework (which seemed to be the key to progress in that field).

Chuck came from one of Minnesota's small cities near the state's western boundary. While Eldon and Chuck discussed their respective backgrounds minimally, they both got along well together. Both worked for their meals at the same restaurant, Carle's Cafeteria. For both, their menial work as busboys—Eldon also spent one of his three hours a day at drying dishes—cut deeper into their consciousness than their schoolwork.

Two other boys from Benson Business College also donned stiffly starched white linen jackets and worked at Carle's three hours per day. As the place did a big business, there were quite a few young women who worked full time and earned their living there in one capacity or another. There was Marie, a short, stocky, smiling Polish girl with dark hair and huge black eyes. She looked very pretty in her white uniform. Marie was quite a tease and would call Milt Andrews a schoolboy. He, rising to the bait, would insist he was, rather, a college boy.

There was another Marie. She worked in the kitchen drying dishes. She was not in the same class at all as Marie the bus-girl. Eldon worked one hour per day with Marie, the kitchen-maid, and did so without problems of any kind. Marie would tell him now and then about "my Old Man," meaning her husband. He seemed to be as immutably related to her as her father. Maybe that's why she called him "my Old Man."

There came a time—a period of a month or two—when this Marie seemed determined to attract Milt to her. When he brought a tray full of empty dishes to the kitchen, she would catch him by the arm above the elbow and try to hold his attention while she imparted some tidbit of personal news. Milt didn't want to be bothered. One time, as Milt was almost out of the kitchen and heading into the dining room, the desperate Marie thrust her hand between Milt's upper legs from the back and grabbed. Milt turned his head long enough to give Marie a furious look. That ended Marie's foolish and hopeless crush on Milt Andrews.

At school there were three sisters by the name of Odegaard. The oldest, Bertha, was blonde with a beautiful face and a short, wavy hair-do which was very becoming and helped to give Bertha the appearance of a finely sculptured bust. Marion, the next younger, was taller than Bertha and red-haired. She cut a more dramatic figure than Bertha but interested Eldon not at all. The youngest sister was older than Eldon but more nearly his age than the others. He never noticed her. She was just a dim blur, a blob, as far as he was concerned.

Eldon was powerfully attracted to Bertha, and vice versa. However, something stood in the way of their getting acquainted and dating. Eldon feared his own passion for this girl and feared she would lure him to destruction. When he looked across the brief space separating his typewriter desk from hers to admire her face and head and hair-do, her neck and shoulders and bust, she would cross or re-cross her legs so as to expose her shapeliness above the knee. The gesture seemed to insist that Eldon forget the trivialities of sculptured beauty, concentrate on fundamentals—and get the show on the road.

There seemed, under the circumstances, no chance for Eldon to be the aggressor. Bertha would usurp that role. He was willing to search and find, but Bertha wouldn't have it that way. She would point out the goal. So the affair of Eldon and Bertha came to naught. They both left school about the same time, and Eldon never heard what happened to Bertha. The red-haired sister got a job and married the boss. That he heard.

Little by little, Eldon got used to the Big City. School was on Marquette Avenue. He lived on South Eighth Street. Carle's Cafeteria was on Sixth Street, just a block away from Benson's Business College, and Benson Business College was less than a block away from a business building in the process of construction. When the riveters let loose on the steelwork with the staccato beat of their air-hammers, as they did in those days, a typing student couldn't even hear the rhythmic clatter of the machine right under his fingertips.

Streetcars ran along Marquette all day, but around four o'clock in the afternoon the clank of their warning bells got louder, shriller, and more frequent. About that time, too, the newsboys at their green, corner stands began to ballyhoo their wares, the news. "*Journal, Star, Evening Tribune*, paper!" Car horns honked, beeped and squealed. The din of street noises reached a climax a little after five o'clock, and then the crescendo gradually died away. The office-workers had gone home. Eldon already had gone from school to Carle's. At seven o'clock his work would be over, and he could leave the domain of white table cloths and napkins to do as he pleased.

Home was not homelike. Nor was it pleasant or unpleasant. It was, rather, a neutral gray. Rents were low; the rooms were electrically-lighted, steam-heated, and comfortable. With more than a hundred young men, mostly students, in residence there was some rowdiness but not a great deal. The neighbor's radio, television, or hi-fi set had not yet become a problem. Indeed, the latter two did not then exist. However, the lodgers lived too much like swallows in the holes of a barren riverbank to suit the taste of an ex-country boy.

Oh, down in the first-floor room just off the entrance, a college chemistry student might be playing the piano endlessly. A graduate student of teaching might be making a stealthy entrance to a maid's first-floor room via the window. A couple of practical jokers might be short-sheeting the bed of someone expected to come home late from a date. These were desperate or puerile attempts to create a substitute for excitement rather than excitement itself.

Devotional services were held every morning in the room with the piano. Reverend Naffsinger who had charge of the so-called Sandstone Hall led the singing and praying. No one Eldon knew attended the morning service. He would look in upon the ceremony as he went to breakfast at Carle's. There usually were a few chambermaids singing lustily but plaintively. Some elderly friends of the Naffsingers might intone "Amen" or "Yes, God" as the reverend prayed. Eldon never felt any urge to participate.

At breakfast, Eldon would load his tray with stewed prunes, scrambled eggs, link sausages (then called "little pig sausages"), toast, and milk. From time to time, R. V. Carle would stare over the counter at Eldon and his companions, Chuck and Milt and Red, and ask "Gettin' any?" They knew what he meant, but they didn't answer. He didn't expect a reply; it was a rhetorical question.

At times, Eldon would spend an evening at a vaudeville show. For a dime he could sit on the wooden benches of the uppermost balcony of the Seventh Street theater and see hours of gymnastics, juggling, tap dancing, joking, banjo paying, male quarters, and ten—count 'em, ten—dancing girls in abbreviated costumes. In addition to two vaudeville theaters and plenty of movie houses, two groups of players at the Schubert and Palace, respectively, gave theatergoers a new choice of drama every week; and from time to time Eldon sampled their fare from a seat in the second balcony.

On his first Thanksgiving in the Big City, Eldon fasted. Carle's Cafeteria, at which he had been gorging himself daily (except Sunday) for two months, was closed for the day. Eldon had put on weight. He was by no means fat, but he felt, for the first time in his life, overfed, sated, tired of food. He interrupted the rhythm of three hearty meals per day. He went to a clean self-service restaurant on Hennepin Avenue at noon where he ordered a roast beef sandwich with potatoes and gravy, a glass of milk, and a piece of mince-meat pie (all for twenty-five cents). That was his meal of the day, and he felt virtuous as well as thankful.

The Christmas decorations that year on Seventh Street between Nicollet Avenue and Hennepin Avenue were impressive. Huge bell-shaped strands made of evergreen twigs and branches, intertwined with electric cords and colored lights, hung above the street at fifteen-foot intervals. Then, just the right amount of soft, flaky snow had fallen and stuck on the twigs and branches. It was beautiful in the darkness of December evenings.

In the daytime, though, Nicollet Avenue was less inspiring. The sidewalks on both sides of the street were clogged with slow-moving, fur-clad shoppers. In front of the entrances to the various stores were bell-ringers soliciting contributions for the poor and needy of the city. The insistent clangor of the hand-shaken bells sounded a discordant note: cried out all was not well. The half-frozen look of the ill-dressed solicitors as they shifted from foot to foot to keep warm made Eldon feel fidgety, confused, ill at ease and anxious to get away from the crowd and the bells. He couldn't be comfortable while any others, apparently, were uncomfortable. Yet what could he do?

During a "January thaw," an acquaintance of Eldon's at the Sandstone Hall offered a $10 ticket for an airplane ride for $5. Included in the ride was a "loop the loop." It seemed like a good chance to see first-hand what airplane rides were like, so Eldon bought the ticket and went out to Wold-Chamberlain Field for the trip in the little orange-red plane. Eldon was the only passenger. The pilot took things for granted and paid no attention to the passenger's buckling of the webbed safety-belt. Looking over the side of the little craft to the ground below, Eldon wasn't so sure he liked the ride. His doubts increased when the pilot banked sharply for a steep turn. When they went into the "loop the loop," Eldon's doubts vanished. This sort of stuff wasn't for him. Then he realized that his acquaintance had decided the same way beforehand. That was why he had offered Eldon his ticket at half-price. The next week the same pilot, in the same plane, crashed.

In April, Benson Business College recommended Eldon for several part-time jobs. One was a simple typing job for a week of afternoons at the sales office of a giant New England manufacturer of paper products, the Bonham Company. The manager, Earl Waldron, and the rest of the half dozen people in the office became friends of Eldon's. His other short-time employer was a lawyer, Mr. McBride, who lived in Minneapolis and had his office in the Pioneer Press Building in St. Paul. Mr. McBride's specialty was collections and bankruptcy. Eldon's work—typing routine please-pay letters and filling in the blanks of legal forms—was done in the evening at Mr. McBride's home. Eldon was sure the lawyer was third or fourth rate, but the man undeniably had a luxurious home on Groveland and a good-looking wife.

One time when Eldon and the lawyer were working at the latter's home, the evening quiet was broken by the shrill, excited, yells of newsboys calling out: "Extry Paper! Minneapolis Club Woman Shot by Robber. Minneapolis Club Woman Killed by Bandit." Eldon had heard many shouts of "Extra" but never had shared the newsboys' excitement sufficiently to buy one of the extras. To his surprise, Mr. McBride rushed to the door, beckoned the hustling newsboy and gave a nickel for the paper (the price for extras was higher than that for regular issues).

"Mrs. Morgenstern. Know her?" "Nope."

"I do—slightly," the lawyer said. "Wonderful woman." Eldon nodded sympathetically; and the two resumed their work.

In the middle of May, Eldon was offered a job at general office work by a St. Paul investment-banking firm. In effect, Eldon was a general flunkey in the advertising department. For the most part, the advertising done by Whitehead and Company consisted of sending prospective customers weekly lists of the bonds they had for sale, the sale-price, the interest rate, and yield. Bond salesmen, of course, were traveling all around the Twin Cities and the state to help the company unload its wares. Eldon's job was mediocre and his pay modest, but he had no complaints. It was an experience just to work in downtown St. Paul.

Eldon decided he loved both Minneapolis and St. Paul, both the twin daughters of the Father of Waters, the Mississippi. And they were so different. To begin with, the twins were of a different age. The elder, saintly city was less Scandinavian than its sister and much smaller. Its polyglot population tolerated more violence and gangsterism. Minneapolis (Minnie) was an opulent blonde of eighteen certain of being found. St. Paul was a skinny but peppy and brainy brunette of thirty looking for a man.

What happened to Eldon in the saintly city could hardly have happened anywhere but in St. Paul. He found a room on Bennington Avenue. The place was a long ways from downtown but conveniently served by a streetcar line. The landlady, Mrs. Gustafson, said "I really wanted to rent this room to a young lady—you see my other room is rented to two young ladies—but I'll let you have it if you like it. You look so much like my brother, I'll do that for you."

Eldon didn't catch all the implications of Mrs. Gustafson's little *spiel*. He liked the room. He took it. Mr. Gustafson worked nights. Mrs. Gustafson was active in church work—not at all partial to Catholics, but then Eldon wasn't a Catholic. The Gustafsons had a son only a few years younger than Eldon but ages younger in some ways.

As soon as the two girls came home from work and occupied their room, Eldon began to catch the implications of Mrs. Gustafson's supposed wish to rent his room to a girl instead of a boy. The rooms were so close together. The hallway was so small. One bathroom served all three. He hadn't had the slightest notion before the girls were there how it would be to have them there.

Everybody was friendly except Mr. Gustafson, but Eldon seldom saw him. The boy, Gussy, was a pain in the neck or lower in the anatomy. He had a way of laughing with his tongue between his front teeth—th-th-th—which irritated Eldon. Besides, Gussy gave Eldon vague intimations that a script had been written for him that was bound to be followed—th-th-th. The cynical insinuation by such a twerp made Eldon determined to prove the ass wrong.

The Elfstrand sisters—Eve and Mabel—were twins. Eve seemed the older. She seemed to dominate and the other to rebel. Eve was fair—very blond, white-skinned, light blue eyes; fair and feminine; blonde and buxom. Mabel was the tom-boy type. Their height was the same, but Mabel was big boned. Her hair was a sort of a greasy yellow. She had blue eyes, too, but they stared at Eldon as if she would as soon kick him in the teeth as her sister Eve.

Eldon might have realized what Mrs. Gustafson had in mind if he had known Eve was so attractive. Indeed, Eldon's first feeling, after meeting the girls, was how frustrating it would be to live so close to such an attractive female—he could already imagine her in a nightgown—and yet have so many people around. The boy would delight in "getting the goods" on Eldon. Mabel would stick close to home to prevent her sister from getting too sociable. Mrs. Gustafson surely would be returning from her church work at the most inconvenient times.

Eldon was all wrong. Opportunities there were aplenty. Neither girl pretended to confine her attentions to Eldon. Both had frequent dates with several different fellows and told him casually enough a little about their friends and fun. It was Eldon who concentrated his attentions on Eve; and the girl proved willing enough. Even after that, however, she let him know he still wasn't No. 1 or Mr. Big. Contemptuous of himself and his low taste, he took advantage of his opportunities to be alone with Mabel in her room, her bedroom. She laughed at him scoffingly. She didn't appreciate him. She knew she was second choice, but she could scoff at this mixed-up boy who thought he wanted to be Eve's Mr. Big.

And Gussy laughed at Eldon, th-th-th. He couldn't have guessed that Mabel, too, figured in Eldon's adventures, but he couldn't have been more derisive if he had known. What he did know he knew as a cynic and not as a witness to any compromising scene. Indeed, everything went on in the household as if the young folks were conducting themselves with absolute decorum and propriety. Though Lexington Ball Park and the Coliseum Ball Room were within easy walking distance, Eldon never took either girl to those places. Neither wanted to be squired around by him. That privilege was reserved for others.

Eldon was always home right after work and dinner. Early in the evening before she left, Mrs. Gustafson would tell him about the Ladies Aid Meeting, the Ice Cream Social, the Church Supper. Gussy might be around for a while or not. One of the girls—very seldom both—might show or not. Eldon was certain to be there.

Eldon made no friends in St. Paul that summer—even at the office. His fellow employees at Whitehead and Company were too old to be companions. The other stenographers, all women, tried to be—and were—nice to Eldon, but as older women to a boy. After the "Minnesota flyer" landed safely in Paris, the cute, Irish telephone operator called Eldon "Lindy" a few times. It was a compliment but obviously had no merit as a nickname. Secretly, Eldon knew he was one of the world's worst flyers.

He was alone but not lonely. The twins were less his friends than his captives, prizes of his home situation. His welcome to their bedroom was to the Garden of Eden, but he wasn't as appreciative of his good fortune as an older person might suppose. He felt he was too young for such delights. As Prometheus stole fire from the gods, he, Eldon, was stealing fire rightfully belonging to his elders. In August he pronounced himself eighteen years old, but he knew better. He was only sixteen.

Eldon's play in the hay with the Elfstrand twins, Eve and Mabel, was an imbroglio rather than a love affair; but his continuing love for the Twin Cities, both of them, was genuine.

In Mid-September, Eldon quit his job with Whitehead and Company, gave up his room on Bennington and registered as a freshman at the University of Minnesota (located in Minneapolis). Though he had been enchanted by the squalor and splendor of St. Paul, his leave-takings were formal and dry-eyed. Incredible as it may seem, he never saw Eve and Mabel again. He never again saw any of his office associates at Whitehead and Company. It was long months before he made a pilgrimage to the heart of the city and walked again on Robert Street from Fourth, past the Bremer Arcade, to Seventh.

In the fall of 1927, it was easy to enter the university of one's native state. Apparently there were no restrictions at all. All comers from within the state were accepted, or so it seemed. It is doubtful if ever a student presented himself at college with less preliminary planning, less conscious of his educational and professional goals, with less support, encouragement and advice. During his stay in St. Paul, he had cut himself off from his family at Drowsy Hollow Farm "to save money and travel trouble." Likewise, he had cut himself off from the few business-college friends he had made at Sandstone Hall.

Eldon was not in the least "taken in" by the pep-talks and green caps of Freshman Week. He promptly made a few friends and more acquaintances. In those days, military training was obligatory for all male students, and Eldon accepted the obligation with good grace (though many grumbled). That is, Eldon liked the uniform in spite of its high, close-fitting collar and those God-awful wrap-leggings. He felt the uniform did something for him, and he wanted to do something for the privilege of wearing it. While he could always count on an A in the course in Military Science, he never learned anything whatsoever in the classes and drills.

To begin with, Eldon had a room near the campus, and he expected to get a job on or near the campus. However, he was disappointed in that respect. The friendly Earl Waldrop of the Bonham Company (the paper products company) gave him a part-time, temporary job and volunteered to use his influence and business know-how in locating a permanent job for the R.O.T.C. cadet. An acquaintance of Mr. Waldrop who worked for Polar-Temp Electric Refrigerator Company said his company needed a night-clerk to answer phone calls, sell parts on occasion, keep certain records, and dispatch repairmen in emergencies. The clerk would have to live on the premises, near downtown Minneapolis. Eldon took the job. The work was onerous but paid enough to make the student wholly self-supporting, which was essential.

At first, Eldon followed a pre-business course, as it was called. English appealed to him, especially poetry. Economics was a conglomeration of words—words without fire, magic, meaning or romance. Bookkeeping was now called Accounting, and he did exceedingly well in it. Next to English, he liked History and took a lot of it. Also on his intellectual smorgasbord were Philosophy, Logic, and Political Science—and, oh yes, Speech. In Speech, as in the magazines and newspapers of the day, the foremost subject was the Farm Problem. Eldon, being less ignorant of the Farm Problem than his classmates, capitalized on the situation.

Two instructors greatly dissimilar in looks and learning would put their respective classes, including Eldon, to sleep and then interrupt their droning lectures to say, "Isn't that right, Mr. Jones?"

"Yes, Sir," Eldon would reply, coming awake but not realizing what he was confirming.

Those two courses were fair examples of others. In one, the instructor gave an objective examination. The other gave an essay type. Though knowing next to nothing about either subject, Eldon scored A's in both courses. There was no one now, as there had been in high school, to say "He bluffs." Still, Eldon didn't take these grades too seriously.

In elementary school he had read "Library books." As a college student, he continued that practice on a limited scale. In addition, he haunted the magazine room in the Men's Union and the periodical room in the Library and tried to find out what writers thought of the Great Wide

World. Some of the periodicals he perused have long since vanished: *Scribners, Century, North American.* Still extant and carrying on are *Harper's, Atlantic,* and *Yale Review.*

His favorite novels at this time were W. H. Hudson's *Green Mansions* and *The Purple Land.* Doubtless they appealed to the farm boy in him. *The Autobiography of Lincoln Steffens* was the first of a number of biographical works he was to like. It told him of the world as it was just before he was born.

It is not certain how Eldon was able to read so much and still do as well as he did in his various classes. His work as a night-clerk for Polar-Temp was considerable. In addition, he indulged in gab-fests and "bull-sessions" with the employees who worked at night with him. The repairman on night duty was changed every week so there always was a new personality to get acquainted or re-acquainted with. His homework was minimal. Eldon was not a speed-reader; nor did he have a photographic memory. His powers of concentration were good but not phenomenal. He did love words, and their meaning seemed to flow from the text to his mind as coffee is poured from pot to cup.

As he got closer to Business School, Eldon shied away from it. He considered Journalism, but the practitioners of the art whom he consulted counseled against it. The lawyers he saw urged him to join their ranks. Thus, one distinguished lawyer, of exceedingly serious mien, insisted to Eldon with a shake of the finger: "If you're good in Mathematics, you belong in the Law."

"I'm not good in Math."

"You belong in the Law, anyway."

Eldon's switch from Business to Law gave him an unexpected bonus. He now had to take a foreign language. He chose French and began it in his third year. He was captivated with the language—the beauty of its sound, the logic of its grammar, the precision of its meaning. Unfortunately, he had to suspend his studies in it when he entered Law School.

Had anyone else claimed to have chosen between two or more professions because of the advice he had received, Eldon would have smiled indulgently, if not incredulously. In someone else's choice of a profession, he would have been well aware of the governing importance of the irrational, inexplicable, emotional factors. He would have realized that the invisible underside of a person's make-up is supreme when major decisions are made. In his own case, however, Eldon supposed his choice of the Law rested on superficial, observable, rational considerations—such as the sound advice of elders in position to know whereof they spoke.

When Eldon was still in Business College, his savings account in a home-town bank was cut in half by the bank's failure. The same type of misfortune had befallen others he knew. When the New York stock-market crashed in 1929, Eldon suffered not at all. He held no stocks. As time went on and business generally got sicker, he had to wonder whether his job would be one of those abolished by Polar-Temp. It wasn't. Indeed, the company even raised his pay.

In summers, Eldon worked on the company's day-shift. In 1929, as a payroll clerk, he participated in the company's institution of a piece-rate pay scale. In the years immediately following, the company made use of the new system for spreading employment and for holding onto the hard core of dependable employees. He also saw how two employees, George Field and Larry Hanson, who were good friends and paid the same salary under the old system, had divergent experiences under the new pay scale. Field's earnings were halved; Hanson's were doubled. Field resigned in disgust. Eldon also saw how two of the dozen or so skilled workers who became salesmen did better for many months than the best of the regular salesmen with training and experience.

Later on, when people asked Eldon what he had done during the Depression, he could say, "I survived." He didn't complain that his earnings were meager. His sex-life was meager, too, but he didn't blame that on the Depression as was the custom of the time.

Polar-Temp had moved its offices from Minneapolis to St. Paul's Midway District. Eldon walked to and from the University, a distance of two miles each way. As he did, he saw the billboards by which the cigarette companies wooed and wowed the women and enlisted them as customers. One proclaimed "A Miss is good as a mile," and showed a good-looking gal giving a well-dressed man a cigarette. Otherwise, the poor fellow would have had to walk a mile for a Camel. Another took its text from Shakespeare, "Coming events cast their shadow before." The shadows of fatness could be avoided if women were well-advised and reached for a Lucky instead of a sweet.

A manufacturer on Eldon's daily route doubled the size of its plant in 1929. Then came the Depression, and the huge buildings stood empty and quiet. God, tempering the wind to the shorn lambs, cut the prices of food, clothing, and shelter. Eldon could buy a big red apple for a nickel.

One evening, Eldon decided he would eat an apple before he settled down to his evening chores at Polar-Temp. There he sat, with his feet on the desk, apple in hand, chewing away, when the Big Boss suddenly appeared in the doorway. Eldon put his feet on the floor and the apple on the desk.

"What's that?" The Big Boss pointed at a compressor which, for some reason, had been left in a corner of the office instead of in the shop.

"A compressor," Eldon told the man who knew it as well as he.

"Oh." The Big Boss left. Eldon began work and forgot the apple until he was sure the boss was not coming back.

In 1931, Eldon received his Bachelor of Arts degree cum laude. He took his rented cap and gown back to Drowsy Hollow Farm so the home folks could see and take snapshots of him in high-falutin' attire. The summer wind from the south was so strong and blew the loose-fitting gown so violently, it wasn't possible to snap a picture of Eldon in placid pose in front of the house. He retreated to the north, back of the woods, and had his picture taken with a field of corn in the background. It was as if the All-Wise Weatherman was pronouncing Eldon's learning and culture pretty corny.

Eldon's brother Abbott now had graduated from high school, and Eldon urged Abbott to try out higher education. Abbott had serious misgivings about going to the Big City. He agreed, though, to take Eldon's place on the night-shift at Polar-Temp for one summer. His work in that capacity was well-liked, but Abbott decided he still wasn't ready to go to college in the Big City. He might try, first, some high-school graduate work at Avondale.

That September, Eldon took a two-week vacation from Polar-Temp and went on a canoe trip with a dozen other college students on the lakes in northern

Minnesota and southern Canada. It was the greatest fun Eldon ever had. The smell of the pines, the beauty of the lakes, the evenings around a campfire with songs by the boys and tales of the North by the guide (and cook), the healthy exercise of paddling and portaging by day, the wide expanse of starlit sky by night, the novelty of pitching a pup-tent and sleeping in it on a bed of aromatic balsam boughs—all these did wonders for Eldon and his comrades. He chronicled the events of the trio and sold a typed copy to each of his fellow voyageurs.

One of the most spectacular sights of the trip was the Northern Lights. The lake and forest by which they camped were lit up one night more brightly than New York's Times Square. It was an eerie light—an eerie sensation.

The car in which Eldon made the trip north to the canoe country was a Ford Touring car (with soft, cloth top and open on the sides) which belonged to a comrade, one of the *coureurs de bois*. On the return to the south, it was so cold as they drove along Lake Superior, they put the cloth and isinglass side-curtains up on the car and bundled in blankets. When they reached Minneapolis late that afternoon, the temperature was over one-hundred degrees—and felt every bit of it.

In Law School, Eldon learned about Contracts and Crimes; about Property, real and personal; about Corporations and Conflicts of Laws; about Taxation and the Constitution; about Courts, high and low. He learned about those abstract, wispy subjects but not all about them like the hillbilly who returned from Law School in a week and took back his old place at the plow handles behind the mule. The father asked, "What's the matter? Don't you 1ike the Law?"

"Naw. Sorry I learned it."

In 1932, the nation went to the polls. The showroom of Polar-Temp was a polling place, so Eldon was able to see the vote in his precinct being counted. The results in the presidential race surprised the pollsters of *Literary Digest* more than anyone else. For the fun of it, he neglected his work for Polar-Temp to watch the count of the feet-long paper ballots which decided various state and local contests and questions. Reporters, party-workers, and telegraph boys kept coming and going from the showroom through much of the night.

In the early spring of 1933, before Eldon graduated, banks began to talk about "frozen assets" and to close. Times were tough. That was the consensus. One law graduate, more or less, didn't seem to count for much—and the Order of the Coif seemed an empty honor.

Eldon considered himself pretty lucky to get a job with the Minneapolis law firm of Morgenstern and Morgenstern. The pay, to begin with, was less than he had received as night clerk at Polar-Temp, but he hoped for improvement. The partners inspired respect as gentlemen of learning and principle. Affection was something the senior partners, father and son, did not give or expect. Marty Nordholm, five or ten years older than Eldon, was a good teacher of law practice and a fine luncheon companion. The firm was a cozy little company of four lawyers of varying ages and two secretaries.

Marty explained the elder partner's stiff reserve. "You know he's never been the same since his wife was shot by a purse snatcher."

"How's that?"

"She resisted a purse snatcher, and he killed her. Then he left the purse intact and ran away."

"How terrible!"

"Yes. Chris never got over it."

"No wonder."

Eldon surmised the son, Olaf, never was the same, either, after that horrifying event. He was affable and quick to laugh, but this ready gaiety always reminded Eldon of the lines:

Why was it that his charm revealed
Somehow the surface of a shield?

Marty, whom Eldon knew best, also remained an enigma. He was so unbelievably gentle, so devoid of the blunt, earthy, forceful, ribald qualities common to most men Eldon had known. He had a wife, whom Eldon had not met, but he nevertheless reminded Eldon of a monk. Marty had read everything and thought about everything but had permitted the life-preserving juices of humor and spontaneous action to evaporate or leak away. Even so, Eldon enjoyed the company and conversation of this lawyerly monk with his vast knowledge and diverse interests.

Marty and Eldon often would have a high-priced but abstemious lunch at a sandwich shop on Second Avenue and then take a long, slow walk along Second Avenue, Marquette, or Third Avenue. Religion was the one topic they seldom discussed. Marty had become, he said, an Episcopalian, and he was perfectly satisfied with his church. He explained, "It doesn't interfere with either my politics or my religion."

Eldon never was to attain such certainty. He wasn't, indeed, willing to be satisfied with such negative virtues. He wanted more from his church than Marty did. In the meantime, he experimented with the Unitarian Church. He had heard the pastor, first on the radio, and had decided the erudite, eloquent, assured churchman was worth hearing in person. In the religious services, Eldon missed the pensive strains of an organ. He missed the galloping rhythms of the evangelistic hymns: Send the Light, Bringing in the Sheaves, The Old Rugged Cross. The preacher made more sense, which was good, but he evoked in the congregation no sense of its own kinship with ignorant, hot-blooded humanity, past and present.

The church had many activities for those of Eldon's age (young adults), and Eldon tried them out. They were a tepid tea, a weak brew. They were less demeaning than the boisterous conviviality of the tavern or the revivalist tabernacle but still not satisfying. He danced with good-looking girls at the supervised church functions and dated several of the most attractive in desultory fashion, but he never lost either his heart or his head to the Unitarian girls or gospel. The doctrines of that church were too intellectual to be heady.

He also partook of the fare at a Baptist church presided over by a learned and distinguished preacher. Once was enough. Nine-tenths of the sermon was devoted to a thoroughly convincing proof that the world was hastening at headlong pace toward war. Then, after this reasoned and detailed demonstration of the inevitability of war within a few years, the preacher denied everything he had been saying on the ground that "once there was a Man!" Eldon was more convinced of the danger than of the rescue—so much so that he never wanted to hear the eminent divine again. He belonged, in spite of himself, to a church that hadn't been built.

Till his church should be built, Eldon had to go it alone. In the meantime, he could have his own individual, if vague and blurred vision of Greatness and

Goodness and measure his actions accordingly. He did just that, and by so doing made others uneasy in his presence. Most of the people Eldon met tried to conform down—that is, to be as common as the next person. This bespectacled lawyer, they thought, is the son of a dirt farmer from Avondale and is just as common as we are. Why doesn't he boast of it, insist upon it (and, so, get more clients)? Is he a snob? From Eldon they got no answer. So far as appeared, he did not even take note of the question. He was simply his complicated self.

There were a number of restaurants in the vicinity of Eldon's office in the McKnight Building which were the hangouts of political crackpots in those depression days, just as certain Paris cafes of the Nineteenth Century were the rendezvous of easel painters and writers. While Eldon was interested in politics, he wanted "no truck" with the kind of politics handed down by the Deity via the good offices of Josef Stalin and the inspired pen of Karl Marx. He never tried to elbow his way to a cheap meal in one of those restaurants. Later he regretted not doing so for the sake of the experience; but then it was too late.

There were more than a few alarms and excursions in Minneapolis in those days—riots, pitched battles with clubs and tools and police guns, bloodshed. One time when Eldon had gone to the Register of Deeds in the basement of the courthouse, some sort of a disturbance took place in the street that led to the use of teargas by the police. Enough of it seeped into the dusty records-office where Eldon was working to cause him to leave hastily.

During these years when restlessness and skepticism were pandemic, Eldon read such books as Leon Trotsky's *My Life* and Emma Goldman's autobiography,

Living My Life. He enjoyed both, especially the latter. However, he couldn't get over the feeling that there were missing links and loose screws in anarchy. His favorite story of that epoch was Melville's *Benito Cereno*. Twenty-five years later he re-read that tale and wondered what he ever had seen in that clumsy chronicle of an imaginary shipboard mutiny.

While Eldon survived the Depression, his brother Abbott did not. Abbott, like many other footloose youth of that time, had made a long trip by "hopping freights"—that is, freight trains. When he was returning and within fifty miles of the home farm, Drowsy Hollow, Abbott met a horrible death under the wheels of the train. He was buried in the earth he had loved and loved to roam, as farm boy and hunter. He was home from his travels.

Eldon, at loose ends and more than ready for a vacation, decided that now was the time to make another plunge into the wilderness of the "border lakes." There, he could let Nature glide "into his darker Musings with a mild and healing sympathy." He pondered arrangements for such a vacation during the day at the office. When he got home, he found a telegram that had been slipped under the door of his apartment. It was from the former lawyer for Polar-Temp, John Daly, who had gone to Washington to take a Government job. He wondered if Eldon would like to go and do likewise. The answering telegram said yes. Eldon's plunge was not to be into the wilderness of Superior National Forest but into the grandeur of the Capital of the World.

III. Mr. Jones Goes to Washington

In the early summer of 1936, a young lawyer named Eldon Jones got off the plane at Washington Airport in Virginia. He had not been chummy with John Daly who had invited him to come to Washington, but he half-expected to be met on his arrival by the older man. No. He rode the airport limousine to one of the hotels on its route, the Roger Gard, registered, and then called John.

John Daly was the son of an extremely wealthy, shrewd, domineering woman who had lost her husband about the same time Eldon's father died. John's success as a lawyer in Minneapolis had been negligible. He was not lacking in intelligence, but he was shy. Now, he was doing all right as the head of a scholarly section of young lawyers in one of the huge government departments. He thought of Eldon as capable of running as fast as anyone in this small group of legal beagles who chased elusive points of law through the bramble-tangle of books as hounds chase rabbits through pasture brush. Starting as acquaintances from the same home town, Minneapolis, Eldon and John Daly became good friends despite an age differential of fifteen years.

Before their six-year association in Government really began, though, it was necessary for Eldon to get "political clearance." This meant the Roosevelt Administration, heading into a campaign for a new lease on the White House, wanted no unnecessary Republicans in its ranks. For that "clearance," Eldon went on John Daly's advice to see one of Minnesota's Democratic congressmen. The congressman, spurred by a telephone call from Daly, gave Eldon a letter so full of indiscriminate praise that Eldon could not bring himself to submit it. He went, without introduction, to a Farmer-Labor senator who wrote: "Eldon Jones is a constituent of mine. Any favors you can do for him will be appreciated." That letter was Eldon's "political clearance." It seemingly certified he was not a Republican.

Then Eldon had to find a less expensive place to live than the Roger Gard Hotel. To begin with, he moved into a boarding house near Dupont Circle, his first encounter with a boarding house. The place run by Mrs. Porteous (for her husband didn't count) rivaled that of Balzac's Maison Vauquer. Otherwise, Eldon wouldn't have stayed as long as he did, till after Christmas. He never recognized the meat in the dinner's main course. It always looked the same, covered over as it was by tan gravy. It always tasted the same. Now and then, from his seat at the table, he would spy a few cockroaches in the kitchen. These didn't embarrass Mrs. Porteous who would say "They're inevitable, you know, in any conveniently located pension."

Breakfast was a thoroughly disorganized meal with everyone coming down at his own time. It was a meal at which Mrs. Porteous never showed up. The colored maid, Jennie, the first Eldon had ever known, took one's order for a boiled egg when he sat down to table. Fried eggs and scrambled were out. There seldom, if ever, was time for two boiled eggs. Jennie doubtless had her orders about that from Mrs. Porteous. Eldon never had cared for boiled eggs—had no skill in shelling them, nor in eating out of an egg cup—and found these particular Porteous eggs the least appetizing in his experience.

He enjoyed his fellow boarders (especially those who weren't fellows). Further, he was within walking distance of his office. Miss Savage was a savage Republican who had been recalled from a foreign post of the Commerce Department to work at home. She was thirty years Eldon's senior, but he thought her charming. Only his sense of the fitness of things kept his hands at home. Bill Mackie, back from a business in Turkey, was called "By Crackie," now and then, to his disgust and Eldon's amusement. An old maid who had been with the Paris edition of the *New York Times* could tell tales of the Left Bank. Bill told her to write them down; they'd make the best bank statements anyone ever read. Someone else commented: "That's right, By Crackie!" The someone else was one of the young men who worked for the Government by day and went to college evenings.

Marie Endicott, the receptionist for a California congressman, was a young beauty. She was dark-eyed and dressed as if she were from India—or dressed to suggest Indian costume. Mrs. Porteous hated her, envied her. Eldon sensed that. David Abosch, a handsome, swarthy, dark-eyed young man, was a constant companion of Marie. Mrs. Porteous took Dave aside one time and told him, "I know you're Jewish, but don't let anyone else here know." Dave moved out in a huff. Marie left, too, in sympathy.

Shortly after Christmas, Eldon read an ad in the *Washington Post* "Room with a French family." He answered the ad and took the room with the Duvals. He no longer could walk to his office, but he liked the Duvals—M., Mme., Jacques, and Antoine. Nothing but French was spoken in the house. Eldon took his meals in restaurants. There was one exception not bargained for. On Sunday mornings, Mrs. Duval would send one or the boys up to Eldon's room with an American breakfast. This was the supreme luxury, breakfast in bed. And the food was so delicious. This arrangement lasted for several years, until the Duvals moved to the New York City area.

John Daly's boss was the Solicitor of the Department, which meant the chief legal adviser to the Secretary. Eldon saw the Solicitor less than the Secretary himself. Both John and Eldon concerned themselves with the law of such abstruse subjects as reciprocal trade agreements between countries, the rates of exchange of currencies of foreign countries, litigation involving tariff rates reduced by trade agreements, etc. One time, Eldon was asked by John to go to Senator Robert Taft's office and justify the rate of duty being applied to certain imports of Swedish steel. In the Senator's ante-room were copies of a picture magazine telling about the Senator's presidential aspirations.

When Eldon was ushered into the great man's office, the latter was as gruff as a lawyer brow beating a witness. A ball bearing producer in the State of Ohio or somewhere was suffering from the unfair competition of the Swedes; and it seemed as if Eldon were personally to blame. With great politeness and deference, Eldon asked if he might bring in some samples of the imports which he had left in the reception room. When the Senator saw Exhibits A and B for the Defense, his manner changed completely. He appreciated Mr. Jones' visit; he had misunderstood the situation.

Eldon seldom saw the key figures of the Roosevelt Administration. He once was invited, however, to attend a welcoming assembly for a group of visiting Latin American diplomats and delegates. They were addressed by Sumner Welles, who in the absence of

Cordell Hull served as Secretary of State. Eldon sat among the dark-haired, dark-eyed, well-dressed, passionate-looking Latins. Mr. Welles was as blond and blue-eyed as a Swede from Eldon's home state. He was as cool in appearance as an icicle—all poise and sangfroid. Yet the Latins liked him.

Some of those Eldon saw at business meetings were unknown then but figured in the news dispatches of later years. Those he saw (but scarcely knew) were the enigmatic Dr. White of the Treasury Department and Alger Hiss of the State Department. The latter impressed Eldon as exceedingly smooth and able. Eldon never suspected either of these two men of shenanigans of any sort. And several others of whom he was dubious, even in that era so free of suspicion, were never mentioned, so far as Eldon knew, by Senator Joe McCarthy or the newspapers of the epoch of that Senator's notoriety.

The congressman who had written so fulsomely in Eldon's favor later broke with FDR and was run over by a political steamroller. Another Minnesota congressman gained a certain celebrity for a one-man stand against the administration when a vote was taken in the House on the Spanish civil-war embargo. Eldon's acquaintance with the hero of this dramatic episode was slight but pleasurable, a spaghetti dinner or so. This unusual figure spoke with a charming accent; and the occasional pauses in his conversation were equally delightful. However, this man's time upon the congressional stage also was brief.

The years from 1936 to 1942 were short but filled with fateful, not to say portentous, events. Government lawyers were involved with side issues such as the right of a munitions-laden ship (the Mar Cantabrico) to leave a "neutral" American port and make a dash for war-torn

Spain, and which side in that tragic civil war owned the Spanish gold shipped to New York. What was the legal standing or nature of the Federal Reserve Bank notes which Japan issued as currency in conquered and occupied North China? Eldon worked on such questions as those in a dress rehearsal for similar problems in a tenser atmosphere when the Germans dramatized themselves as villains in the theater of Europe.

In 1938, Eldon sailed for Europe on vacation. In those days, a crossing by transatlantic steamer was the most common way to go to Europe. One could already fly across the ocean on a huge propeller-driven plane, but ordinary tourists commonly sailed, as Eldon did. One more sensitive than he, or more prescient, might have gone on a different ship than the Bremen. But that was the ship he took, tourist class.

Sitting in a salon, sipping tea, Eldon spied the label in the light coat of the young woman at the adjoining table. It read, "Dayton's Store, Minneapolis." Eldon, who hadn't been in Minneapolis since he left in 1936, leaned across the space between the two tables and asked innocently, "Pardon me, haven't we met—in Minneapolis?"

"Maybe. That's my home. I teach art at the University of Minnesota."

"Oh, that's my alma mater, class of '31. I didn't study art there, but I often visited the Art Institute. Maybe we met there."

"I'll bet we did."

Eldon noticed his new-found friend, Angela, slipping her wedding ring off. She said, "I'm going to France on a fellowship to study art at the Louvre."

"The French language is my long suit. I plan to spend much of my time in Paris and most of that at the Louvre."

"How wonderful that we meet on the way, before we get there."

"Yes."

He and Angela Morgan had a good time together on shipboard and in Paris. Both were amazed at the grandeur of Versailles, restored by an American philanthropist. Eldon was not the kind to take a cab to the Louvre and tell the driver to wait, but there was more there to see than he could savor. He enjoyed visiting Notre Dame and other cathedrals with Angela, but there was always something about those ancient stone structures he couldn't grasp or assimilate or appreciate. He left them with a feeling of chill.

When he went south to Avignon, Eldon went alone. On the train, he sat opposite, for a while, a young French army officer in uniform. The young man said, "After France, the United States is the country of my predilection." Not to be outdone, Eldon said France was his second home.

The papal palace at Avignon seemed to be, as indeed it was, a relic of the distant past with no present-day utility except that of evoking the bygone era. The countryside, with its unearthed Roman ruins, the chirp of crickets, the sight of sheep, was wonderful but less homelike than Eldon might have given the army officer to understand. Then, in an aluminum mining district there were people living in caves and listening to radios. Truly, France was a country which united past and present in an unbelievable way.

Eldon went to Nice by a bus which travelled along the Mediterranean seashore. From Nice he again went by bus to Grenoble by the route Napoleon had taken on his return from Elba. Nice and Cannes had seemed as different from Avignon as Grenoble and Chamonix seemed from the southern cities. The same people who worked so lazily around Avignon and played so frivolously at Nice went in for alpine stocks, climbing boots, and the strenuous life at Chamonix.

At Nice, the proprietor of Hotel Mercure had asked Eldon what country he came from. "Guess," Eldon replied.

"I can't...Hungary?"

"Why do you guess Hungary?"

"Because you wear rimless glasses." "No, I'm from the United States."

"Is that so? I'm from Brooklyn, myself. I married and stayed here after the war."

After France, the rest of Europe, even Britain, seemed anti-climactic. However, the Swiss Castle of Chillon impressed Eldon, as did the castles along the Rhine and the medieval buildings of Oxford University. And in London in 1938, Eldon saw a televised program of ballet dancing. He was not to see television in his own country till after World War II.

While seeing the sights of London, Eldon struck up the acquaintance of a prim young lady doing the same. She was from New Zealand. Like Eldon, she had been in Paris. She had been shocked, she said, by the number of nude statues in Paris. "Why, we wouldn't stand for even one statue of a nude in New Zealand," she declared. Eldon marveled that New Zealand could be more puritanical than his own country. Most of all, in Paris, he had loved the wonderful, free, white marble statues in the Tuileries Gardens.

Eldon returned to the New World on the Empress of Britain which discharged its passengers at Quebec. From there, after sightseeing, Eldon went to Montreal. In the latter city, he had apple pie with his lunch. If not yet home, he felt close to it. How good that apple pie tasted.

On his return to Washington, he realized, too, how homelike that city was. He had a new appreciation of the beauty of its buildings, plazas and parks, especially woodsy Rock Creek Park. Mount Vernon, not far away, belonged to him as he belonged to it. The White House was a whiter symbol than it had been. At their next blooming, the cherry trees around the Tidal Basin and Haines Point were more glorious. Nearby Virginia had never seemed so pleasantly redolent of history, American history.

A year after Eldon's return from his European vacation, Hitler's armies invaded Poland. The European war seemed to be a brooding omnipresence in the sky. It was part of Eldon's duties to skim the *Congressional Record* every day to see if any pending bill, legislation, drift of opinion, called for action by the Department. In spite of himself, Eldon would read the screams about the transfer of 100 destroyers to Britain, would read the alarming speeches about the Lend Lease Bill. He had a part, if slight and negative, in delaying the departure of the ship in which he had crossed the Atlantic the year before. Despite the delayed sailing, the Bremen eluded the British ships set to intercept it. It made its way to Norway (where it dared not and could not leave and was immobilized—a sitting duck for bombers—for the duration of the hostilities).

John Daly was thoroughly committed to the American policy of every assistance to Britain "short of war." He realized, however, that to Eldon such a course seemed to be chafing at the bit to get into the war, and John never tried to push his views down the throat of his assistant. The times were tough, for Eldon's private opinions were not in harmony with the official line. It wrenched his conscience to feel the law had to be stretched and twisted to serve a warlike policy. It didn't help that the policy was called "short of war." Never, after that, did the law seem as holy as it once had, always had.

The Japanese attack on Pearl Harbor "got him off the hook," as the saying is. He had come back to Washington from horseback riding in Virginia with a friend, Jim Ryan. They were sipping beer while waiting for their lunch in a restaurant on K Street. They were thirsty, hungry, and, temporarily oblivious to each other, were each on his own trying to make sense of the confusing reports coming over the radio. Finally, the two looked at each other, almost in disbelief of the news. How could this monstrous thing be true? But it was, and they knew it.

Within a week, Eldon volunteered for duty with the Coast Guard in Hawaii. His experience and qualifications were needed there, but he was turned down because of his poor eyesight. His work with John Daly seemed easier now, and he took it more easily. He would be drafted fairly soon. He had been neglecting a cute blonde of his acquaintance, Inge Johnson, too much lately, and she was from Minnesota, too. For years, he had been seeing black-haired and dark-eyed Sharon Scarlatti from time to time. He could tell she was destined to be a white-haired old maid, but now he would take her more often to concerts and the theater (to see, say, Robert Sherwood's smash-hit play about the grotesque Russian-Finnish War). He even met a new gal, a beautiful, blue-eyed brunette who did interpretive dancing for clubs, night clubs, theater, restaurants.

For all his night-clubbing and theater-going, Eldon found time in the hectic months between Pearl Harbor and his rendezvous with the military to read Tolstoy's *War and Peace* and Jules Romains' *Verdun* and to listen to recordings of Beethoven's symphonies. Nor did his frenetic activity after business hours signify any loss of his sense of humor or of his customary good humor. A snide caller by telephone one evening asked, "Am I calling at an inconvenient time? Did I get you out of the arms of someone?"

"Out of the arms of Morpheus."

In the meantime, Eldon was carrying on some perfectly futile negotiations which required him to go to New York with a colleague for a few days every two weeks or so. (In those days such trips were by train, as a matter of course.) He knew the talks were futile, but, presumably, no one else did. One time, while there, he received a telegram from his draft board. He telephoned the board, and in those days long-distance calls were not such a casual affair as now. "Oh, it's not urgent," he was told. "Come and see us when you get back." Well, that was the beginning of a new career for Eldon. He was going to war.

IV. War and Peace

In 1942, at age 31, Eldon Jones became a soldier. Fifteen years before, as a college student, he had been an ROTC cadet, which, he now discovered, was quite different from being a draftee in the war-time army. Nobody seemed to care now about the perfection of his shoeshine.

At Camp Lee, Virginia, he was given his uniform. To his surprise, it was a fit. It was comfortable and good looking. He also received his first set of immunization shots. After the shots, the platoon reassembled outside and stood in ranks. First one sat down and then another, till Eldon and two others were the only ones still standing. The sergeant pointed at someone and shouted, "You, there, sit down before you fall down." Eldon took the hint.

A friend of Eldon's, Bill Holloway, was a lieutenant at Camp Lee. He called Eldon and said, "What do you want to do, Eldon? Where do you want to go? Maybe I can help."

"Thanks, Bill; but let's just see what happens."

What happened was that Eldon, the lawyer, was assigned to the Medical Department, to a hospital unit being organized at Camp Custer in Colorado. He and two dozen other draftees from Camp Lee who shared the assignment were placed in charge of a Brooklyn boy who was made Acting Corporal for the duration of the trip. Ernie Kodert, who surely didn't invent gunpowder, took his duties very seriously. The only casualty, which wasn't Ernie's fault and wasn't discovered till some time later, was that one of the draftees took advantage of the half-hour between trains in Chicago to have a kiss-me-quick affair that resulted in his acquiring an unpleasant disease. Otherwise, the contingent arrived at Camp Custer without mishap.

Though not a reluctant conscript, Eldon was not an enthusiastic recruit, either. The well-ordered world of his past six years as a government lawyer in Washington was no more. He was lost in this new world of soldiers, of young men in uniform. He reached out, as it were, to find a friend or two. He failed. He failed to find a friend. All were his comrades, but all were about the same. Seemingly it was so for everyone. They got along together, working, drilling, marching, training, but friends they were not.

In the beautiful, small city of Sonora Springs, which was near Camp Custer, Eldon found a friend, a girlfriend. Her name was Mildred Quam. He saw her first at church on Sunday but learned her name, no more. That was enough, for he met her again during the week at a USO dance in the City Auditorium. A romance was begun between Eldon, the displaced civilian, and the young school-teacher-musician. Millie played the cello.

To Eldon as a civilian, Washington had seemed a great melting pot. The government's civil servants were drawn from all the states of the Union. The war-time army was an even more representative cross-section of the nation. Here, the soldiers came from all ranks of life, all levels of society. Here, by some strange alchemy, they were fused into a unit. A few were discharged as totally unfit for service (Section 8'd). Some were transferred to different, more suitable units. Those remaining were transformed—or, at least, partially transformed. They put themselves into their roles, much of themselves.

If Eldon spent his strength on a mountainside during the day gathering rocks with which to line the gutters of Camp Custer, he renewed it in the evening by going on a date with Millie Quam in Sonora Springs. If he knocked himself out pounding stakes with a heavy mallet and helping his unit put up a hospital tent, he found relief and escape by taking Millie to a dance. She seemed to understand, though he couldn't tell her what there was to understand; though she couldn't possibly know what there was to understand.

After three months or so of basic training, Eldon applied for OCS (Officer Candidate School). The colonel in command of the hospital unit called Eldon in to dissuade him from going ahead with the application. "The unit," he said, "is just beginning to shape up. We need every good man we have. We can't afford to lose any." This was the first time in Eldon's military experience that he had been called a "good man" even by implication, but he refused to be diverted from his chosen course. He didn't consider it for even a moment. His application was referred to a board, which, he learned later, was so impressed by this soldier so little impressed by himself that it made a special report on Eldon to Third Army Headquarters.

Eldon carried on with his regular, routine duties as a private wholly unaware of the board's special report. Then, one day, he was told he was to be transferred to Third Army Headquarters in Texas and that he was to leave the next day. This sounded good, but he didn't know. His first wish was to tell Millie Quam. He had lived over thirty years without knowing her and now, all of a sudden, she seemed indispensable. On the eve, then, of his departure for Texas and unknown adventures, he promised to return in June, and Millie Quam agreed to become his wife at that time.

From the crude cluster of barracks at Camp Custer to the regular army nest at Fort Sam Houston, with green grass, trees, and stone buildings, was a breathtaking change. He was still a private, though, and acted as shipping clerk until a new and different assignment could be made. He learned that a new OCS was to be set up for those who had been lawyers in civilian life and so were eligible to become Judge Advocate officers. Eldon withdrew his pending application for other schools and made an application for the Judge Advocate School. Then he waited and waited.

In June, Millie Quam became Millie Jones, wife of Corporal Jones. They honeymooned in the wonderland that is Colorado in June. One day as the couple was having a picnic in the park known by the grandiose name of Manitou's Playground, a neighborhood boy came with a letter which had been addressed to Corporal Jones at the Quams. The corporal was to report to OCS in a month.

The school was at Ann Arbor, Michigan. Though wives were not welcome, Eldon took his with him. Millie did not live far from school, and Eldon managed to see her fairly often. Ann Arbor's grass was even greener than that at Fort Sam Houston. And in the fall the foliage was so flamboyantly red. The time there seemed to pass with the sudden violence of armored columns. Corporal Jones—or Candidate Jones, rather—became Lieutenant Jones and a few months later was ordered overseas.

Eldon bought a house for Millie to live in while he was gone. It was in Sonora Springs near the home of her folks. The baby, when he came, also would have a comfortable home till his father returned from campaigns in Europe. When Eldon had made these arrangements for his wife, he returned to Fort Sam Houston for the "processing" preliminary to going overseas.

During this waiting or preparatory period, Eldon went into the post barbershop during duty hours. There he was in the barber chair, as big as can be, when General Hodges, the Commanding General of the Third Army, entered. He looked directly at Eldon, said "Hello, Lieutenant," and sat down in the other chair.

After this wait at Fort Sam Houston, Eldon went "as a casual," i.e., alone, to the "port of embarkation," i.e., New York, where he waited some more at Governor's Island. He crossed the Atlantic in the Queen Elizabeth, which had become a troop ship. After that, Eldon waited some more at a Replacement Depot (Repple Depple) near Birmingham, England. By now it was April, but, in the absence of heat, very chilly. Eldon caught a dilly of a cold. For the first time in his life, he tried a remedy he often had heard recommended. At bedtime, he drank plenty of water, took a generous dose of aspirin and emptied a half-pint of whiskey he had toted along for just such emergencies. The medication was effective.

Eldon spent three months at an army post in the southern part of England (Gloucestershire). The countryside was beautiful. By a remarkable coincidence, the Commanding General this time was born in Minnesota near Eldon's own birthplace. He knew people who had been friends of Eldon's father. General Connor, though quietly and absolutely domineering, was a fine man and seemed to be especially considerate of Eldon. He made a nice little ceremony of announcing Eldon's promotion and pinning on his captain's bars. He resisted the efforts of Third Army Headquarters to have Eldon assigned to Staff Section X for certain special, unspecified duties. When Eldon said he would like to return to the Third Army, General Connor put through the transfer without delay.

Eldon reported to Section X on July 4th, 1944. He landed in Normandy on July 14th. It was only after this that he learned that his son, David, had been born on May 28th. On that date, according to Eldon's best recollection, he had been on a weekend trip in Wales. Those deceptively peaceful weekends, with trips for the sake of travel and recreation, were gone for quite a while. That he knew.

Two weeks later, the Third Army, now commanded by General Patton, hurled itself against the enemy. For Eldon and his comrades, there followed a series of changes in bivouac areas in apple orchards, woods, and forests. Not until October did they sleep under a roof. By then, much of France had been liberated. About this time, Eldon chanced to meet a lieutenant he knew who had come to the headquarters on some business of his infantry division. Lt. Puckett said "This is great here where you are. Up front with my division, it's rough."

Eldon didn't doubt that what Lt. Puckett said was true. However, Lt. Puckett added, "I'll meet you for breakfast tomorrow, and we can talk a little before I go back to my outfit. I'm billeted at Hotel Americain, and right now I want to take advantage of that." During the night the Germans shelled the small city with a couple of big guns. One of the shells landed squarely where the wall of the Hotel Americain met the ground. It did little damage inside, but it must have ruined the sleep of everyone billeted there. Lt. Puckett did not show up for breakfast with Eldon as he planned. He was on his way back to his division.

A few months later, in a little city of another country, Luxembourg, Eldon had a chance meeting with another friend from a different infantry division. He took Lt. Riley to his billet for a talk before going to mess. The owner of the house, a widower of, say, fifty, invited the two of them to dinner. "We're going to have rabbit," he said. Both accepted the invitation though each was secretly skeptical about rabbit. It was delicious. After dinner, as the evening wore on, Bill asked the host, "Would you mind if I rolled out my sleeping bag in the snow along your walk?"

The host laughed, "You're sleeping in a bed tonight, young man. The maid is already heating water to put in the bathtub." Bill made some feeble protestations to the effect he wasn't used to beds but was firmly overruled.

In Luxembourg City, one morning, Eldon was crossing, on foot, a seldom-used bridge when he met a young priest. The cleric asked Eldon if he would accompany him to an American field hospital nearby. His brother was in there wounded, but the priest, being a civilian and unable to speak English, had been denied entrance. The two were admitted without any trouble at all. It was Eldon's only visit to a hospital after a major battle. He was impressed: by the number of seriously wounded soldiers, by the height and sight of the pile of removed bandages, by the sounds of pain, by the quiet efficiency of the nurses as they went about their duties. Death had stricken two comrades of Eldon's, just over a hedgerow from him, before the Third Army galloped south out of Normandy, but that had been so sudden and final, so different.

Eldon and his colonel, though in Luxembourg City but a short time, became friends of the Cure of the Cathedral. He, perhaps thinking they were more important cogs in the American military machine than they were—or perhaps indifferent absolutely to such things—invited Colonel Embry (a Catholic of sorts) and Eldon to a small dinner where they met the Prime Minister and Foreign Minister of the delightful little country, "le pays des anges," the country of angels. It was the high point of their various evenings with the Cure.

They had plunged into Germany but had not yet crossed the Rhine when Eldon, now Major Jones, was ordered to take a "rest leave." He wanted to remain till the Rhine had been crossed. No. He preferred to go to Paris. No. He was to be on a plane that was taking a group of "restees" to Cannes. The sojourn on the Mediterranean Sea was a wonderful change. The opportunity to relax was good for Eldon, too. He knew a sergeant who had gone to pieces, nervously, and been evacuated through medical channels. When Eldon returned to Headquarters, the Third Army was across the Rhine.

One time as Eldon and his driver were hot-rodding on a mission in a jeep, along one of the superhighways called an autobahn, they passed a woods. "Look," Eldon said pointing to a line-up of planes half-hidden under the shadow of the trees, "no propellers."

"Those are jet planes."

"What?"

"Jet planes the krauts invented. Don't you know? Got no propellers."

"Oh, yes. Never saw any before this. They look like that—like a headless horseman."

Then it was decided that Bavaria, not Berlin, was to be their objective. As everyone knew, the war in Europe was hastening to a close. Eldon was to meet Colonel

Embry in Regensburg (Ratisbon in French) on the Danube late in the day on May 8th. As the colonel descended from his jeep, he said, "This is it." Eldon knew what was meant. The Germans had surrendered. It was VE Day.

General Patton wanted to lead an army against Japan. Before he went home to see President Truman about such a command, he told his staff: "I promise you this. If I go, you go." President Truman turned thumbs down on the General's proposal. Eldon had been less than enthusiastic about the "promise" anyway.

Incidentally, Eldon had been in Paris a month or so before VE Day. He had gone as a courier to deliver a message to General Eisenhower. He was not, as he had supposed, to see General Eisenhower and personally deliver the message. He did deliver the letter to a general at Ike's Headquarters who said, "I'll take it."

Early the next morning, around six o'clock, Eldon was walking toward the officers' mess for breakfast. Few people, civilians, were on the street, but Eldon sensed that something was wrong. For one thing, a number were reading newspapers as they walked. Then he caught a glimpse of the headline: "Roosevelt Est Mort." That was the cause of the stunned grief he witnessed about him. He wondered if his own countrymen were as deeply touched by the President's passing.

The Third Army became an army of occupation. Everybody was marking time until it was his turn to go home. Eldon heard the Munich Symphony play Dvorak's "From the New World." He managed to get to Salzburg (by way of Berchtesgaden) for an evening of festival music. He saw the theatrical facilities at Oberammergau (but not the passion play) and looked over the resort city of Garmisch-Partenkirchen. He made a cursory inspection of Marshal Goering's captured art collection. He thrilled to the fall change in the color of the foliage in the Alps. His duties, alas, took him a number of times to Dachau, one of the Nazis' infamous extermination camps. He beheld General Patton's enforced good bye to the Third Army and attended General Truscott's first staff conference as Georgie's successor.

Then it was his turn to begin the homeward journey. The first stage of his trip was a Replacement Depot in a desolate mining region of Northern France. While there, Eldon went to Luxembourg City, to make sure, maybe, his friendship with the Cure had not been a dream. On his arrival in the city, in a central marketplace, a number of unknown women, of varying ages, lavished kisses on the surprised Eldon. It turned out he was the fortunate recipient of the love and gratitude those women bore America. That day a large contingent of Luxembourgeois had arrived back from German prison camps.

When the Cure saw Eldon, he kissed him on both cheeks. They were friends all right. Those evenings together some months ago were not a dream, after all. They were real.

A troop train bore him, them all, to Marseille. There these soldiers of the Republic, these veterans of European campaigns, boarded an army transport ship. Their course took them westward on the Mediterranean, through the Straits of Gibraltar, across the broad Atlantic to land at Boston. Another troop train continued the westward trek, dropping cars at big cities as it went along. At Denver, Eldon and his Colorado comrades got off. The train went on.

The soldier was home, free to see his wife and his eighteen-months old son. He was home, and he was free but not yet a civilian in the same sense he had been one some three years before. That would take time. A farewell to arms is a slow process, not a quick wave of the hand.

V. The Descent into the Maelstrom

The year 1946 was a year of beginnings for thirty-five year-old Eldon Jones. He was back from the Crusade in Europe—back in the civilian clothing he had doffed in 1942—back in the Capital City on the Potomac that he had left as a draftee.

He had left these familiar surroundings as a bachelor. He returned with a wife and an eighteen-months-old son. Previously an apartment-house tenant, he now was a suburban householder with a GI loan. Once a humble civil servant who drank beer with his colleagues before he went home, he now belonged to a car pool that departed for the Maryland suburb promptly at five after five o'clock. There were millions of veterans, but, Eldon, in spite of himself, had a reputation as a war hero.

Eldon was still a lawyer but no longer a government attorney. He had a new job, Secretary of the Glick Art Museum, a foundation set up by a retired millionaire brewer from Cincinnati. The founder had bought a grand residence on Massachusetts Avenue just off Dupont Circle, installed his art collection in it, called it a museum (mainly for art students), endowed the institution, and left the peculiar business in charge of Gil Carreau, the Director. There was a Chief Curator, too, a respectable gentleman named Clell Putney, who formerly had been Mr. Glick's valet. Eldon, the third man of the triumvirate, was chosen for his vague duties by Gil Carreau.

Once, as a teen-aged busboy at the Oslo Cafe in Minneapolis, Eldon had been vexed by the dearth of dishes to be stacked in trays and carried to the kitchen. He had quit the job in favor of one with the busy Elgin Marbles Cafe. But Eldon had come a long way since then. He now made work for himself: consulted with Gil on the slightest pretext and pointed out the potential legal dangers in everything around and about the Glick Museum. Waxed floors in the galleries? People slip and fall on them. This necessitates careful procedures lest the Museum be sued. The books are full of "slippery floor cases." Gil agreed. It was easier that way, and it kept Eldon happy. Gil didn't expect Eldon to leave the Glick Museum as he had left the Oslo Cafe. No other place would pay so much for so little. Eldon knew that too, and now he had a family to support.

Eldon piddled on some lawsuits, but Mr. Glick's own lawyers had the chief responsibility for these. An ex-wife of Mr. Glick claimed the old boy had wronged her somehow when he transferred his art collection and money to the Glick Art Museum without getting anything in return. Because of the Glick's restrictions on public attendance, the taxing authorities of the District of Columbia kept challenging the Museum's tax exemption. An artist discharged before his term of employment expired sued for breach of contract. It seemed Mr. Glick had signed him up for a year's service as an educator before learning the inacceptable fact that the brilliant Mr. Podesta was a Socialist with polygamous tendencies. Trying to be helpful, Mr. Putney indiscreetly told a little old lady from Louisville (in a letter) that the masterpiece she purchased in London was a fake, the frame of which was worth more than the picture. She sued. But Eldon did his part in these and other suits by giving off-the-cuff ideas and suggestions to Mr. Glick's lawyers when they called on occasion from Cincinnati.

At home, things went quietly, too. The Joneses now had a new son, Lloyd. They had a beautiful brick home on Endicott Street, which signified the house had been intended for Eldon from the beginning. His middle name was Endicott, though he seldom used it. He usually signed his name E. E. Jones. It was surprising how often people would ask, "What does E.E. stand for—Extraordinarily Excellent?"

Eldon couldn't get used to the strange world in which he lived. It was taken for granted he was a war hero, although he had said nothing to start that legend. He now began to doubt he had been decorated as the army's special orders read. Further, he was being paid more for negligible services than cabinet officers were paid for the onerous duties cast on them by the Cold War with Russia. Gil Carreau, whose abilities were inferior to Eldon's, was paid more by the Museum and cut a wider swath in society. Without wit or a sense of humor, and absolutely devoid of originality, Gil was made to shine on the TV quiz programs of that era. He also won rich prizes that way. Gossip columnists who calumniated others praised Gil as an authentic genius.

Eldon ceased to be comfortable alone in his private office. He feared some unknown enemy might brush aside his secretary and enter suddenly unannounced. He wasn't at ease, even when his secretary, demure and deferential, came in to take dictation. He was finding it increasingly difficult to draft a memorandum of procedure for the shipment of paintings or sculptures on loan with the same care as if the memo were an important state paper.

At home, he couldn't explain the difficulties of the day. Difficulties in a job almost without cares, not to mention crises? Then he began to have trouble sleeping.

He would awaken in a cold sweat—and would find his wife awake, afraid. He started seeing a psychiatrist. Thanks to the doctor, he suffered less from sleeplessness, but his sleep was haunted by nightmares. His days were calmer, but he made no effort to pretend there were important things to be done. He was too drained of strength and vitality to make the effort. His calm was that of exhaustion.

In the summer of 1949, he was feeling better. His wife took the two boys, David and Lloyd, on a vacation trip to see her family. Eldon was to join them later. Gil Carreau and Clell Putney—both of whom were ignorant of Eldon's malaise and supposed their able colleague was as stable as an elephant—took their vacations, leaving Eldon in charge of the Glick Museum for a month. The Jones's house on Endicott Street had only one house near it—the Johnson residence. The Johnsons, whom Eldon knew fairly well, had left for the seashore. Eldon was alone—quite alone, physically and emotionally.

He now was mocked in all his leisure moments—not at the office, fortunately, for he was temporarily kingpin there as Acting Director. He attended a performance by college players of *The Tempest,* and the monster Caliban was modeled after him, Eldon Jones. He would have to tell the psychiatrist that on his very next visit. After the theater, home alone, he remembered the awful scene in *King Lear* when one of the characters—he couldn't remember which nor find it in the text—had his eyes gouged out. He was sure that scene was in *Lear,* and he was certain his own punishment here below was predicted. Then there was Othello—a black man. Surely the English poet-playwright had looked down the centuries and foreseen E. E. Jones. Eldon's skin was white but by no means blond. In his ancestry somewhere—according to Shakespeare with whom Eldon agreed—there had been infusions of Negro blood. He had blue eyes? African violets are blue. Such dizzy, crazy, disjointed thoughts flicked, skittered, through his mind like scenes from one of those early, silent movies; and he could not sleep.

It is a wonder Eldon was capable of driving his car over to the psychiatrist's office the next morning, but he succeeded in keeping his early appointment. He told Dr. Langley of his newly-discovered identity, Caliban. The doctor wanted to think his patient was joking, but, alas, Eldon's intensity and conviction prevented any such suppositions: his intensity and conviction and his pitiable abasement; his plea for mercy.

Dr. Langley said, "But doesn't your good sense tell you better?"

"No."

Dr. Langley put in a long-distance call to Eldon's wife: "Come back." He called a local physician with whom Eldon had worked and gone to school years ago in Minnesota: "Come over." There was no struggle to get Eldon to a hospital. He was as aware he was sick somehow as he was convinced he was Caliban—and an African violet.

At the hospital, Eldon was given a physical examination by a young doctor whose verdict was "You're in perfect physical shape. I can't say the same for your mind." The patient, realizing he couldn't come and go as he pleased, supposed he was locked up for some heinous crime. He tried to imagine what that was, could be. He did not accept the doctor's pronouncement that his mind was awry, although he could see plainly that his fellow patients were quite erratic. He wasn't at all sure the young doctor was a doctor and not a prison official.

His wife called on the phone once in a while but seldom came to see him. "Doctors" went through the halls but at first scarcely noticed him. He was herded with other patients about the extensive, green grounds of the sanitarium. He saw beautiful fields of corn such as he had seen as a boy on the Minnesota farm. He saw a wondrous river like the one that had run along the boundary of Drowsy Hollow Farm, his boyhood home. It was a serene dream, in a sense, but was it to be endless? He demanded to see a doctor, any doctor. "Why certainly, Mr. Jones."

Dr. Hinton listened but said little. It was as if he had no more authority than the hospital attendants, those husky, white-suited young men who shepherded their charges in the wards, at meals, on the excursions around the hospital grounds. So Eldon was obliged to wait—to enjoy those pin-point sprays of alternating hot and cold water shot at him from a distance and called hydrotherapy. He bided his time at occupational therapy where he played around with high-speed power saws in the carpentry shop and contemplated suicide by sawing the arteries in his wrists. He felt certain his captors desired his self-destruction. In the leather-working shop he turned over in his mind projects for hanging himself with a rawhide thong from one of the building's overhead, horizontal steel beams. However, neither wrist slashing nor hanging appealed to him as a means of exit from his situation.

To drown in the river which ran along the edge of the hospital grounds—that was the way to take his leave. On a Sunday walk with other patients and the ever-present attendants, Eldon made a break for it. He was caught just short of the river's brink. No one asked him what he intended to do. They knew. A panel of doctors was assembled to ask him why he sought to do anything so final, so permanent. As if they didn't know, thought Eldon. As if they didn't want just that. Or, did they, perchance, covet for themselves the infliction of the fatal blow?

The next day two attendants escorted Eldon to a room which was empty except for a narrow hospital cot. They told him they wanted to tie him to the cot and give him a shot of insulin. "No." He refused to cooperate. Some more attendants arrived on the scene, and the struggling Eldon was tied down on his back—with feet and arms spread. "This is it," Eldon said to himself. "This is the end."

After this first, experimental or test shot of insulin, Eldon submitted to the others which were given every day for more than a month. At least, he had breakfast in bed when he awakened from the deep coma; and what good breakfasts they were; and what delicious fruit juice. After breakfast, all the insulin patients showered, which was all right. Lunch came soon afterward, and before long Eldon was beginning to feel overfed and sluggish. Accordingly, he objected to taking the pill that was offered just before lunch. "What's it for?"

"To sharpen your appetite." It was the pretty, short, blue-eyed nurse who spoke. However, a pugnacious-looking but little attendant was hurrying up.

"I already have a good appetite."

Now Eldon's arms were seized from behind by an attendant he hadn't seen coming up. The other attendant, the slight bantam rooster, said, "Now take your pill!" The nurse put the pill in Eldon's mouth, and he, giving up the fight, swallowed it.

Toward the end of the course of insulin treatments, the thick fog, the all-enveloping gray mist in which he had moved and had his being during the past months began to dissipate and rise and clear away. He commenced, too, to see one of the hospital doctors regularly. He told Dr. Haigler, "My nose is tender, and a little blood comes out."

"Yes. That's from the electric shocks you're given."

"I thought I was getting insulin shock."

"Yes, both."

Later, on one of his periodical visits to Dr. Haigler, he complained, "One of my ribs hurts. It feels like it's broken."

"Yes. One of your vertebrae is broken from the shock treatment. I think it will be all right. Let me know if it doesn't get better."

Spring had come. He had the freedom of the hospital grounds unattended now. He could wander along the river and watch the swans gliding on it. Daffodils tossed their heads "in sprightly dance." Birds sang. Nature exulted.

A few visitors came to call. Eldon's wife, Millie, made several calls. She was tense, nervous, restless. She had undergone great hardship with Eldon away. Their money in the bank had melted away—much of it. His salary, thank goodness, had continued. She even had received a kind note from Mr. Glick. Gil Carreau, on his way to a weekend with some TV celebrities, stopped by. "I suppose you'll be getting out soon," Gil said, as if Eldon had been serving a term in the state penitentiary.

"I hope so."

"I'm sure you will. You're looking tip-top."

"Thank you."

When Eldon saw Dr. Haigler, he asked, "Will I be allowed to go home soon?"

"Maybe. There are a few things you ought to know first."

"What?"

"For one thing, you won't have a job."

"I just saw Gil. He didn't say a thing about that."

"He asked me to tell you."

"I see."

"That's enough for today. You think about it."

The two discussed Eldon's leaving the hospital on a trial visit at length during several consultations. Eldon insisted he was ready to leave.

"What about a job?"

"I'll get a new one. I want a new one, anyway."

"It might not be easy to get one."

"It won't be easy. I know that."

"How long has it been since you've seen your folks in Minnesota?"

"Several years."

"Will you go and see them if you're given a trial visit?"

"Yes."

"I told you once there were several things you needed to know before you left the hospital on a trial visit."

"Yes."

"One is that you don't have a job."

"Yes."

"But we haven't yet talked about your wife."

"What about her?"

"I think she wants to leave you. I discouraged that idea, but I don't think she was convinced. She had consulted Dr. Langley and another doctor he suggested. She's talked it over with a few friends. I have a hunch everyone advised her to stick to you. I don't know what she's finally decided; but you ought to know she might not be there when you get home, or the children, either."

"I haven't seen the boys in all this time."

"I know."

"I hadn't figured on this."

"I know."

In the middle of May, Eldon went home on a trial visit. The house was full of furniture, but his family was gone he knew not where. There was no note on the mantle, no note anywhere. He figured he'd find out where they were in God's good time. He went to Minnesota. He came back in two weeks. He got a new job, though not right away, though not at high pay. He located his family that fall. He made a comeback, but not without delay, anguish, and heartache. But all that is another story.

Few descend into the maelstrom; fewer return. Eldon Jones did both. None of those who escape is ever the same afterward. Nor was Eldon. It didn't matter. He had come up from the depths. That was enough; enough for hallelujahs.

VI. Father and Sons

When Eldon Jones had recovered from his nervous breakdown sufficiently to be released from the hospital conditionally "on a trial visit," he found himself without a job, with his wife and two sons fled to parts unknown, with a crippled bank account. For the time being, he lived in the family residence on Endicott Street in one of Washington's Maryland suburbs. He had been in the hospital for almost a year, and the grip of old habits and old associations and friendships had been loosened if not broken. Naked came he into the world, and now he was starting again from scratch.

He found a job in the least likely of places—the Internal Revenue Service. He never really understood how it was that the hard-headed officials of that Service would take a chance (really not so great) on him. He was an egghead, which was against him, was in his late thirties whereas the System's recruitment was aiming for young men, young lawyers. Finally, he had a medical history which was enough to alarm the most timid (which is to say most) employers. Dr. Haigler, his doctor at the hospital, had recommended him for the job without qualification. That he knew. Friends of his in the Service may have said a few kind words. Maybe somebody up there liked him. Anyway, he went to work in August, 1950.

On the Labor Day weekend, he made a trip to Lexington, Kentucky, the capital of the horse country. He cared very little about race horses, but he had a hunch he might find his family in that vicinity, for his wife had friends there. He was too late. They had been there but had gone to Colorado to be nearer her folks and further from him, Eldon. Well, he knew where they weren't and where, in all likelihood, they were. He went back to Washington and his job.

At Christmas time, Eldon made the trip to Sonora Springs, Colorado, by railroad day coach. He stayed at a motor court just a few blocks from the house which he had bought years ago. His two sons—David, six and a half, and Lloyd, four—were overjoyed to see him. They often came to his place to see him, bringing with them the only police dog, Jeff, Eldon ever really knew and liked. Jeff would sleep outside Eldon's first-floor door overnight (according to the proprietors of the motel) and not leave till morning. It was a happy reunion in Sonora Springs.

Grandpa was now in the hospital, but David and Lloyd would not permit their father to visit him there. Eldon understood. A hospital had accounted for their long separation and the boys weren't going to take any chances that this hospital in Sonora Springs might detain their father as had the one in Maryland.

It took Eldon a year to wangle a transfer to the Kansas City office of the Internal Revenue Service. At the time, that was the closest office to Sonora Springs with a job for Eldon. How Eldon appreciated the tax-gathering service which, by the oddest chance, had employed him. His visits to Sonora Springs still had to be rare and relatively brief, but he was much closer to his sons than before the transfer, and he felt closer.

Eldon stayed in Kansas City a year. During that time, his wife, Millie, obtained a divorce. By agreement, Eldon deeded to her the house in which she had been living with David and Lloyd and gave her the custody of the boys. He retained only, as the decree put it, "the right to visit them at reasonable times and places." With no wife now to cumber his title to the former family residence in Maryland, Eldon sold it and put the money in a selected list of stocks. He was homeless but not penniless.

Toward the end of 1952, the Truman Administration created a Revenue District Headquarters in Denver which needed several lawyers. This was a magnificent opportunity for Eldon to be still nearer to his two sons if he could be appointed to one of the positions in the Denver office. He pleaded his own case and won. He was transferred to Denver with the title of Chief Trial Attorney. The title was splendid, but trials were so few that he was the chief of only one trial attorney. Furthermore, the election of a Republican president in November made it doubtful whether the Denver District Headquarters created by the Democrats would be long-lived.

In six months the Eisenhower Administration abolished the Denver District Headquarters. Eldon refused to be transferred, and in another six months he was forced to resign. No matter. He had established a pattern of weekly visits to his sons in Sonora Springs—every Saturday—and he would let nothing disturb that arrangement. He opened an office for the practice of law in Denver. Clients stayed away in droves. His practice was a dud. He kept at it with a borrowed typewriter, a second-hand desk, a piddling collection of books.

So far as David and Lloyd knew, their father was "in the chips." When his fees were particularly meager, which was often, Eldon would liquidate one of the stocks he had purchased in Kansas City. As a rule, he waited before selling a stock until it was quoted at double the price he had paid. In this manner he made his slim portfolio last a number of years.

It was Eldon's custom to drive up to the boys' home in Sonora Springs at nine-thirty each Saturday morning. One fiercely stormy winter morning, he didn't arrive till about a quarter of ten. When he finally entered the driveway, David came out of the house and declared with disapproval, "You're late!"

On several occasions over the years, Eldon said, "I'm sorry I don't see you as much as other fathers see their sons." David or Lloyd would reply, "You do. You see us all day on Saturdays. That's more than other fathers do." They wouldn't admit they were in anyway underprivileged and evidently didn't consider that they were.

Eldon didn't feel at home in the house which had once been his. On his visits to the boys, they spent a minimal amount of time there. In the summer they would play baseball, play in a park, play at tennis. In the winter, they ice skated and (as the boys grew older) played hockey. Later they took up skiing—by no means an inexpensive sport. They went to the zoo. Eldon taught the boys to play ping pong and pool. He provided golf clubs and all types of sports equipment.

Once, on a Saturday morning, David found a letter addressed to him in the mail. It was a check from a newspaper syndicate for certain snapshots of animals he had made at the zoo. "Aw, shucks," he said. "I hoped it was an invitation to the newsboys' circus party."

Late one winter afternoon when about an inch of snow had fallen and the streets were slippery, Eldon's car collided with another. No one was hurt, and neither car was badly damaged. The three teenagers in the other car, however, were so nervous over the accident they couldn't write their names. When the police officer arrived, he asked Eldon to sit in the police car while he made notes for his report. David and Lloyd came up to the car in distress, and Lloyd said, "Well, Dad, you could at least give us bus fare to get home."

Eldon laughed. "Why I'm not going anywhere. You guys get in the back seat." He opened the back door of the police car for them. They got in with relief. The tension was released, broken.

Not often, but at intervals, one or the other of the boys would ask their father, "How should I be different?" Eldon began by treating the question lightly and singing "Stay just as you are." Since the question was repeated, he realized his answer wasn't satisfying. The next time the question popped up, he replied, "Oh, I guess if you, Davey, were more like Lloyd and Lloyd were more like you, that would be OK." After that, the question was forgotten; it never recurred.

Lloyd asked, "Dad, if you suddenly got a great big fee—a million dollars—what would you do then?"

"Oh, I don't know. But remember this: If I get dough, you have dough!" Both Davey and Lloyd understood. They all three laughed.

One summer day when Eldon arrived in Sonora Springs, only Davey was home. Lloyd came up a few minutes later with a neighbor boy. Eldon put his arm gently around Lloyd and, after a pause, said, "Lloyd, you know you're too young to smoke."

"I know it." Lloyd moved away. Then he asked reflectively, "How'd you know I'd been smoking?"

"And you smelling like a smokestack?"

In the middle of one May, Davey said, "Dad, do you know what I did yesterday afternoon?"

"You were in school, weren't you?"

"No. Clyde Fitchett and I and Duane Carter walked along Florissant Creek."

"Oh." Eldon made no further comment. He appreciated Davey's frankness and was sure his older son wouldn't make a practice of playing hooky.

At an afternoon baseball game in Springer Stadium, these three musketeers were spectators. Lloyd noticed, among other things, the bulging cud in the cheeks of some of the players. "Dad," he said, "you wouldn't mind if I tried out a plug of tobacco some time, would you?"

"You mean you just want to find out what it's like and then quit?"

"Yes."

"No. Go ahead. Find out what it's like some time and then quit."

"I will."

Two of Davey's sixteen-year-old friends, Clyde and Bob, joined the three of them one time on a trip to a ski area, twenty-five or thirty miles away. They sat in the back seat with Davey. As the car—without snow tires or chains—climbed the snow-slick, winding mountain highway, Davey's friends kept talking endlessly about girls and sex in vivid, concrete, earthy terms. Eldon suspected they were trying to elicit some comment from him, but, preoccupied with keeping the car from going over one of the steep banks, he didn't know just what to say. Finally, he interrupted their palaver. "That's right, fellows, go ahead and talk sex. Talk, talk, talk. A good fuck would kill you." The boys laughed uproariously for minutes. Then they turned their conversation to other subjects, and the car continued its steep, slippery, hairpin course to its destination.

In time, Eldon's clientele dwindled to one retainer: a Wall Street financial house, Skinner-Wetmore, which consulted him from time to time by phone or mail about the Denver aspects of its transactions. The retainer was not a living. While Eldon never said so, the boys apparently realized it. Lloyd, who seemed to speak for his brother as well as himself, kept saying such things as "Skinner-Wetmore is a big outfit, isn't it? Skinner-Wetmore sends you a lot of money, doesn't it? Next year, you'll probably get more from Skinner-Wetmore, won't you?"

Eldon answered his son's questions as best he could to allay fear. He didn't have fear himself. Yet, he knew, too, he couldn't go on indefinitely with only one good, regular client. He had sold all the stocks he owned and, by this time, had surrendered most of his life insurance policies for cash. He applied for a modest, supremely modest, job with a publishing house in the small city in which his sons lived with their mother. He got the job and moved closer to his boys than he had been in the ten years since his release from the hospital.

Davey was now in high school. He was a handsome, blond boy. To look at him was to see, in the mind's eye, the tow-headed tiny tot he once had been. When Lloyd became of high school age and began to grow, he seemed to cast off many of his chief physical characteristics. He always had been rather short and heavy-set. He became tall—taller than his brother—and thin. He remained brunet, but his face, once almost swarthy, seemed paler. Davey always had been first in his class at school—always. Not until Lloyd was in college did he realize the same honor could be his (at which time he reached out and seized it).

Davey came often, after his high school classes, to visit his father. Only when he was in college, about fifty miles away, did Lloyd show a similar appreciation of his father's company. Then he took advantage of every opportunity to visit. By that time, Davey was a student at Harvard College on a scholarship. Lloyd was destined to go to a distant eastern university for his post-graduate work (on a fellowship). In a remarkably short time Eldon was the father of grown sons. His burden of care and support, which really hadn't been a burden, was less, but the joy of leading and teaching two healthy young boys of intelligence and good will—that immense and inestimable joy—had vanished forever.

A Case for Commitment

How often do I go to the library? About as often as I go to the Notions section on the second floor of Gosling's department store. Buttons, needles, snaps, frilly pieces of ribbon and the like just don't ignite my engines, if you know what I mean. Now, a hardware store: that's different. I could spend hours looking over the necessary tools and implements needed to keep things working like they ought to. Things like chisels, T-squares, trowels, plumb bobs, and the many other indispensible tools needed to get the job done.

But the library: even the building repels me. The Sonora Springs library is housed in a cold, gray stone structure that looks like a small fortress, the kind you might see in Europe somewhere, with worn granite steps leading up to its huge wooden doors with massive bronze door handles and hinges capable of deterring any unwanted after-hours intruders. (As if anybody would ever want to go there at that time). Inside is just as forbidding. Solid oak. A large front desk with oaken card-catalogue file cabinets on either end guards the entry. And the librarian, a middle-aged woman with a stern look of utmost seriousness, keeps watch on the comings and goings. Behind her, a large chandelier casts a dim light over two long oak reading tables with their wooden straight-back chairs and green table lamps. Off to the side in a dimly lit cavernous room are rows and rows of bookshelves, laden with musty tomes seldom read by even the most ardent pedant.

The occasion of my rare visit to this vault of knowledge, this fortress of wisdom, was to read about a little known court case during the Dachau trials brought to my attention by Seymour Minefeld, my partner in the law firm of Minefeld, Spookes, and Smith. When I say little-known, I mean less well-known to most people than the famous Nuremburg trials, but I knew a lot, in fact too much, about them. You see, I had been there—Dachau, I mean—during my years in the army as a member of the Judge Advocate General's Corps. Minefeld said that I should definitely read what he found to be a particularly amusing account of one particular hearing that referred to events in Dachau shortly after the war. "You might enjoy reading about it," he said. "I doubt it. I don't really enjoy reading about Dachau," I replied. But, to appease my trusted partner in law (I almost said "crime"), I decided to spend an afternoon at the library.

After searching the card catalogue in this asthmatic chamber of knowledge, I found the book I was looking for: *A Layman's History of the Dachau Trials and Related Events* by Dr. Magnus Marigold. I started scanning the weighty book, and after a half hour or so, I found the hearing recommended by Minefeld. As I read amidst the tomb-like silence, despite Marigold's irreverent wit, drowsiness quickly numbed my mind, sending it into a realm of dreamy sub-consciousness. Nevertheless, periodically I pulled back briefly to full consciousness, only to realize the need to re-read the last several paragraphs. I read on, taking mental notes to help me digest Marigold's account of the gristly meat of the case. To the best of my recollection, it started out thusly:

His Honor was looking over the report of the Lunacy Commission and the stenographic transcript of the testimony of witnesses a little wearily. With an election campaign looming on the horizon, he begrudged even the meager attention he was required to bestow upon these relatively unimportant matters. He had no choice under the law but to approve the report of the Commission. But then the attorney for the unfortunate person could ask for a jury review of a commitment order. Besides, there was the possible necessity of a conservator of the incompetent's property—a question which the state legislature in its wisdom had not delegated to any commission but had vested securely in the County Court itself. His Honor Hendrik van Fossil, the judge of the court, would be the last to shirk or minimize the task of appointing a worthy conservator.

Yes, the Commission had found, with that liberal sprinkling of whereases which take the place in legal documents of the hems and haws of social conversation, that the defendant, Dr. Franz Lieber, was by reason of mental illness and distraction unable properly to manage and take care of himself, was likely to be imposed upon by artful or designing persons, and ought, therefore, to be committed to a hospital for care until such time as he regained his competency. Yes, the respondent did have property; and Judge van Fossil blinked a bit when he saw the estimated value of it. He'd have to be careful in appointing a conservator of the estate.

In view of the limited responsibilities in cases of commitment, Judge van Fossil was in the habit of doing no more than peep at the transcript of the testimony before the Commission. This case was different; it claimed the attention in spite of all. For some reason, the importance of the impending election campaign and the host of decrees and orders waiting to be signed vanished completely from his mind. He pored over the questions and answers before him with even more avidity than he reserved for the detective stories with which he bemused himself at home.

Dr. Lieber, it appeared, had been born in Germany in 1906. He had studied medicine at Heidelberg and had finished his internship in Berlin not long after Adolf Hitler was called to the helm of the unhappy country in 1933. Dr. Lieber married his childhood sweetheart, Maria Earhardt, and took his bride with him to the new post as a staff physician at the Dachau Concentration Camp. He had fled from his official station, leaving his attractive, childless wife behind him in 1936.

Earnest Jones, who was Dr. Lieber's attorney, questioned and cross-examined an expert witness, Dr. Goobers, about the defendant's mental unsoundness. Jones could always be counted upon to do a workmanlike job for his client.

Q. Now, Dr. Goobers, you consider Dr. Lieber's inability to carry on with the responsibilities of the post at Dachau as a significant symptom of his emotional instability, do you not?

A. It is but one of the circumstances on which I rely.

Q. Is it your opinion, Dr. Goobers, that the camp and station at Dachau in Bavaria represented such a perfect society that any man of sane and sound mind in Dr. Lieber's position should have made an effort to swim with the current of the social stream?

A. I would say that an endeavor to get along with his environment would be evidence of a more stable temperament than flight from the situation. Besides, it must be remembered that Dr. Lieber not only fled from his professional assignment, he also left his young and attractive wife.

Q. Is it not true, Dr. Goobers, that leaving an unhealthy and unfavorable setting is one way of adjusting to it?

A. Yes, that's true in a sense.

Q. It is true, is it not, that this country was largely inhabited in colonial days by people who had made that kind of adjustment to their European surroundings?

A. I'm sorry, Mr. Jones. But I do not believe I'm qualified to testify about national history. I came here for a different purpose.

Q. Do you know Maria Lieber?

A. No.

Q. Is she dead now?

A. So I've been told. She was killed in an aerial bombardment while visiting Munich. No, I believe Dr. Lieber said Nuremberg.

Q. Did Dr. Lieber tell you why he left Dachau without taking his wife with him?

A. He said she didn't want to go. She preferred to remain.

Q. Did he say why his wife wished to stay?

A. He thinks she was having an affair with a pal of Goering's who lived not far from Dachau. This suspicion of his wife and with the propriety of her relations with this much older man, Arnold Hanft, fits into the pattern of distrust of society and impatience of the authority of age and the established order which characterizes one who is suffering from Dr. Lieber's type of illness.

Q. You don't know that Mrs. Lieber's attitude towards Arnold Hanft was above reproach, do you?

A. And neither do I know that it wasn't.

Q. Was Hanft an official superior of Dr. Lieber at Dachau?

A. That's not what I've been told. If Dr. Lieber is to be trusted here—I mean credited—Hanft was not connected with Dachau at all in the thirties. He was married to a woman, Elsa, much younger than he. He owned a factory for making contact lenses—for the eyes, you know—at Halle or Kassel or someplace up there in northern and more or less eastern Germany. He and his wife had a summer home at Tegernsee in Bavaria. He met Dr. and Mrs. Lieber while he and Elsa were spending a vacation at their summer home.

The judge pondered as he read. What was the name of the hated German official at Leyden, in the Netherlands during the war, that his own Dutch relatives had told him about when he visited them last year? Wasn't that Hanft, and wasn't he a buddy of Goering? Of course, the German occupation of the Netherlands had begun four years or so after the Liebers separated. What a coincidence if the Hanft and Maria in this case were the same Hanft and Maria of which his relatives had spoken. Judge van Fossil adjusted his pince-nez, rimless glasses and turned back to the transcript.

Q. You have diagnosed Dr. Lieber's trouble as that of a split personality, Dr. Goober?

A. That's correct.

Q. Something like Dr. Jekyll and Mr. Hyde?

A. Yes, something like it. If you wish a literary reference, I should say that Dr. Lieber oscillates between reacting like Don Quixote and behaving in the manner of Sancho Panza.

Q. I take it, Dr. Goobers, that insofar as Dr. Lieber resembles Sancho in his relish for folk sayings and in his concern for the creature comforts and the edible, earthy fruits of life here below, he is quite sane and sound?

A. Oh yes, no doubt of it. He is quite well adjusted to that extent.

Q. But he resembles Don Quixote with his lack of adjustment as he attempted simultaneously or alternatively to live in the clouds?

A. That's one way of expressing it—in the cloudland of the past, like Don Quixote.

Q. Don Quixote foolishly imagined that the age of chivalry was not dead, as I remember Cervante's novel.

A. Precisely—that it was not past and that he was living in it.

Q. In what way, superficially, has Dr. Lieber followed the example of Don Quixote?

A. In more ways than one. For example, he labors under the delusion that his wife, Maria, wronged him by giving herself to Arnold Hanft, a well-to-do married man. Nevertheless, Dr. Lieber made substantial remittances to her from this country from 1936 until about the time of Pearl Harbor or perhaps a little earlier when it became impossible to send money to Germany.

Q. Dr. Lieber's irresponsible desertion of Maria, as you put it, is, in your opinion, one of the evidences of his incompetency, is it not?

A. I have so testified.

Q. The financial arrangements he made for her, after leaving Germany, likewise are symptomatic of mental or emotional illness on his part.

A. That's right.

Q. He has a guilt complex?

A. That's part of it. He has a deep sense of personal worthlessness and a powerful urge, at the same time, toward a feeling of dignity and self-respect. Such conflicting tendencies are not uncommon in patients suffering as Dr. Lieber does.

The judge smiled. He was accustomed to having each of the adverse parties stress how some of the various, assorted, stray bits of evidence pointed to a conclusion in his favor. The medical profession, or at least the psychiatric branch of it, had improved on this technique used routinely by lawyers. In that specialized science, apparently, contrasting pieces of evidence, the various different footprints in the sand, all pointed in the same direction. The desired conclusion drew evidence to it, instead of *vice versa;* it was like the deflection of a compass needle from true north by the hunted, ferrous ores beneath the surface of the earth.

The judge meditated. There were more points of similarity between law and psychiatry than he had thought. Psychiatry dealt with conflicting tendencies. He did too. His own headaches often were caused by conflicting decisions of the higher courts, which he had to reconcile and apply. Finding these decisions in the first place necessitated considerable research into the murky, musty, buried past, and then his reconciliations, like those of other judges, had to be woven from the sheerest, insubstantial gossamer filaments only obtainable by flights into the airy realm of abstraction—a sort of legal, and therefore legitimate, counterpart of what Dr. Goobers had called cloudland. Rattled, the judge made a brusque return to the transcript.

Q. You have considered Dr. Lieber's failure to mesh his gears, figuratively speaking, with those of Nazi

Germany as a symptom of his insanity, have you not, Dr. Goobers?

A. Certainly.

Q. You consider his sense of guilt as a symptom?

A. Yes.

Q. But if he lacked a feeling of guilt, he would be out of tune with all the good folks who, individually in some instances and collectively in others, make a religious duty and a ritual of confessing their guilt and sense of sin?

A. I assure you there's a difference, Mr. Jones.

Q. Wouldn't Dr. Lieber be out of harmony with the spirit of the times if he did not have a strong feeling of his own worthlessness which requires self-effacement and compliance with the social dictates of law, custom, and convention?

A. Dr. Lieber fails to see his way out of the abyss. The ordinary hobo on skid row realizes that a new suit of clothes, money in the bank, a salaried job, and above all a new car, would do wonders for him; would put him on a pedestal of social approval; give him a value as an individual which would make him an object of envy to all his old comrades. Dr. Lieber lacks the vision, the perception, the simple understanding of the hobo. You see?

Q. The value you mention, Dr. Goobers, is not in the poor pilgrim himself, but in the clothes and so forth, isn't that right?

A. No. In your profession, Mr. Jones, the law is always right; in politics, the voice of the people is the voice of God. *Vox populi, vox Dei*. In the field of mental health and sanity, what we call society is the supreme arbiter of value. I am held and firmly bound as the lawyers say—yes, committed, you might say, Mr.

Jones—to that view of things, to that theory of psychological science.

Now, in the eyes of society, cars and clothes make the man. The value of clothing (whether it be a natty sport coat, a judicial robe, or a woman's flowered hat) is imparted in a mysterious way—and I am sure that science will explain away the mystery in time—to the individual who wears it. It's as simple as that.

Judge van Fossil nodded his vigorous agreement. His own value had been demonstrated emphatically time and again at the polls. He felt a new assurance about the results of the forthcoming election campaign and, simultaneously, a resurgence of the fighting spirit he needed to win the battle of ballots and to prove his own worth to himself. He put the transcript into its file jacket with his decision. He could ignore any corroborating testimony; that guy Goobers was a master—he had made his point clearly. It was an absolutely plain case for commitment, but signing the order could wait. He tossed the file onto a work table and, lugging the folds of his robe close to his sides, the judge turned abruptly, almost violently, toward the statistics on his desk which showed the number and variety of petitions filed and acted upon since the last election.

I must confess that I was interrupted by a sharp rap on the table that startled me, waking me from what must have been a sound sleep. Standing over me, the librarian motioned to the large grandfather clock and said, with no hint of humor, "The library closes in five minutes." I set the book aside, pulled on my coat and scarf, and hurried outside into the fresh air. During the walk home, I pondered what must have been a dream: a judge, a defendant, a prosecutor, Dachau. Dachau—good grief! A feeling of nausea came over me. It would be a long time before I returned to this hall of knowledge to complete my chosen task. I'm sure that Marigold would never know and Minefeld would understand.

Cathcart at St. Helena

All the tenants were given notice to move on or before January first. This was not unexpected, and the eviction letter was sent out in mid-October, so there was plenty of time to look around for a new apartment. The change would be harder on Allen Cathcart than on the others, because he worked for the landlord, in a way, and was getting a special rate for that reason. It would be difficult for everyone, however, for the Meriwether Apartments were the most conveniently located of any in Sonora Springs.

The building had been owned for the past five years by a church congregation, and it had been marked during all that time as the site of a new church as soon as the financing and other business arrangements were settled. Now, those details were in order, and the landmark would have to come down to make way for the city's first church construction on the edges of downtown in fifty years. Sonora Springs was growing, and not only in the suburbs.

Allen didn't bother to look around much. He had been in the Meriwether Apartments for five years, but he knew where he wanted to live, he knew values, and he had made up his mind about the maximum rent he would pay. He decided to try out the St. Helena. It was centrally situated, spacious, reasonable, and had a car port. The neighborhood wasn't perfect—a nondescript conglomeration, which included huge, ancient residences, some converted into rooming and boarding houses and some still family homes. The St. Helena was old, but it rubbed shoulders with buildings so new as to be completely air-conditioned and to have the stairways visible through glass according to the current, inexplicable fashion and taste.

The adjoining buildings were so close, in fact, that the residents of the St. Helena who did not have a front or back exposure received very little daylight. Allen Cathcart decided he could overlook that disadvantage. He would be at the office during the daylight hours, anyway. Soon after he took the apartment, however, the Sunday School weekly for which he worked decided that it would be unnecessary for so dependable a member of the staff as Allen to fight traffic morning and night, day after day; it would be enough for him to come in once or twice a week. For the rest, he could make use of the mails.

Allen's most valued contributions to the Sunday School paper were tiny little tales, sometimes for children, sometimes for grownups, which pointed a neat moral. He also wrote, primarily for his own satisfaction, nonfiction articles extolling the importance of immortality and, now and then, these articles would be included in the missionary monthly. The subject of life after death was a favorite with Allen, and he deplored that the theme had lost its old-time fascination, popularity, and esteem.

Allen lived on the first floor of the St. Helena. There were six apartments on each floor of the three-story structure and one in the basement, at the rear. His was apartment four, on the south side between two and six.

He made no inquiries, before he moved in, about his neighbors. Afterwards, he learned that the tenants in apartment two had made their home there for twenty years. The man was a mechanic at a garage, his wife an employee of some sort at a hospital. The inhabitant of six was a partially disabled veteran of World War II, about Allen's age, fortyish. He was a bachelor, like Allen, and he told Allen that he supplemented his VA pension by the telephone solicitation of new female pupils, not necessarily volunteers, for a studio which gave lessons in ballroom dancing.

Allen could see from the names on the mail boxes at the front entrance of the building that a Mr. and Mrs. Haskins dwelt in number one. Evidently, Mr. Haskins' better-half had taken special notice of Allen and was quite satisfied with him and his respectability so long as he had followed the practice of going to the church's publication office every day to cudgel his brains and do his regular stint with pencil and typewriter. Her husband's habits were similar. When Allen began to stay home all day and to go and come at irregular hours, from the back door or the front door as it suited the whim of the moment, Mrs. Haskins must have been either beside herself with rage and curiosity or frantically determined not to let a rare romantic opportunity slip by for lack of initiative. He figured this out little by little.

Simultaneously with his ceasing to leave for the office by the front door about eight-fifteen each morning from Monday through Friday, his mail box began to bulge with mail after almost every daily delivery. This fact, presumably, did not escape Mrs. Haskins' attention. She would crack her door open, noisily, as soon as he had mounted the front steps, passed the threshold, and was retreating down the corridor looking over the morning haul and sorting mail from the office from other junk mail. He speculated that Mrs. Haskins speculated that he was engaged in a mail-fraud scheme. The janitor who lived in the basement apartment "chanced" to be coming out of the Haskins' abode a number of times as Allen's footsteps in the hallway proclaimed that he was going to take inventory of what the postman had left that morning.

Allen realized, of course, that he could have put an end to the inquisitive interest in his affairs by the simple expedient of catching the janitor by the lapels of his coveralls and pouring out his heart to the fellow. He did not choose to do so. The wiles of the amateur detectives disgusted and annoyed him more than they amused him, but he refused to take the steps which would have ended the farce.

He spoke of the situation to a friend or two. One of them, a man of the world, suggested that the crude, ambiguous gestures made by Mrs. Haskins, or carried out by stooges at her prompting, did not signify suspicion at all. Maybe, being home all day herself, Mrs. Haskins hankered for a little extramarital adventure. Maybe she had an unmarried sister for whose stock a market remained to be discovered. Allen's own, special lady-friend smiled knowingly when he told her of his neighbors, but she was noncommittal. If she understood their motives, as she implied, she wasn't going to give an explanation and risk being proved wrong by subsequent developments.

One evening, Allen's telephone rang. It was Stella Sanders, who lived in the apartment just overhead. "Do you live right above me?" Allen asked. He had wondered mildly who it was who lived there. He had supposed it was the tall, spare, dry-skinned old maid he had seen from time to time descending the back stairs en route to the carport. For some reason, he considered the name of his caller, Stella Sanders, as confirmation of the tentative identification he had made.

"Mr. Cathcart," Stella went on, "I just received the strangest telephone call. Someone just called me and said 'Check on your neighbor downstairs.' I was so flabbergasted, I didn't know what to say. I said 'Wha-a-at?' and the man replied 'All right, I'll repeat it: Check on your friend downstairs.'"

"Did it sound as if your caller meant that the neighbor on the floor below might be sick or in need of help?" Cathcart queried.

"No: it sounded as if he meant that something might be going on down there that ought not to be going on," Stella said.

"Did you ask who was calling?"

"No, I didn't. I was so flabbergasted I didn't know what to say. I've tried to call the Haskinses, but they aren't home. I tried to telephone the caretaker, too, but nobody answers there. Do you know if the caretaker is home?"

"I have no idea whether he is home or not. Didn't you ask what number your man was dialing?"

"No: as I say I was so flabbergasted, so frightened by it all."

"Well, of course, you were frightened—such a mysterious call. No doubt the guy got a wrong number. I wouldn't worry about it unless the fellow calls again. If that happens, get details. As it is, forget it. Don't worry about it."

The next day was Friday, the day Allen generally went to the office to get his pay-check and to have his confabs with his colleagues. The weather was so wonderful that he chose to take the bus this time and to walk back (which was downhill). When he returned from his errands, via the front door of the St. Helena, he stopped to pull a particularly large load of junk mail from its lodging place: nothing but junk. Hearing the Haskins' door opening, he involuntarily brought the bundle to his chest and, in spite of himself, concealed what he had in his hand under the flap of his opened jacket as if it were a precious secret he cherished mightily and dared not reveal or expose to others even slightly.

The head of a young woman was stuck out of the Haskins' doorway. "Oh, Mr. Cathcart," the stranger exclaimed, "are you going out? I've double-parked in the alley behind your car, but I'll get away in two jerks if you say so." Allen looked the girl over for an instant. She improved the shining moment by thrusting a chocolate into her mouth. "No," Allen replied with finality, "not right now." Then, like an old fraud, he continued down the hall, hugging to his chest a partially-hidden bundle filled exclusively with bank notes of the larger denominations.

A rapid shuffle of slippers coming to his ears told Allen that Mrs. Haskins had joined her friend at the doorway to watch after him. He increased the jauntiness of his gait and the swing of his hips and nonchalantly whistled the few bars that he remembered of an old song, "Love on an Island."

A Close Call

It was a beautiful June evening, just about dusk. Mr. Smith was walking north on Millimet with both hands clasped around the bottom of a bag of groceries bought at the supermarket on the edge of downtown Sonora Springs. Mr. Smith's younger son, Duane, was home from college for the summer and used the car in his work. As a consequence, the father occasionally had to do the family shopping the hard way. Everybody worked, including Mother; and, except for Dad, whose office was within walking distance, each breadwinner required a car to go to and from the job.

As Mr. Smith approached the inter section with Dale Street, he saw that two teen-age youths were doing likewise from the opposite direction. They would reach the curb on their side of Dale a bit before he arrived on his side. He couldn't, therefore, avoid a meeting with the pair by making a turn onto Dale. He didn't think of jay-walking across Millimet. He was uneasy about the approach of the strangers but not frightened out of his wits.

Just the same, Mr. Smith did not like what he saw. The taller of the two roughnecks was several inches less than average height. Both were slight. Their pants hung low on their hips and bagged around their ankles so that if their heels weren't tramping on the cuffs of their trousers, it was a wonder. They slumped along rather than walked, and, as they slouched, each smoked a cigarette as if he were experimenting with an unfamiliar and difficult art.

Before the new freeway was built, Millimet had been the main north-south thoroughfare through the small city of Sonora Springs. At times it still handled a lot of traffic. This was not one of those times. It was virtually deserted. Nevertheless, a pedestrian acquainted with the neighborhood, as Mr. Smith was, could be excused for not expecting to meet on an errand or a leisurely evening promenade a couple of young ruffians. There they were, all the same, headed his way.

Just as the two got to Dale Street, a car going east pulled up and paused for the stop sign. The taller of the two pedestrians called out, "You're a bloated bastard, you!"

Without a word, the driver of the car, with a quick effort, slid out from under the steering wheel to stand on the pavement. He was big, but by no means fat; and he was as tall as he was stout. Mr. Smith was surprised that a fellow so ordinary looking when sitting should be of such fierce and formidable proportions when standing. The half-pints were astounded as well.

"Heh, heh," the leader of them laughed nervously, "we were only kidding, just joking." Even in the twilight, they were pale to their long, hairy sideburns. Instead of going by the front of the car and so continuing their course past Mr. Smith, the frustrated partners hustled westward on Dale Street. The passenger in the car made a gesture as if to get out of the car but apparently gave up the project as not worth the exertion. The bull of a man called after his retreating adversaries, "Yeah ?" but, receiving no reply, he got back into the car and closed the door. Now, seeing Mr. Smith, and surmising the latter had witnessed the whole incident, he shook his head. Mr. Smith responded by shaking his head. The car drove away.

When Mr. Smith got home, Duane was already home, back with the car.

"That buggy would have come in handy for me a little while ago," Mr. Smith said.

"How is that?"

Mr. Smith told what he had seen. His son was silent for a minute. Then he said, "If you'd been driving, you might have been the one called a bloated bastard."

"Yes," Mr. Smith laughed. "As it was, I came damn close to insult, if not injury, if not to being robbed."

"The way you described them they were just a couple of punks," Duane said. "They couldn't have given you much trouble."

"It's precisely the punks who are dangerous," Mr. Smith argued. "It's the little fellows who travel in pairs and threes and who carry a knife or a gun."

"Still, you made them seem more pitiful and pathetic than anything else," Duane insisted.

Mr. Smith was surprised at the tack the talk had taken. "Hey, whose side are you on, anyway? Here your father had a narrow escape from a couple of amateur, abject thugs and you carry on as if I'm making a mountain out of a molehill. But for that Tony Galento coming along when he did, I might have been stabbed, beaten up, trampled upon. Do you realize that?"

"I know, Dad. I'm on your side, of course. But those guys are abject all the time, permanently; and they only wanted you to be that way momentarily. That you could do. You're strong enough to stand that."

Mr. Smith changed the subject. He was bewildered, but Duane spoke with an unusual, quiet conviction. As they gossiped now of this and that, Mr. Smith forgot his own experience and remembered that of his son a few years ago. Then, after starring in a high school basketball game, Duane was going to his old jalopy of a car when he was surrounded by a bunch of players from the losing team. The gang slugged his slim son in the face and made him admit the losing team was the better of the two. For a year or so after that, Duane had tried to keep a tire iron between car seat and foot pedals, close at hand, for protection.

Gone now were the jalopy, the tire-iron, the fears.

"Coming back to that business on Millimet, Duane, you were right," the father said.

"Yeah," the reply came easily, "I think I was. Justice is two-faced. I'm glad, though, the thing turned out as it did."

"Yes. So am I. All's well that ends well."

Coffee Break

The hottest thing in the news that day was the kidnapping of Roscoe Roberts III, the middle-aged son of the town's wealthiest real-estate operator. The sudden collapse of another television favorite and the impending Olympic winter games in California were as nothing compared to this dastardly crime in our own backyard. Generally, we skipped from one conversation piece to another during our brief, though expandable, coffee break, but not this time.

As usual, we were at Schubart's café, right across the street from the bank building in which the offices of Campbell & Carruthers were located. Hilda was visibly pregnant, and while we paused for the coffee to be brought, there was a bit of preliminary banter at her expense about soon having to give up skiing as well as the job. Claude and I, old timers with the firm, did the teasing. Emery Bohannon just listened and smiled. He was new.

Claude was the son of our Old Man Campbell, and, though younger than my thirty-seven years, was already a partner in the accounting firm. He it was who had hired Emory. He had confided some misgivings to me about the young man's being so strangely tense and "bottled up" but pointed out that it was the firm's policy to fill all vacancies occurring in its staff of juniors from the latest graduating class of the local school of business administration. Emory was one of the few who had finished his course of studies at the end of the fall term and the only accountant who had not made employment arrangements before graduation. With the busy income tax season just ahead, there hadn't been time for Claude to get replies from the fellow's out-of-town references.

"Here's your embalming fluid," the waitress announced briskly and carefully as she set down four of Schubart's sturdy cups and saucers. She slapped down an equal number of separate checks and left as quickly as she had come. The three of us waited for Claude to set the pitch for our table talk: not the topic, but the pitch. He knew as well as we that nothing but the Roberts affair would be a suitable subject under the circumstances. It was a matter of unwritten law, almost.

Claude hesitated briefly in the face of our expectancy and then said: "The family has had no word from the kidnappers yet. I called the city desk of the *News* just before we came over."

"It's awful," I said.

"With the FBI in the case," said Hilda, "the kidnappers haven't got a chance."

"That makes it worse in a way," said Claude. "Those thugs might kill Roscoe. Kidnappings often end in murder. Look at what happened to the Lindbergh baby."

"Or the Grenfell boy," I added.

Hilda nodded. Claude went on: "Every minute of delay without a contact made between those desperadoes and the family is dangerous. Flight with the victim would be next to impossible, and they can't hole up or hide away forever."

"Yes," I said. "The family offered ransom right away. The delay is unnerving: enough to chill the blood."

"And if you feel that way, think what it must be like for the guy's wife and kids," said Hilda.

"I'm afraid they've already killed Roscoe and are trying to make a get away," said Claude. "What do you think, Emory?"

A spray of coffee came from Emory's lips at the question. I turned my face just in time to catch the stuff in the back of the neck. I wiped at the moisture with my handkerchief. Emory was coughing. "I'm sorry," he said. Then he regained a semblance of composure. He faced into the frowning curiosity of three colleagues.

"You've touched on a sore point with me," Emory began. "I don't know what to think. I've never known. I went through hell when the Grenfell boy was stolen. I was living with my folks at the time. I didn't know Freddie well, but our house was close to the school he was taken from.

"I was introduced to the crime early in life. When I was real small, my step-father would joke about having kidnapped me. It made me shiver and raised goose-pimples on my skin. It paralyzed me so I couldn't talk. I almost believed him and wondered if that was the way Mother got me in the first place. When I got a little older, I used to hope somebody else would kidnap me—and maybe even shoot me.

"I wish it had been me instead of Mr. Roberts…." His speech came to a chopped-off halt. He was dry-eyed, but he sniffled as he paused for breath, half recovered now from the agitation with which his outburst had begun. He looked around at us doubtfully.

"I wouldn't have asked if I'd known," said Claude. "I guess everybody mixes up his wishes, fears, and thinking when he talks about things like this. Let's get back to the salt mines and everybody forget who can."

He grabbed for the checks without interference. "I'll get these," he said.

The Crisis

Once upon a time, during the second administration of President Eisenhower, there lived, in the populous and growing city of Sonora Springs, a fine fellow by the name of Rudy Grimkin. Now, Rudy wasn't a particularly distinguished citizen of the great republic, but in the eyes of those who knew him best he long had enjoyed the supreme distinction of being as average and undistinguished as it is possible to be.

In his youth, Rudy had gone to war as a matter of simple duty, not against the Kaiser or anyone special, not as a reluctant conscript, not to make the world safe for democracy. He went because he was eighteen years old at the time, and Uncle Sam wanted him, and all the boys his age were going. Call it duty. There'll be enough later to sift through his career for obituary praise. Rudy is facing a crisis, a severe test, right now, but he isn't dead yet, not by any means. He still has quite a few years to go before he exhausts his biblical span.

The crisis is a recent thing. Its nature can't be put down in a word, but it isn't an outgrowth of ageing or ill health so much as it is a product of circumstances.

When Rudy returned home from his stint at Jefferson Barracks after World War I, he married a cute little girl and got a job as a mechanic, in reverse order. He expected to live happily ever after those remarkable events, in accordance with the immemorial, pleasant practice of his predecessors on this planet, and he wasn't disappointed, not for a long time. He cleaved to his wife, and he clung to his job with a praiseworthy pertinacity. Two children, both boys, were born to him and his wife. One is "high up" in the civil service in Washington, and the other is making a career of the military.

Six months ago, Rudy's wife died suddenly of a heart attack. This was, no doubt, according to the rules and regulations, but not the rules of any game with which Rudy was familiar. His sorrow was all the greater because he knew no language in which to express it. There were certain words which came to his mind, even at times to his lips, but he knew they didn't really fit: unconstitutional, illegal, unexpected. The word which he had to suppress most often was "unconstitutional." Somewhere along the educational line, which ended in the tenth grade, he had picked up the notion that the unique Federal Constitution was a sort of Great Barrier Reef which insulated American citizens from the problems common to other peoples. He knew that proposition didn't hold water, but it had an effect on him nonetheless.

Preachers have words that do fit occasions of grief and great loss, and Rudy knew the apt expressions. He knew them because he and his wife had made the decision to be “saved” before their first child had been born. The trouble with the preacher's limited, repetitive, consolatory vocabulary was that it wasn't Rudy's. It didn't reach to his center. It had an organic connection with everything else (which was nice so far as it went) but none with him. He felt at ease with the commercial twang of the signs in front of the church during the week (“You ask so much of God; you give so little”), but that was because it dove-tailed with his thinking about customary or periodic events such as the trade-in of an old car for a new one. For him, at least, the religious slogans connected with the commercial more than the crucial. The predicament in which he found himself now was different, more like that of a mountain climber on the brink of an abyss offered rescue by a preachy chap with an engaging tremolo in his voice but too short a rope.

Before his wife's death, in fact some years before, Rudy had lost his job as a mechanic. The airline for which he worked hadn't fired him but had, instead, transferred him to the parts department. This was a safety measure taken in advance of a slip of a wrench, in advance of need, in accordance with the dictates of good, sound business administration. To be an airplane mechanic is to be proud in proportion to the number of years spent at it, which in Rudy's case was many. He loved the intricate, metal mechanisms as dearly as flesh and blood, but, of course, one can't quarrel with good sound business administration or with safety. Rudy took his transfer in his stride. It wasn't unexpected. Besides, even planes have a calculated rate of obsolescence.

It was some months after his wife's death that Rudy began to notice some peculiar symptoms—not in himself but in the world about him. The solid earth beneath his feet was less stable than customary. It gave way under him in the fashion of "rubber ice," in the way a trampoline or a peat bog does. He put down this curious impression as the result of reading too much science fiction. He let up on that and thought he noticed a little improvement. He ceased poring over the latest experiments in space travel, and the Earth was well-nigh back to its normal steadiness.

One morning as Rudy was shaving with his electric razor, the mirror in front of him went through some antic gyrations, and Rudy had a distinct premonition that all was not well. The sensation was so certain that he didn't bother to hurry. The news would be in the morning paper. He would get to that after breakfast. Indeed, fear of the worst made him sluggish: impelled him to put off and postpone picking the paper up at the front door or turning on the radio for a summary of the latest developments.

There it was: the unexpected. The American plane shot down over Russia was not a weather observer which had strayed off course at all. It was on a spying mission. This was now admitted by the highest authorities and justified, without regard to niceties, as necessary in the interest of national security. He would hear a lot about the incident at work, on the radio, on TV, everywhere, but he wouldn't understand. That is, he understood, and he didn't. Automobile accidents happen to other people to furnish new items for the daily papers; acting with an eye single to national safety was for other nations only. The law had always been on the side of survival of him and his, though indifferent to those so unlucky to have homes across the seas. Always! He couldn't square the official admissions and confessions with this invariable, inflexible Rule of Life, and he was upset.

Maybe he had been coming down to Earth lately, too. The designation of the spy plane, U-2, seemed to point that out, to point directly at him. The ground had been wobbly before because he wasn't used to it. Perhaps he had been walking, up to now, on a pretty, pink, aerial, legal, coral reef erected by the Dreamer of Dreams after he had finished his work on the castles in the air-space over Spain. These ideas flitted through his mind in the twinkling of an eye in order to accommodate themselves to the time Rudy had budgeted for getting ready to leave for work. He was due at the parts department window at 8 a.m.

He backed his car out of the garage at 7:30 a.m., which meant he was around five minutes ahead of schedule. This was fortunate, for though he was unaware of it at the time, he was to encounter a brief, unusual delay. A traffic light en route switched from green to amber. Rudy wasn't sure whether he should stop or go through before the amber changed to red. He kept going.

A police officer who had been lying in ambush on a side street swiftly put his car in motion. He was determined to second guess Rudy's decision to go ahead rather than to brake to a sudden halt. The policeman said "I'm going to give you a ticket for running the red light."

Rudy explained, "But I didn't run a red light." He didn't go on to explain. All palaver was useless anyway. He looked the officer over: the dark blue uniform, worn but not threadbare; the dark sun glasses; the coarse pores of the guy's skin. The cop was conscious of the inspection. He said: "I'll tell you what you do. You tell your side of the story to the judge, and I'll tell him you ran the light."

All his life up to then, Rudy had regarded himself as a law-abiding man above all. At the cop's remark, Rudy recoiled involuntarily. The policeman was satisfied: the man to whom he was giving a ticket was an enemy, but one who shared the officer's own contempt for giving the name of Law and Justice to those hit-or-miss processes and procedures of the traffic court which were at best a lottery. The two had an understanding. Rudy couldn't complain that Officer Knowlton—he could read the name now on the citation—had put thoughts in his mind. The disrespectful thoughts were there. His quick, visual inspection of Knowlton had been part of an accusation more damning than the ticket he himself had received. Knowlton hadn't answered the unspoken charges but had "passed the buck" to the judge, as it were.

The police car pulled away to hide where it had been before and to lie in wait where its chances to sneak up and prey upon the passing public were pretty good. Knowlton took off his dark glasses and held them before him with both hands as if they were binoculars and he were a soldier secretly surveying enemy troops as they defiled before him. He was a heroic sniper. (He was regaining the importance which seldom came off without his uniform but which had dissolved under the gaze of that insolent Grimkin). He waited for one of the enemy forces to become, by certain chance, vulnerable to his fire. To be sure, his weapon, the ticket book clamped between metal covers, was not as deadly as a firearm, but in warfare, to wound is better than to kill. A wounded man is more trouble to his people than a dead one. He clamped the glasses back on his head and spun his rear wheels as he shot forward in his patrol car in pursuit of a new victim.

In the meantime, Rudy continued on his way to the airport musing on Knowlton's failure to proclaim or even to suggest in any manner whatsoever the essential decency of his own role and that of the traffic court. He didn't want to be an accuser. He didn't want to receive implicit confessions of guilt, of contemptibility. On the contrary, he wanted support for everything he had believed in the past, for everything he had built his life on. The foundations were crumbling, and those in charge of shoring them up simply said "So sorry; they aren't worth fixing."

He came to a stop in the employee parking lot in ample season in spite of the setback. Later he would have to go to City Hall and pay the fine (because, of course, he wouldn't waste the time going to court). He dreaded the experience but knew that the charge of a "moving violation" required his personal appearance. He wasn't especially concerned with shelling out a fine of ten or twenty dollars, whatever it might be. What he feared, hated, flinched from was the terrifying possibility that the flunkies in the Traffic Bureau would say "This is a den of thieves, specializing exclusively in polite piracy. Checks are acceptable in lieu of cash." He was sure they wouldn't put it so bluntly, but he was all ear lately and took in strains that trumpeted the truth behind the false façade of fair dealing. If the employees only could be counted on to say somehow by their manner, "We are honest and upright men. We are not in league with Officer Knowlton and his Honor."

A set of knuckles rapped on his windshield. It was Joe Parsons. "Come on, Grimy Old Boy," he said, "or you'll be late. Say Man, you look pale this morning; are you all right?"

"Sure, I'm all right. Can't you see I'm okay? I didn't kick the bucket, Joe, I just turned a little pail."

"Putrid. It stinks…kicked a little pail…Ha, ha, ha. Yeah, there's life in the old boy for sure if he can come up with such a stinkeroo so early in the morning. Gosh, that's a good one. I'll have to tell that to Hank and Jim. See you later, Grimy." They were punching the clock now.

To work all day, to work for two days after this before he could respond to the summons the cop had given him and find that out about the people in the Traffic Bureau. That was to walk forever on the rim of the crisis. He would give all he had for a Grand Inquisitor at whose feet he could throw himself down immediately and confess all. Damn the destiny which had torn from him the protective cloak of the compulsion to conform and comply. Damn the miserable, petty officials who were ashamed of themselves and their hatchet work. Damn the fate which had decreed that this ageing, stiffening veteran ex-mechanic should face a crisis for which he had no preparation, no preparation at all except birth.

The Dilemma

"Men and women! I have an important announcement to make. An unknown young man, riding a horse, was struck by an automobile yesterday afternoon on Toboggan Hill and nearly killed. The driver did not stop after the collision and is also unknown. However, the motorist who happened upon the scene immediately after the accident, and who stopped to give aid to the injured, has told the police that the driver and passenger of the hit and run vehicle appeared to be boys of high-school age and build.

"The police are investigating the affair. They have asked for the school's cooperation in discovering the identity of the hit and run pair. It is, of course, too early for any accusations, and none is being made. At present, in fact, there is not a shadow of suspicion resting upon any individual in this room. If any person here knows anything whatever about the matter and wishes to come forward and reveal his information, the chief of police himself will be at my office tomorrow morning at this time to receive it. In the meantime, I will listen to anyone who chooses to talk to me about the situation. The chief wishes me to warn you, though, that no reward of any kind is being offered. There is no immunity from punishment or even of leniency for any offender. And, finally, there is no threat of severity or anything else if anyone having information does not care to volunteer it.

"This notice will be posted on the bulletin board in the hall, but I wanted to bring it to your attention personally first. That is all."

The superintendent of the high school, Mr. Horace White, stepped down from the platform and left the room. There was a brief silence of amazement. The students were awed by the solemnity of Mr. White's words and manner. There was a challenging ring in his intonation of the unfamiliar phrase "Men and women," and an ominous atmosphere suddenly had enveloped and stifled the innocence of the weekend just past and the week getting under way. The stunned hush gave way to something near pandemonium as the assembled students got ready to go to their respective classes.

The news of the accident was flashed to the general public soon afterward by radio. Gossip would spread it far and wide before the single afternoon edition of the town's only daily newspaper was on the street corners. Things were usually pretty quiet in this mountain town of Cathedral Rock during the fall and winter. The hustle and hubbub of tourists faded swiftly away after Labor Day. Activity revived slightly, but only slightly, after the first of the year when skiers overflowed the towns nearer to the runs and lifts and spilled a bit of their business into Cathedral Rock's two year-round motels. As it was, the misfortune on Toboggan Hill was big news, rating more attention from students and townspeople than the season's first snowfall. The latter event was mentioned only as having impaired visibility and thus set the stage for the highway tragedy.

In schools there is a curious process of news osmosis and fermentation comparable to the exciting telegraphy of drums among jungle people or the spreading and metamorphosis of rumors in an army. In this way it becomes common knowledge, soon after Mr. White's announcement, that the victim was Hank Farinas, a regular hand at the Crystal Creek Ranch. He was not nearly as badly hurt as at first supposed. Two horses had been involved in the misadventure. Hank had been leading one, an ornery wild maverick which had refused to be driven with the rest of the string, back from the summer pasture, when the car had hit his mount. This extra animal on the road shoulder, perhaps, had accounted for Hank's being further on the traveled portion of the roadway than otherwise would have been the case. The haltered horse had escaped injury when Hank's horse had been hit, and Hank himself had been catapulted over the steep, eight-foot, snow-covered bank at the side of the road.

Toward the end of the noon recess of Cathedral Rock High School, a sophomore student by the name of Rudolph Hokanson appeared at Mr. White's office. Rudy, a handsome, husky, red-cheeked, dark-haired lad of sixteen looked considerably less sturdy and granite-like than usual. It was evident that he was pretty shaken up over something.

"Come in Rudy. Did you want to see me?" Mr. White called.

"Yes, I did. About tomorrow morning. You can tell Chief Ainsley he doesn't need to come over then. I'm the one he wants, and I'm ready now."

"But you don't drive, do you Rudy? I've never seen you with a car."

"No, sir, I don't drive, but I'm the one."

"It isn't the passenger in the car the Chief especially wants, Rudy, so why don't you just wait till tomorrow morning. That'll be soon enough, and Chief Ainsley will be here then. The guest of the driver didn't do anything so awful, you know. He wasn't necessarily what you'd call an accomplice or partner in crime. Tomorrow morning will be okay."

"I'd like to keep the passenger out of this, Mr. White. That's what I was thinking, that the passenger wasn't nearly as guilty in the eyes of the law as the driver. I'd like to keep the passenger out of this deal altogether, if I can. You sure don't think I'd snitch to Chief Ainsley on my guest, do you Mr. White?"

"No, I certainly don't, Rudy. But let's let the business go over till tomorrow anyway. The Chief will be here then, and he'll know exactly what to do."

"I was hoping we could clear the whole thing up right away today, Mr. White."

"I know, Rudy, I know. But Chief Ainsley wanted to have until tomorrow, I guess, so we better leave it that way."

"Okay," Rudy murmured, and he went off, leaving Mr. White shaking his head with a baffled expression on his face.

The next morning, Rudy was at the superintendent's office before Mr. White got there. He waited in the hall. Chief Ainsley came along alone. "Did you want to see me?" he asked. Rudy nodded.

"What's your name?" the Chief asked.

"Rudy Hokanson."

"Oh yes. I know your dad. Does he know you want to see me?"

"Not yet. I thought I'd tell him later."

"Well, we'll see. I reckon I'd better have a chat with Mr. White first. He told me there were two boys who had asked to see me."

"Two boys? There couldn't be."

"There couldn't be? Why not? Maybe one was the driver, and the other the passenger."

Just then, Mr. White came along with Rudy's good friend Karl Bartelt, a junior who was tall, spare, serious, old-looking. "Here's the boy that wanted to see you, Chief," he said. Karl and Rudy looked at each other wonderingly. "And, Rudy," Mr. White went on, "you and I can have a word together while the Chief is busy with Karl."

"Yes, sir," said Rudy. Chief Ainsley and Karl went into Mr. White's private office and closed the door.

"We can talk in Miss Renfrew's room across the hall, Rudy. She's with a class right now." They entered, and Mr. White half sat on and half stood against the front of Miss Renfrew's desk. Rudy stood in the doorway.

"I wanted to keep Karl out of it," said Rudy.

"I know, and he wanted to keep you out of it," said Mr. White. "Only trouble is, Chief Ainsley won't believe there were two drivers and no passengers in the Bartelt car at the time of the crash."

Rudy was blinking rapidly to hold back his emotion. "It's awful," he said, "to pile all this on Karl. He was so panicky he couldn't stop at the instant. It was snowing hard right then, and we didn't either of us see the horses until it was too late. Neither of us, and Karl didn't see the man at all. I thought there was a man, but we didn't want to go back afterward with the other guy being there helping, and the police sure to come. It's hard enough on Karl just to know he was driving at the time and might have killed somebody. I couldn't possibly snitch on him. Besides, I was more to blame than him, more than a passenger ordinarily is. The law doesn't know that, and Chief Ainsley doesn't know that, but I do."

"I can see your dilemma, Rudy," said Mr. White. "You couldn't heap trouble on your friend's shoulders, and you couldn't feel at fault and still stay mum. Is that it?"

"Yes, that's it."

"Well, the horse that Hank Farinas was riding was hurt so bad he had to be killed, but Hank isn't so bad as the doctors thought at first. He says he's more to blame for what happened than the driver of the car."

"Does he really?"

"Yes. And did I tell you that Karl also wanted the name of his passenger kept out of the affair?"

"Yes."

"Well, you go back to your classes, Rudy. Chief Ainsley isn't a man-eating tiger, you know."

"I know," said Rudy. "He knows my father." With that, the boy smiled slightly, tentatively, and turned and took off. Mr. White remained where he was, half standing, half sitting, facing the doorway. And shaking his head thoughtfully as he listened to Rudy's retreating footsteps in the hall.

Doctors and Patients

It was early evening when Ed Grimly gingerly took his customary place at the bar, joining his three companions, the twins Ian and Liam O'Malley, and Frederick von Friedhof, or Fritz as he insisted on being called. The four drinking buddies had been coming to the same tavern after work at the state mental hospital across the street, sitting in the same seats, drinking the same ale, telling the same jokes, and playing Sheepshead for nearly fifteen years. They took special pleasure in telling stories, usually about people at work—patients, doctors, nurses, other staff members like themselves. It's not a stretch to say they knew each other pretty well.

"What's a matter, Eddie? You look gloomier than usual," says Ian. "Did your mistress finally leave you? Did your dog chew a hole in those new elk hide slippers?" "Yeah, Eddie, did your wife finally move back to her mother's place like she's been threatening to?" chimes in Fritz. "Naw, I'll bet it was the tennis pro she finally moved in with," says Liam with a hearty laugh.

"No, oom, I gotta toothache. Really bad one, too. Oom. Can't see the dentist until next Wednesday."

"The nerve of those dentists. Can't they tell when a man needs help? Makin' you wait a whole five days. It's unconscionable," says Fritz.

"Yeah, oom. Unconsiona-whatever. Oom. I can't talk much; it hurts. Oom."

"Joe, bring Eddie a pint. Maybe that'll cut the pain," shouts Liam to the bartender who was already on his way with a tall mug of the hallowed beverage.

Ian says: "Lemme tell you about the last time I went to see a dentist. It was 12 years ago, and I hope it's the last time, too. It played with my mind, I'll tell you."

The Dentist

I went to the dentist that day. As usual, I had the impression that I was regarded there as a victim rather than as a patient. Besides, my troubles with my teeth provide an opportunity for financial plunder. But, I had little recourse because I was having trouble with my lower left teeth in general and the eye tooth in particular. Dr. Beckwith it was. His office is fairly close to here. I spoke first to Dr. Beckwith's assistant. I couldn't remember what he calls her. First, I thought of Shelley (as a young man in Sheboygan I knew a girl with that last name) and then Sherry. It actually is Garry. I wanted to make her more feminine: more dear (*cherie*, as the French say).

Dr. Beckwith and his girl played around with x-rays, an electric current, ice. The ice was so shaped as to remind me of a mother's tit; also, somewhat of those rubber finger-ends that file-clerks use. This is to say the ice resembled a nursing nipple, being hollow even.

I was left alone for some reason, and my throat became dry. I spied a glass and filled it with tap water from the sink. Soon after, I was seized by extreme chills. I shivered and shook. I was terrifically nervous and in a hurry to get out of there.

Dr. Beckwith, having returned, took my temperature. "He has a fever," he told Garry. They gave me a prescription for achromycin, and then Dr. Beckwith gave me some aromatic spirits to drink right there. I almost collapsed before I got home. In the meantime, I was shaky, gasping for breath, nearly in the grip of a seizure like those of epilepsy.

For the next few days I didn't sleep well, though I kept to my bed a great deal. My vague, obscure dreams were questions: What is real? Ah, I thought, my better half will tell me when she comes home from visiting her sister in Omaha. I lay in bed thinkin' that sometimes the theme proceeds as far as a tentative answer. Reality may be tit-for-tat treatment. It may be a process of consumption and excretion.

The what-is-real theme was awfully upsetting, virtually a nightmare. It occurred to me that this experience and these dreams are reenactments of early infancy. I reject the milk bottle and its cold impersonality. I spurn the validity of the scheme of tit-for-tat: you get well fed if you stifle your anger and sobs or get this if you do that. Ah yes, I felt like weeping at the dentist's office.

In taking the drink of water in the dentist's office, I projected myself back and took care of myself in infancy. All I got was water, but that was what I wanted. I determined what I wanted, saw the glass, and got the water. Symbolically, I returned to childhood and trampled over substitutes for father and mother. Slew my parents and supplied my own wants.

I was in a hurry to get away. I had come out there on my own two feet. I wanted to get away, be alone, call Mazie and tell her of my sudden illness. Despite my discomfort, I walked home.

My eyes burned for days after the seizure. I discovered this when I put a wet towel on my forehead; the coolness felt good to the eyes. Before that, I knew my eyes hurt, and I kept them closed much of the time. I trotted around our dim apartment without any glasses.

For a couple of weeks, I couldn't sleep. I was a bundle of nerves. That night, the chicken I had for dinner was slow in digesting. Sleeplessness had not plagued me since I started working in hospitals years ago.

As for the process of consumption and excretion, I had an incipient, involuntary bowel movement at the dentist's office. I noticed the odor and thought it came from Dr. Beckwith's breath."

"Okay, okay," interrupts Liam. "I've heard enough."

"Oom, me too," mutters Eddie as he winced while taking a swig of his second pint of ale. Somehow it wasn't as soothing as he had hoped. And he really didn't need to hear more about dentists or, for that matter, his dear friend's excretory glitches.

Hoping to change the subject to something more light hearted, or at least less gloomy, Ian shoves into the conversation. "That's all fine and dandy, but let me tell you about Dr. Jackal and Mr. Lamb."

Fritz interrupts: "You mean Dr. Jekyll and Mr. Hyde, don't yous? C'mon. Everybody knows that story."

"No, of course not. I mean Lamb, not Hyde, like baby sheep, not sheep skin."

"Oom. Go 'head," says Eddie as he held the mug of ale against his jaw, hoping vainly to tame the savage microorganisms ravaging his beleaguered tooth.

Dr. Jackal and Mr. Lamb

Mr. Lamb had been having a time of it with a cold for over a month; and his wife had been after him to see a doctor; said she and the kids sure would catch it from him if he didn't get rid of it. The darn thing had hung on in spite of all Mr. Lamb's home remedies. When he chased it from his throat, it just retreated to his head and vice versa. The poor guy finally gave in before his wife's insistence and his own growing despair and agreed to visit a physician. This was an unusual step for Mr. Lamb. He hadn't seen the inside of a doctor's office for years. He didn't even know whom to see, except that it should be someone handy. His wife got the name of an eye-ear-nose-and-throat man from a friend who was a nurse and that left practically no reason at all for just going along as usual—unless there'd be a long wait involved. Mr. Lamb had told his wife he wouldn't put up with that.

By an odd coincidence, Dr. Jackal was at his office early and would see Mr. Lamb right away, meaning, of course, as soon as the patient could get there; as soon as the office nurse could get down on a card all the information she needed; and as soon as Mr. Whitecoat could speed another patient on his way. That part was much less painful than one would expect. Everything ticked off like clockwork.

Dr. Jackal had no more than taken a quick peek at the patient's throat when he became vaguely communicative. "There's a TV program," he said, "which talks about the seven sinuses. Actually, there are about a dozen of them." By this time, the efficient office nurse had put in her employer's hands a couple of wires cut on the pattern of the sparklers kids light on the Fourth of July. Without hesitation, the doctor rammed these things up the nostrils and into the patient's head as far as they'd go and departed to keep a date with a sufferer in an adjoining cubby hole.

In time, the pseudo-sparklers were removed, and the gentleman in the white coat asked "What do you do, Lamb?" When he was told, the expert in the healing arts commented sharply, "It wasn't on the card. Are you trying to keep it a secret?" This drew from the victim a laugh which was close to a scornful snort. The nurse said, "I didn't ask him."

"Do you have hay fever, Mr. Lamb? Any allergies? No? How about the family? So? It's pretty good, isn't it, for children so young to learn that citrus fruits disagree with them, when many people go for years without suspecting they have an allergy." There was a trace of a suggestion that Mr. Lamb undoubtedly had some allergy, probably hay-fever even, but was too dumb to realize it or too stubborn to admit it.

While this conversation was going on, the ever-ready nurse had placed herself behind Mr. Lamb. "Hold on tight," she said, "we're going way back." The chair in which the patient sat had, in fact, begun to do stunts, and in a twinkling the surprised Mr. Lamb found himself standing on his head still in the chair, of course, and holding on for dear life. The doctor had disappeared again. "Say cookie," the nurse said. "I'm going to pump you out."

Mr. Lamb didn't have to wait to get an idea what was meant. A sort of milking machine had been applied to his nose. It was evident that if his visitor had any secrets, the doctor intended to pull them out or know the reason why not. Confused recollections of the Spanish Inquisition, the third degree, and a picture named Les Supplices which he had been looking at just last night chased one another through Mr. Lamb's mind. He wasn't used to thinking, however, in an upside-down posture, and nothing came into focus clearly, and he couldn't remember for sure whether Les Supplices meant tortures in some alien tongue.

The doctor came back, and the nurse righted the marvelous mechanical chair and Mr. Lamb with it. "Who sent you to me?" the physician asked. "Ursula Packer," the patient answered. "Yes, it's on the card, but who is she?" Regaining his senses slowly but surely, though he was after the topsy-turvy rigmarole, the patient noticed the quickening pronunciation which signified that the glorified detective was expectantly counting on the new line of investigation to bring confirmation of his wild, unspecified surmises. "She's a nurse at St. Anthony's Hospital." In a voice that indicated that, though delayed, he still felt on the verge of an important discovery, the questioner followed up. "Ah, did you just get out of the hospital?" From the suspect came the disappointing negative "No, but I know her."

"Open wide and breathe out your mouth." Dr. Jackal had taken up a stance like that of a fencer before an opponent. The instrument in his hand was a cross between a sword and an artist's brush covered with red paint. Quick as a flash, the soft brush made contact with the back of Mr. Lamb's throat. A push toward a receptacle with running water accompanied the words "Now spit."

The nurse placed something resembling a soft, brown caterpillar caught in a pair of tongs into the Chief's hand.

The moist, furry object slipped from the tongs into one of Mr. Lamb's nostrils. Then the process was repeated for the other orifice. "Now we'll ask you to face the fire," the doctor said as the nurse flicked the switch on a heat lamp. "See if you can keep facing it pretty close," he said, "and hold this drip-pan on your chin. I'll be back before long. The heat from the lamp was so gentle, Mr. Lamb wondered why the busy man hurrying to the compartment next door had doubted the patient's ability to "face the fire."

Returning finally to remove the foreign substances left in the patient's nose, the doctor said, "You may want to come in every once in a while, as others do, to get cleaned out." He wore a slight smile, as beatific as that of a Buddhist priest, as if profoundly pleased at having relieved his patient of dark and guilty secrets and a fluid burden of sin from the sinuses. "I'm not going to give you a shot of penicillin," he added. "You know the bugs are getting more and more immune to that. Here's a prescription for a different antibiotic. Call me in a few days if you're not a lot better. As I said, come in whenever you feel you'd like the works again."

And that's the way Mr. Lamb got rid of his cold. The prescription worked wonders.

Liam clunked his mug down on the bar counter, laughing: "What a stupid story, brother of mine."

"Yeah, oom, har har har," exclaims Eddie as he pushed the mug against his jaw after another swill. He smiled for the first time that evening: "Oom. It hurts when I laugh."

Fritz settled back as Joe deposited another round onto the already crowded counter in front of the four comrades, and says, "Well then, you'll be reachin' for the pain pills when you hear this story about doctor and patient. It's real funny, I tell yous. But it's true. I heard it while working on the third floor."

Ian laughed and said, "I'll bet you dreamt it while sleepin' in a broom closet on the third floor."

"They got pretty good broom closets on the third floor, oom. Lotsa room to drag a chair into and take a rest," joked Eddie.

"Okay, okay. Listen up," says Fritz impatiently.

The Last Class

This was it. Dr. Hinton had been telling him for some time that the end was near; and now it had come. Only it wasn't Dr. Hinton, but Dr. Roning. He kept thinking of his mentor as Hinton because of the good doctor's habit of avoiding an explicit statement whenever a hint or a suggestion could be made to do instead.

The office nurse, Miss Ebaugh, came out of an inner room, saw him sitting there in the waiting room, smiled, and said "You may go in now, Mr. Catesby. The doctor is ready for you." He nodded but couldn't quite manage a smile in reply. He got up and went into the consultation room.

Dr. Roning was standing in front of the capacious brown leather armchair at the opposite side of the room, by the windows, as he always did. "Good morning, Tom," he said.

"Good morning." Tom let himself down into the comfortable depths of the nearest chair, a replica of the one on the other side of the smokers' table, except that this one was a dull dark green. It was his usual seat.

Dr. Roning waited for Tom to begin. The latter took a look around, as a tenant takes note of an apartment he is vacating. There were fresh assorted gladioli in the two-foot high, slender, gray-blue vase on the floor—garden flowers supplied by one patient for the vase made by another. The copper plate which hung on the blue-plaster wall had been fashioned, somewhat crudely, by Dr. Roning's only son, a teen-ager. The lamp on the desk was turned off, because Tom didn't like to have an artificial light competing with the daylight from the windows (and with his own natural illumination). The appointment book lay on the desk beside the lamp's base. It was unopened but was nevertheless a gentle reminder that Tom was not "the only pebble on the beach" of Dr. Roning's professional attention; not the only claimant of his time.

Still no further word came from Dr. Roning. Tom didn't expect any opening remarks this time, although on many previous meetings some little hint had been used to start the conversational ball rolling—some hint or, quite often, a simple question like "What are you thinking, Tom?" It was up to Tom to call the turn in every respect on the occasion of his last confab with Dr. Roning. He knew it; and, of course, he wanted it so.

"Ever since my last visit," Tom said finally, "I have had a most unusual song on my mind. Although I was brought up in a predominantly German community, I don't know that I ever really heard the song. It's *Der Vaterland, Der Vaterland....*" He peered at his confidant to see what kind of an impression this strange information was making. The latter's face registered interest but nothing more.

"My mother was born in Germany but immigrated to this country with her parents when she was still a child. My father was a native-born American. My fatherland is definitely America, not Deutschland. My father was born at a place called Clearwater, and I often think of my father's native state and my own as the water land. There are so many lakes there." Again Tom looked across the smokers' stand to see what kind of a reception his words were getting.

"Michigan, I believe, has the words 'Water Wonderland' on its car-registration tags."

"Yes," Tom replied, "but Minnesota has many more lakes. When I was a young man and lived in that part of the country, there was great rivalry between the two state universities—not about lakes but about football, swimming, hockey. Both states are waterlands."

"I noticed," said Dr. Roning, "that you pronounced *Der Vaterland* as Dear Vaterland."

"Yes. It is dear. I mean, it is pretty satisfying to have a motherland and fatherland at the same time."

"Do you think you have a tendency to confuse Father and Mother?"

"No. It isn't confusion any more. At last, it's fusion, rather than confusion; at last, my parents appear to me as merged and unified, fully cooperating."

"There ought to be fission, too, in that waterland you speak of," Dr. Roning said.

"Yes," said Tom, "fusion and fission." They both chuckled.

"During the war, you fought against Germany as a soldier, didn't you?"

"Yes, I did, but if that song that's been running in my mind means anything at all, it means the war is over. As I said, I can't remember that I ever heard the hymn—it's the German national anthem, I guess—but it seems to me that it begins on the same tune as America, the Beautiful!"

"You love your former enemies?"

"Yes."

"Maybe your own private war with your German mother is over, too."

"Yes."

"And with your deceased father."

"Yes. And going back to that idea of merger and unity again, do you know that I often associate water, in the back of my mind, with..."

"Yes; with what?"

"Well, the female, the womb—as if I had a recollection of life before birth."

"Yes. Water sounds like Father and suggests Mother. It's a good thing my name is Roning and not Walker, or you'd have me walking on water!"

"I suppose I would, as sure as Daudet is daddy. And in French the word for mother has the same sound as the one for sea."

"Yes, that's right, *la mer* and *la mere*. And to be at one with things is a darned good feeling, isn't it?"

"Yes. It seems to me that to merge the opposites of land and water, male and female, Father and Mother, friend and foe, Germany and America, is to unify myself, myself and my double, so to speak."

"What we sometimes call integration, maybe?"

"Maybe."

"Or thesis, antithesis and synthesis?"

"Could be."

"*Der Vaterland* is a pretty sentimental song?"

"In this case, for a peculiarly sentimental celebration."

"Music isn't your long suit?"

"No."

"But you resorted to it this time?"

"Yes. And just this instant another song from my childhood, my earliest days, flashed into my mind: 'Are you ready, Mr. Gallagher? Absolutely, Mr. Shane.'"

"A musical answer to the question you expect me to ask: Are you ready to get along without me?"

"Yes."

"A happy wedding of words and music, situation and idea, youth and age, I'd say."

"Thank you."

"Don't thank me. Besides, I'm so well-adjusted, you can depend on a bill."

"Thank you, anyway."

"Thank you, too. Never did a teacher learn more from his student."

"Which speaks well for Herr Professor."

"Thank you again."

They were shaking hands now, and without further words they parted. It was their last class together.

"Ach, Fritz. Das war ein gutes story," says Ian as he reached for his newly refreshed pint. "Those head shrinkers are funny people."

"Ya vole, they sure are," adds Liam. "They're crazy as loons."

Fritz asked "What's so crazy about loons? All they ever do is sit in the water and sing."

"Oh, everybody knows that loons are crazy. It's a proven fact. Just ask Joe."

Joe, who just happened to be dropping off another round at the time, hastened an answer, "Yeah, sure. Everybody knows that. Really crazy they are. But not as crazy as the dumbo octopus. They're just plain nuts."

"C'mon," says Liam. "Octopuses aren't crazy. They're real smart. They can count to eight 'cause that's how many arms they got."

"Legs, not arms. They got eight legs," chimed in Ian.

"Oom," moans Eddie. "I've heard enough. I gotta go home. Maybe sleep will help. Oom. But wait, it would be a shame to leave a mug that wasn't empty." With that, Eddie settled back on his stool as Liam shuffled the deck of cards. The ale was starting to ease the pain—enough for at least one hand of Sheepshead and the remainder of the half-full mug.

The Garden of Eben

Eben was returning from lunch. He had eaten alone, his usual luncheon companion having been occupied with errands. From a bookstore on his route, Eben had purchased a paperback novel and, as he ambled along, he swung in his hand, back and forth, back and forth, the yellow-colored paper envelope-bag which contained his purchase. He had taken off the white smock, which he wore in the air-cooled laboratory, when he ventured out under the cloudless sky, so now he was clad simply in short-sleeved sport shirt and light-weight slacks.

He had passed the Sonora Club, the noontime rendezvous in Sonora Springs of the well-heeled and well-dressed, when he spied two familiar figures approaching from the corner. A new, red-brick, prosperous church, with its grounds, adjoined the sidewalk between him and his two acquaintances. The few sprinklers on the grounds were revolving lazily. The water pressure was weak, owing to the season's prolonged drought. To the parched grass, the feeble spray was as a crumb to the needs of a famine. The air, nearly as devoid of humidity as that of the desert to the south, vied with the soil to see which could absorb the more moisture.

The two men coming toward Eben were silhouetted against the trees and houses at the end of the street beyond the intersection. Still beyond that, and above, were the mountains—not snow-topped now but pink-gray in the barrenness above timberline. The older of the two men was attired in a suit nearly the color of the upper reaches of the mountains. That is, the suit was gray, but the reddish-tanned face and hands of the wearer blended with the color of the suit to create a pinkish-gray ensemble. This was L. J. Samsome, the owner of Purdue laboratories for which Eben worked.

The man with L. J. was Harry Eubank, president of the company. He was president, but not Number 1. L. J. was definitely Number 1. Harry was wearing a dark suit. His eyes were protected from the sun, and his full blonde face nearly hidden from view by a pair of black, over-sized spectacles. He was taller than L. J., and, whereas L. J. was relatively lean, Harry's middle appeared soft, bulbous, and bloated. He was new to the presidency, though not to the company. He had risen slowly, step by infinitesimal step, through the ranks of the bookkeeping department to Chief Accountant, Comptroller, President. It was only after he had become president in name, and glorified stooge in fact, that he had fallen victim to the grossness of overweight. To be sure, such a dual role isn't an easy one.

From a distance, as if fearful that Eben might speak first and set the tone of the greeting, L. J. called out to Eben, "Would you like a shower? There's one!" He indicated the nearest sprinkler with a jerk of his head and a restricted, lame, abortive gesture of the hand. Harry, in the meantime, seemed to shrink into his new-found plethora of flesh and to withdraw behind the dark facade of sunglasses. From his tight lips came no sound.

"Yes...Nice day." In his reply and afterward, Eben labored to make sense of L. J.'s curious greeting. He didn't know whether the Old Man meant a shower bath or a rain shower. It could be, indeed, that the eminently successful businessman was implying that if the brilliant researcher expected his successes in the laboratory to bring forth a shower of gold, he, Eben, would be grievously disappointed. His reward would be as meager and ineffectual as the listless sprinkler on the church lawn. Furthermore, the Old Man could rely on his fat shadow, the Lord Keeper of the Books, to back up his decision. At that, at least—seconding L. J.'s resolutions—Harry was pretty good; at that, and at figures on cross-lined paper, i.e., costs. People: they're something else again; *oui, en effect, c'est autre chose.*

The home of Purdue Laboratories, a block from the red-brick, low-church temple, is scarcely the latter's architectural rival. Its lines are simple, straight and severe, but the austerity of line and color and the economy of its flat, gray, concrete composition are mitigated by a luxurious border of flowering myrtle and by the soft greenness of ivy stretching up the walls. Inside, everything is fluorescent-lit, comfortable, efficiently arranged, adequately appointed. In a sense, these precincts, like those of the nearby church, are holy ground for the researchers and scientists within these walls, standing and sitting with their backs to the antediluvian mountains outlined through the windows of the north, who have discovered marvels, produced wonder drugs, revealed hidden designs of Nature, and divined secrets of healing dating back to Creation.

Purdue sells the products of its laboratories to the medical and dental professions. The exchange which takes place, however, is more than the simple, secular give-and-take of the marketplace. Some of the holiness of Purdue rubs off on its customers, and then, Purdue benefits in turn from the reputation of these modern medicine-men who are its customers and whose miracles of surgery, freezing, and transplanting are so often in the news. The commerce is holy, wholesome, and profitable for everybody. Such, at least, is the popular wish; and yonder rocky peak will sooner yield to the miner's pick than that hard-shelled wish to any inquiry or challenge, be it scientific, parliamentary, or otherwise.

When Eben had got back to his desk and resumed his smock and the seriousness of a scientist at work, he learned that something new had been added: two new colleagues. One, Joamilla, was a native of India who had defected from the antiquated wisdom and the material, if not spiritual, nothingness of his village birthplace to graduate from Caltech. The other was an American Indian from the desert country to the south. He was nearly as dark as the other new arrival, but, needless to say, their physiques were in marked contrast. To the two tongues of his childhood, Spanish and Navaho, Henry Wetclay had added the strange, marvelous, scratched or written language of science, learned during his doctoral studies at Harvard. It remained, however, for him and Joamilla, both to learn the time-clock routine and rigid discipline of working for Purdue's. As for Purdue's, it had completed its case and proved that its hiring practices have nothing to do with color-consciousness.

There had been more than a little dissatisfaction lately at Purdue's. The congressional investigation of profiteering in similar businesses had stirred up and nettled L. J. and Harry and the host of others in the organization concerned with the mysteries of costs, administration, public relations, selling, accounting.

What the public hearings had turned up hurt. What the government inquiry had fallen just short of uncovering—those unwritten, perhaps illegal, understandings with competitors—had dealt an even more serious blow to L. J.'s pose of righteousness and peace of mind. It had done all this without even coming close to the problems which put their legs around the neck of Eben and soon those of Wetclay and Joamilla, like so many Old Men of the Sea.

Probably no amount of dollars, francs, piasters, or rubles could solve problems so shadowy and indistinct (though real): remove burdens fastened on backs out of sight; relieve weights and pressures felt but not seen; remedy woes indescribable. Just the same, Eben's colleagues usually began and always ended their complaints, whether voiced to their supervisors or muttered to each other, with a stern, vehement, desperate insistence that their salaries were too low. Even the old-timers were touched by these new, fierce winds of restlessness with their repetitive, mesmerizing murmur of money, money, money. So, Doc Slosson, the old-timer who had broken-in Eben and who for years had been company-man first-class, had become vociferous, testy, and demanding. The Chief, in the manner of the dying Caesar reproaching Brutus, had had to caution his long-trusted lieutenant not to be a trouble-maker.

Now, Eben was told that Doc Slosson was to train first Joamilla and then Wetclay in the rites and habitudes of Purdue's. Doc had done the same for others before Eben, but there was something different about his mission this time. Eben knew it, if Doc didn't, and seemingly he didn't. Eben's apprehension reached to his bones, their marrow, their irreducible ash. Old memories of World War II in Germany and of those wartime, earthen flower pots at Dachau never destined for plant life, revived in him and made him shudder.

Doc's huddling with Joamilla and then Wetclay fitted into the whole, crazy, jig-saw puzzle of the burned-out, legislative inquest and the current uneasiness at Purdue's. He couldn't get over the sense of *déjà vu* over the movie-goer's realization that "This is where I came in." In this quiet, cloistered, small-city scene of research, learning, dedication and concentration, there it is: concentration camp. Doc Slosson, all un-knowing, was training his own replacement on the staff.

The Great Guinea Pig

Sure, there's probably much to be said for a husband and wife takin' separate vacations, but listen you to me, Brother, I've been through the mill. I've done it both ways and used to think it was six of one and a half-dozen of the other. Last year, though, I had it. You can go ahead and do what you like, but I'm tellin' you what happened to me.

Everything went along fine at first, even in the evenings. I got along without television for a change and read some of the magazines that were layin' around the house; wrote letters to relatives; told my wife by mail how I missed her, course I hadn't begun to really, but you know how it is. Toward the end of the first week that had begun to wear thin; don't have a lot of relatives and never was much of a one for readin'.

I went back to lookin' at television. That's a wonderful invention, and I wouldn't take a tick from it. But have you ever noticed that the programs aren't made for just one person? That's why they're dumb as all hell—just plain dull. I swear they're awful that way. When two of you are lookin' at 'em, you feel kind of superior or something. It's okay then. If you have friends in, you don't even realize how shallow and silly the shows are. But listen, this was August, and all my friends were on vacation.

Usually I ignore the doorbell in the evening if I'm not expectin' someone or don't have a pretty good idea who's ringin'. By the middle of the second week of my wife's visit to her folks, I began to hope for anyone at all to nibble away at my lonesome. I welcomed strangers like long-lost brothers. It was something different at least.

One guy was collecting signatures on a petition for a liquor license at Sixteenth and the Avenue. He was brisk and businesslike—didn't have time to come in and visit—would have to quit by nine o'clock and was paid by how many signatures he got. A good-lookin' Oriental who said he was a veteran of the nasty mess in Korea was better company, until he learned that I had no intention of subscribin' to either *Colliers* or *Woman's Home Companion* or of renewin' for *Time and Tide*. Then he dropped me like a hot potato.

It was no fun, I tell you. I didn't want to call the little woman too often. A matter of pride. Then, for the first time in my life I would awaken at night and hear the whippoorwills callin', or thought I did. I never realized before that we had them in this part of the country. To tell the truth, I'm not real sure of it now. A guy can be wrong about those things, you know.

But what I wanted to tell you about was that God-awful gal who was takin' a survey. That beat everything. It was partly my fault, I'll admit, 'cause I asked her to come in. But how did I know what she was gonna ask? She had a rough, long horse face, which was bad enough without the questions. Besides that, a doubtful smile would come and go as she looked at me, like she doubted whether I was tellin' the truth, knew what I was sayin', or had enough good sense to catch her questions straight. If that smile on Mona Lisa gets you, you shoulda seen Horse Face. You'd know what I mean—on top of the questions, mind you.

She was gonna write a thesis, so she said, comparin' middle-class beliefs with those who lived in the tenement districts, in low-income housing and such. Well, she put me in the middle class just like that, and bein' a fool, I let her get away with it. I ain't never been a guy to stay in a pigeon hole, however, and I guess she found it out soon enough. I hope the darn tarryhootin' bothered her as much as it did me. That I do.

She asked me if I believe in America. I said "Sure thing, gal. It's all around me. I can see it. Seein's believin'." She said "You didn't understand me. I mean its heritage." I came back with "Where'd you think I came from? My daddy and his daddy and his daddy before him were born in this country. How's that for heritage? I don't just believe in it. I know it." She replied "Well, let's skip that, and we'll come back to it later." She never did, though.

The next question was "What about democracy?" I answered "What about it?" She said "Would you vote for it?" I gave her question for question. "When's the election?" She said "If you had a chance to vote, if there was an election....Which do you think is perfect, democracy or communism?" I put it this way, "Listen, gal, there ain't nothin' that's perfect. Not here below. Suppose two countries got what they want. Who'm I to complain? I like it this way. I don't want perfection, Sister; wouldn't suit me at all." I don't know what she put down.

That's when the gal got personal. "What's your religion?" she asked. "You Catholic, Protestant, or Jew?" I shied a bit at that. "Ain't I got no other choice? Do I have to say it in one word?" She began to look at me funny. She was impatient, too, but whether it was my answers or just to hurry things along, I don't know which. "Can I put you down as Christian," she asked, "and let it go at that?" I said "I'm no Indian, but you can put it down with reservations, if you want." She started to mumble something but gave it up. I didn't like the answer any better'n she did, but what you gonna do?

"Do you favor Capitalism?" She was lookin' at me kind of fishy, with that doubtful smile I told you about. I could see she reckoned my answer would be a dead giveaway, but what did I care what Horse Face made of things. "Well, I don't know," I said. "Why shouldn't I support Capitalism so long as it supports me? Just the same," I told her, "I'm not a capitalist." I thought I'd give her back a bit of her double-talk, but that did it. I guess she was sure, then, she'd found a genuine communist in the middle class. She left in no time flat, mutterin' something about there ought to a law.

I haven't got over that one yet. Afterwards, I never did get any time away from the business. My wife had her little change of pace, and I didn't. Figger that. As if it wasn't bad enough to be a great big glorified guinea pig for a college twerp without an ounce of brains in her head, I missed out on my vacation. Just let that be a lesson to you, Brother, what I mean.

The Great Judge

I chanced to be in the vicinity of the Federal Building down on Bidwell Street the other day when a sudden, fierce shower came up to bless the parched pavements and thirsty earth of my home town. As it was about lunch time, I sought shelter from the welcome downpour by slipping into a convenient cafeteria.

Cafeterias have the same easy informality, that casual familiarity, so characteristic of cross-country buses and the day coaches of trains. This is even true at Walton's Cafeteria, though the prices there are such as to limit the democracy to those of the upper middle classes. Nevertheless, at Walton's as at the others, a stranger is always at perfect liberty to share any person's table during the hectic, noonday hours when, as often happens, there is a dearth of unoccupied tables.

On this particular occasion, the rain had made this bustling restaurant even busier than usual for that hour of day. It was not surprising, therefore, that I was no sooner seated than a middle-aged man of a quietly cheerful demeanor politely asked leave to sit down at my table. I assented willingly and as a matter of course. I was facing the rain and exulting in it. He chose to face toward the line of hungry customers at the counter.

The stranger proved to be an affable and engaging talker. His accent was that of the region; his pronunciation was perhaps more slurred and careless than the ordinary. Yet there was lacking in his speech the rude slang and repetitive exclamations of the street and tavern as well as the current clichés of the market place. I had no hesitation in concluding that my chance acquaintance was a self-educated man. I still had lingering doubts about that and my other speculations concerning Mr. X, however, and wished for the confirmation which would flatter my powers of observation and deduction.

When I asked my companion where he had gone to school, he answered with careless ease, "Right here in town; afterward, I finished at the state institution." Then, casually changing the subject, he inquired, "Do you see the tall man there in the line?" I turned slightly to look and saw a tall, firmly built man in his fifties. He stooped slightly at the shoulders but had a good figure notwithstanding. The two deeply-etched, frowning lines between his eyes suggested either habitual, studious concentration or a brooding melancholy over his own lost illusions and the follies of mankind in general.

"Yes, I see him. Do you know him?"

"That's Judge Krutch of the federal district court," the man replied.

"Oh yes. Now I connect him with the pictures I've seen in the papers."

"There's a great judge," the stranger asserted with unexpected emphasis.

To me, Judge Krutch was as much of a stranger as the man across the table. Indeed, as a man he interested me much less. Yet the subject of greatness is one which long has fascinated me, at least since the time years ago when I read the elementary principles of greatness in *Jonathan Wild*. I like to compare notes with Fielding to see whether the standards have changed in any respect in the last two hundred years. Accordingly, I was disposed to encourage a stranger to carry on the conversation along the lines which he had chosen. Besides, in what way could he tell more about himself than by discussing the greatness of another?

"Do you know him well? Are you a lawyer?" I asked.

"I'm not a lawyer, but I've given quite a bit of study to the law and to judges, mostly state judges. However, I have read about this judge; I have seen him a number of times, here in the cafeteria and in court. I have heard him give talks. I feel I know him well. He's a great judge."

"Can you say that of a man who is still living?" I demurred. "You know, the major museums have passed a 'death sentence' on the work of artists. They say no one can tell whether a painting is a masterpiece deserving an honored place in a museum until the artist has been dead for some time, say twenty years. Don't you think it is also impossible to determine a judge's greatness in his lifetime?" I asked.

"With some of them, perhaps, but not all. This man is a great judge. I'll tell you how I know.

"It is not much over five years since he was appointed judge. I knew there would be a ceremony of some kind at his chambers when he first put on his robe. I made it a point to be there for the occasion. Those present were his friends, guys from the D.A.'s office, reporters, photographers, and a few like me who just like to be on hand for such things.

"You have seen the man. He's six feet tall, and big. You think he looks a bit stiff and arrogant maybe. But you should have seen him that day. Before he slipped into that robe, he appeared a dejected, if you looked close, as a thoroughly wet chicken. Humble isn't even the word for it. He was positively insignificant, and he knew it. As he was helped on with the robe, he changed. Then he was worthwhile. But he knows the robe made him that way; that without it, he is nothing. That is one of the reasons he is a great judge: he is humble; he knows what he owes to others.

"I've seen him sitting as judge in criminal cases. He may not know much law: probably doesn't; anyway he doesn't seem to pay it much heed. As we all know, a man isn't prosecuted in federal court unless he's pretty surely guilty of something—something more than being unfortunate. That being so, he should be punished. Ninety-nine times out of a hundred, the accused man, who resembles the rest of us, feels that way himself. A lawyer with his preachings of the law only confuses the poor fellow struggling in the net; gives him false hopes of escaping by means of a meaningless, despised technicality or an accidental loophole, the punishment he deserves, knows he deserves and often wants. Judge Krutch understands all this and does whatever he can, which is more than a little, to bring about a jury conviction whenever the accused is foolish enough to plead not guilty.

"I've said the judge knows what he owes to others. Besides that, he appreciates, deep within him, what is owing to others. I read in the papers what he said in a civil tax case. Some farmers near here should get back the taxes they paid. They live in an arid part of the country, where farming is a tough job. The government tax lawyers live way back in a humid, eastern city and don't know nothin' about farming out here. That's what he said. I saw it in the papers. Doesn't that read well? And the judge means it. Remember he's a federal judge and doesn't need votes. He sympathizes with our farmers, realizes they need tax relief, even if he has spent his entire life in a city. He could make a big fuss about the law first and afterwards decide the same way, but why bother? There's no need of method in his kindness. He's not technical.

"Have you ever heard him talk or read a report of his speeches? His talks are wonderful, so common and down to earth. That's another reason he's a great judge. He's so human. The average guy don't know about truth; it's too complicated. What is truth?" Here the stranger shrugged his shoulders ironically as if to say you can plainly see the answer is beyond us both. Then he continued: "Judge Krutch is too practical, too human, too simple for that sort of thing. Even the college professors leave that kind of stuff for the sparrows. The judge looks for the plausible and talks in that vein to people concerned only with the same. Do you see what I mean? He's not dumb; he knows his limitations and those of others."

The stranger paused and gazed quizzically at me. I was silent. Finally, instead of commenting on his description of the judge, I blurted out the question which had never fully left my mind during his plausible dissertation on greatness: "Are you an author by any chance? What's your line?"

He smiled. "In a way I'm an author. I live by my pen under a nom de plume. I don't write books, however." Then he added in a sweetly mild, disarming, candid way, "I write checks."

Judge Niven Sums Up

It wasn't the pressure of official business which impelled Judge Niven to go to his chambers in the post office building a few days before the New Year. His retirement as federal judge was to become effective December thirty-first, and he had finished nearly all the work which remained to be done by him. On this trip to his offices, the judge merely wanted to be present in the familiar surroundings without a thing to do—and without doing a thing. Now that he was leaving the career which had absorbed his energies the preceding twenty years, he wished to take one long, leisurely, reflective glance back.

It was Saturday and most of the offices were empty. As he walked down the dimmed corridors, he could see lights here and there through the closed glass doors, signifying that some of Uncle Sam's vast horde of clerks, investigators, agents, and prosecutors were on the job. Their hours of work were rigorously regulated, but always certain deviations from routine were occasioned by the whim or idiosyncrasy of an individual employee or by the emergency needs of the various government bureaus.

The interior of the judge's private office or chambers was dominated by the picture given him years ago by the Western Slope Railroad. It was a photographic view of sturdy, beefy-looking, white-faced, red cattle (mostly steers) standing in a meadow against a background of a dark, rocky, timbered mountainside. Today, as the white-haired, reddish-faced judge slumped rather wearily into his chair, the scene smiled upon him almost as serenely as usual. As was his wont upon entering the office, the judge gazed at the picture in silence for a few moments.

Surely none of those customers whom the railroad had favored with an identical tableau could have been more appreciative of the gift than Judge Niven. In the many years that the rustic scene had hung facing the judge's old-fashioned, oaken roll-top desk, the pictorial unity of beast and landscape never had failed to fascinate the rugged, heavy-set jurist. Moreover, nothing else had done as much over the years to pacify the turbulent emotions which the conflicts of the courtroom had stirred up in his breast.

The judge unfolded the morning newspaper which he had brought with him. There on the front page was a brief story of his retirement under the caption "High Judge Steps Down." Details of the testimonial party given for him at the Sonora Springs Club the evening before were on page seven. His hand felt a slight twinge of pain as he read, as if it were experiencing once again the hearty, congratulatory grip of one of the many civic leaders who had come to wish him luck in the luxurious surroundings and the properly exclusive atmosphere of the Sonora Springs Club. He tossed the paper aside without perusing the laudatory editorial he had been told was located still deeper in the journal.

Judge Niven's fingers beat a slight, nervous, impatient tattoo on the desk as if he wished to dismiss from his mind all recollection of the affair of the previous evening. He had done his duty in attending. The party was over and done. He had conducted himself with his usual dignity. It didn't take much imagination to realize that the grave decorum of his mien and bearing had been the subject of many an admiring remark after the event, especially by those of a less sober temperament or discipline. Well, it was a thing of the past, and that was that.

This business of being a judge, it had been satisfying enough, no doubt. He had sought the honor with all the resources at his command while at the peak of his successful career at the bar. In the two decades which followed he had never really regretted his efforts nor the success which crowned them. He hadn't been utterly disappointed. Still, he had to admit that the life of a judge was not what he had expected it to be.

He glanced at the black robe which hung, almost hidden, behind the half-closed door of a closet. He had expected that the warming glow of power which the robe imparted at first would continue. It had faded away imperceptibly. Then he had become conscious of the restrictive way in which the gown clung to him. Even after he left the court building he would, particularly when tired, imagine that the garment weighed on his shoulders and flapped around his knees. It was easier to reconcile conflicting rules of law than to feel the power of one's high office while clad in the raiment symbolizing it.

The length of the robe had irritated him. Why, even women now were emancipated from the tyranny of dragging skirts. The color had displeased him, too. Staid wisdom's hue it might be for the poet, but his concerns had been of a different nature, more practical and partial. How could one settle greedy, stubborn quarrels over this world's goods with the dark, brooding, other-worldly insights of a man in black? Other-worldly, that was it. The color suited better the frock of a priest, for the dissemination of celestial wisdom pertained to his calling, not to that of a jurist.

It was senseless, of course, to be so agitated over such a trifle as the apparel of his station. The feeling of angry frustration had diminished in time but only to be succeeded by a surprising resentment at the very essence of the law itself. He couldn't remember now whether or not the seed of the latter feeling had been a rough reversal of one of his judgments by the higher court. It didn't matter what caused it all. The fact was that there had been so little room for movement and maneuver in his work. That was the important thing.

He had lacked freedom as well as power—and he a high judge to whom everyone spoke with exaggerated courtesy and deference. He had been a high and mighty slave, that is what he had been. Hadn't Ibsen said that the pillars of society are the tools of society? He couldn't be sure. Anyway, there seem to be some things each individual has to discover for himself without the help of Ibsen or whomever.

When he had been an advocate, he had enjoyed the hunt for the statutes and ancient decisions which contained the rules of law which governed the newly-risen disputes. Whenever he had located a particularly favorable case, he had rejoiced as much as if he had been handed the stone tablet of the law on Mt. Sinai. In his capacity as a judge, however, the pleasures of the chase had been lost on him. He was obliged to rely on briefs of counsel to supply him with precedents.

It is all right, he had thought, for the court reporter to copy exactly what is said by the witnesses at a trial. But am I, in my place of power in the courtroom, to have as little latitude for independent judgment as the stenographer? Am I to take dictation from those judges whose only claim to preeminence is that they belonged to an earlier age, a dead, departed one? As he mused, Judge Niven had half forgotten his forthcoming retirement and was thinking of these last questions as if they were still presented for his personal, if unofficial, decision.

The judge shifted his bulky frame in the well-worn chair. Just the same, the little things had been as annoying as those more fundamental. There was the matter of sitting, sitting, sitting. His mind may have become a bit rusty with the passage of time, but it remained alive and vital. He felt his age more in the posterior than anywhere else. No wonder. The advocates who appeared before him stood on their feet like men, and like men they addressed the court and spoke their piece. His had the passive role of listening and forever sitting like the superhuman Delphic oracle of antiquity. Good grief, he was no oracle; nor had he been cut out to be a mechanical receptacle like that gadget which receives the pennies of diverse, childish customers in return for a tiny, printed forecast of their future.

His eyes returned to his favorite picture. This time, he confronted it rancorously. These many years he had shared the pictured herd's contented vision of good pasturage, and he at least had mistaken the vision as one of something vastly better than it really is. Had he been betrayed, or had he betrayed himself? No matter. One thing was sure: he was not being turned out to pasture now. And he was through looking at copies, even photographically exact copies. There would be time for him himself to look at the real thing; and he'd do it, standing up.

He gave a bitter chuckle and mused out loud:

When a lusty man pursues phantoms
And finds at last what they conceal
It's no consolation his companions
Insist that shadows are the real.

His reverie was interrupted by the sound of a hand on the door knob. His friend, Paul Corvo, the District Attorney, entered. "Well, well, Judge, is the court sitting on Saturday?"

Judge Niven rose to his feet quickly. "Not by a long shot. From here on out, I'm standing."

"Standing on the sandy banks of the good old, swift Echo River, I reckon. You've earned it, Old Timer. There's no denying that. It ought to seem pretty nice, though, to sit a little now and then and enjoy some pipe dreams and build some castles in the air. You've earned a chance at that, too." As he turned to leave, the visitor added, "I'm certainly going to miss you in this wonderful, spacious, comfortable office."

"I'm not gone yet, Paul. I'll be here again Monday. See you then."

The District Attorney left. Alone in the hall, he smiled. The old guy can't fool me, he thought. He dotes on power and hates to leave it. Can't say I blame him He's had the power and freedom of a big shot for so long. He's bound to miss it.

A Lonely Lunch Hour

I never was a one to make friends easily. All the people I know real well I've known for a long while. The way some folks can hook up in a short time is a wonder. I envy them. It isn't that I have trouble talkin' to strangers. I don't at all, but we're still strangers afterwards or, maybe, acquaintances that don't mean a thing to each other.

Like the other day. Most often I have lunch at home in my downtown apartment and then stop by to see the neighbor who lives on the floor just below me. She eats alone, too, but then we have coffee together, and I walk her back to her office before I go to my own. She is awfully cute and plump and nice, and I like her a whole lot. The way she can make coffee is nobody's business. I don't get lonesome at all when she's around. We were friends back before I moved into the apartment.

That's the way it usually is. But the other day she was away on vacation as she is yet. After a sandwich and a cup of instant coffee, I went and sat at the edge of the park between the Capitol grounds and the Civic Center to smoke my cigar and soak up the sunshine summer breezes. There was a guy there who had just come to Denver from Oregon, and we had a cozy chat, about how he always was lucky gettin' a job and had fallen into one here right away as a dishwasher at Cedric's

Café on Colfax Avenue and would have to have his membership in the union transferred from Portland and how he liked the Colorado weather and a lot of things of that sort.

But, as I was sayin', nothin' ever comes of my meetin' up with people easy-like. At the end, I threw away what was left of my cigar with a little wave to show I don't need to get every last puff of smoke out of the things and said, "Well, I'll have to be lopin' along." He nodded understandingly and folded his paper up and says, "It's a little too breezy to read a newspaper here. Guess I'll toddle back to the room. I live over there on Twelfth Street." He jerked his thumb in the direction of Broadway.

That's the way it goes. Maybe, as I get older and leave my forties behind, I can make friends quicker. Tain't no trick at all for some folks, I know. Like those two I saw a few days later. That time I sat more in the middle of the park. It was a perfect spot, some wonderful light-green branches shadin' and filterin' the sun a bit. A little distance off there was a young couple sittin' on the grass under a tree, watchin' their two tiny tots playin' around and laughin'. The little girl, about five, was older than her brother and had the prettiest blonde hair you ever seen. Now and then the father would catch the boy or girl, whichever came near enough, lift them up with a gentle roughness they liked, and let them go again, while the mother looked on it all with a contented smile.

The other couple, the one I'm talkin' about, sat on a metal bench that was fastened to another with a wire so as to make a double business of it. I saw them as I came up and took a place at the far end of the bench. I wondered if they were father and daughter at first. Even so, I could see they weren't very relaxed if they were—

not at all. They looked awfully tense, pent-up, and held-in. She was a plain-lookin' girl, without a trace of rouge or powder on—between twenty and twenty-five years old, I should say. She was dressed sensible, too, not going out of her way to call attention to her bosom. I know 'cause I didn't notice it at all, and I would have otherwise. Only once, while I sat there and while she was talkin' to the man, did I notice her knee, and that wasn't on display so much you could say she was teasin'. She wore a kind of a small-checked, black and white dress, which gave a gray effect. You can see how it all was.

The man I didn't size up as well, except that I saw at once that he was upwards of fifty and dressed in a good suit. Real erect he was: tense-like, as I said, interested in the girl. As soon as I sat down I realized from what they were sayin' that they just had met. They talked some about the children runnin' around the tree on the other side of the walk in front of us. She said her four younger brothers did a lot more playin' than she ever had or could. The guy told her how his kids had grown up and gone to California and his wife had gone out there later, too. The girl spoke about her husband, but I couldn't make out whether he still was her husband or only once had been. The same with the guy's wife. I didn't want to show I was listenin'.

As it was, I stayed long after I had finished my cigar and was due back in the office. I pretended to be dozin' in the softy sun and not even noticin' they were there. They had moved nearer together and were talkin' real personal. The couple with the children had gone. Most of the conversation I couldn't hear, but the girl was laughin' more than before, a nervous laugh she couldn't control; and the guy, though sittin' maybe a foot or two away, was leanin', swayin' toward the girl, quite close at times, like he knew the proper distance in this public place but couldn't keep it. I didn't hear nothin' real romantic from the man, nor see the girl givin' what I'd call the come-on. Suddenly like water burstin' from a dam, the guy says to the girl in a husky voice, "Would you like to see how nice I've got my room fixed up—just over on Lincoln?" And they got up, and he put his arm tight around the girl's waist, and they left me there all alone, watchin' them go.

It's not that I need the knack especially or miss it often, but somehow, right now, I do envy the guy who can make friends fast. I don't know why I should, all in all. It's one of those things, I guess: a kind of warm weather madness that comes over a guy when he happens to have a stretch of lonely lunch hours.

Loudly Sing Cuckoo

"Men without women" may be a good title for a book if the book is by Hemingway, but otherwise it doesn't make sense. Nature doesn't abhor a vacuum more than men miss the company of women. If the circumstances are right, the first thing they do is corrupt the sexual purity of the gathering by introducing some females into it. Under less favorable circumstances, the gals are promptly given top billing in the conversation. So true is this, that talk of women is one of the chief competitors for the attention of men that a woman in the flesh has.

The manner in which the fair sex clambers onto the stage when none of its representatives is present varies considerably. On this particular night of nights, Red McEwen gave an intentional assist, but all the time he was talking about opera to three fellows who knew nothing and cared less about music. Having tickets for a performance of *Manon* later in the week, Red had been reading the story from which the libretto was taken. He was amazed, he said, at the degree to which the hero of the book, Chevalier Des Grieux, was constantly being cuckolded. Does the same thing happen in the opera? Surely not: such things couldn't happen today, even on the stage.

There was a pause while the three who were enjoying the hospitality of Red's club and drinking his whiskey were mentally stripping the opera and the book, which they regarded as so much surplus clothing, from the subject, which appeared to have more potential than the growth stocks which they had been describing in detail up to then. The club was across the Potomac River from the nation's capital city. All the men had served in the Corps Headquarters which, during the late Great War, had borne the code designation of Buffalo. All now lived in Washington save Jim Stickney whose visit to the East from Sonora Springs was the occasion of the reunion celebration in progress.

"Well, I don't know, Red," said Jim. "I think it would be better to say such things can't happen to the likes of us. Romances of that sort are no more dead, though, than is romance generally. I've heard tell of quite a few instances, and some have impressed me as true. As a matter of fact, I know from personal experience of an affair bearing a close resemblance to old-fashioned cuckoldry.

"It was this way. A guy from my home-town, who works for the same company as I do, expected to go to Kansas City on business for a few days so he wrote a college chum of his, who lived there, to expect him the coming Saturday. Before the guy left Sonora Springs on the trip, he received a wire from his pal in K.C. to the effect that the latter had been called to the West Coast suddenly and would be gone for several weeks. The telegram went on, however, to urge its recipient to stay in the sender's apartment at the Charing Cross Hotel. Everything had been arranged with the hotel.

"The guy, call him Joe, accepted his friend's invitation and made himself at home in the hotel suite. After he came back to the apartment at the Charing Cross from a solitary Saturday-evening dinner, the telephone rang. He answered. It was Florence, the friend's best girl. She had heard so much of Joe that she'd like to meet him, she said. Perhaps they could see a little of the town together. She had a car. Maybe Joe knew better, maybe he didn't. Anyway, he bit on the girl's proposition.

"I needn't tell you that one thing led to another and Joe took advantage of his friend as well as his hospitality. Since then, which was ten years ago, the girl and Joe's friend have married. The two get along as well as any couple, probably, but both are disappointed at not having children. When Joe happens to think of the episode he will laugh and say to himself: "The devil pulls us toward another man's wife, but we pick our own for ourselves."

There was a variety of brief, chuckled, grunted responses. Then Lance Linkletter picked up the ball. "I had a case a couple of years ago which beats anything I ever heard in this respect. The Federal court, which doesn't pay anything to the attorneys it appoints, asked me to represent a fellow from the Midwest who had been arrested and brought back here for trial. He was charged with tax evasion by claiming as a dependent a child whom he and his wife had abandoned and who had been legally adopted by some folks who were giving the little girl a good home.

"The charges were true. Catesby, however, was delighted at the opportunity for legal services without expense to himself, and he insisted on pleading not guilty. Besides, I suspect, he wanted to sound out the possibility of beating the rap by legal magic, a failing which is pretty common among individuals of infinitely better character than Catesby. The first time I ever saw the fellow in jail, I had a mental image of a limp celery stalk in a garbage can. He lacked starch, stiffness, backbone. Talking to him was like trying to pick up mercury or gelatin pudding with the hands.

"Of course, the truth or falsity of a criminal charge doesn't always signify what verdict the jury will bring in. There's always the unexpected, the side issue which pops up accidentally and tips the scales one way or the other. In this case, the facts of the unexpected favored the prosecuting attorney. It developed during the trial that while Catesby was overseas during the war, his wife was convicted of prostitution and served a sentence of imprisonment. This was news to me. The chance revelation about Catesby's wife hurt Catesby more with the jury than the bona fide evidence on the tax evasion charge.

"But that's not all. It is all the jury learned, but one of the Treasury's special agents came over to me when the evidence was in and while we were waiting for the jury to return with its verdict. He said he had worked on the phase of the investigation which took place in the Midwest. He said 'Now the case is out of your hands and our hands. I can tell you something I'm sure you don't know. Catesby's wife wasn't fooling him when he was away; she worked at the same trade when he was around. He rustled up customers for her.'"

There was much head shaking among Lance's listeners, not of disbelief but, rather, of distaste for Catesby. Then Bernie broke into a nervous laugh and exclaimed, "Was that a T-man or a tit-man told you that?" They all left off some noisy snorts and guffaws at this remark.

"Yeah, maybe the poor guy didn't know there are some things just can't be done by proxy or by agent," said Red. "Maybe he had heard more about such devices than he understood."

"I guess it's time for me to go into opera," said Bernie Slocum, "and nobody has less business there than I do. When I first came to Washington as a young bachelor, I had a job in one of the government departments. I had one of those cubbyhole offices along one of those dim, interminable corridors. I shared it with my secretary, a beautiful darling about my age. She was wonderful, and she had everything: big blue eyes, dark hair, splendid figure. Only trouble was, she was married. This made things pretty hard for us. I can realize, looking back, that she had a more difficult row to hoe than I had. She wasn't getting along with hubby, but neither he nor she believed in divorce. The husband, a private detective, was away a lot. Nowadays, he'd probably get out a little business card, 'Have gun, will travel.'

"The girl's name was Tracy. I told you she had a knockout figure, and I know. As time went on, we used to play tennis together often, with her in one of those cute tennis costumes. She was enough to make a guy's blood boil. People at the office began to suspect things before they happened. I left the government service, and Tracy transferred to another department. We continued to see each other. Finally, I could see a war was coming on, and I got into the army and was sent away from Washington. It was the only way out."

"Gosh," said Red, "I had no idea I might be starting a confession session when I spoke about *Manon*. But now that the party bus has taken that turn, I'll tell one. Mine isn't a tale of love and romance, unfortunately. I wish it was.

"You may wonder how I could make a cuckold of a guy without love or something akin to it figuring into the situation. It isn't easy; it takes some doing, but I managed it, all right.

"When I got out of the service after the war, I had no definite notion what I wanted to do, except that it should be different from what I had been doing in the antebellum days. I answered an ad in the paper. I had an interview with the fellow who ran it. His name was Bill Wassoon. He had started a management consultant agency: had procured a few clients, hired a few clients, and was hoping for the best.

"Talk about a Nervous Nellie. Wassoon was it, was the prototype of them all. He was impressed with my experience; apparently rated my abilities above his own. I could see he wanted to take me on as an assistant in the worst way but was afraid that if he did, I would take his clients away from him, gobble up his business, and leave him nothing. The idea was utterly ridiculous, but in spite of myself I began to throw out vague hints and threats that I had exactly that in mind. In spite of himself, he hired me, as if he wanted the worst to happen.

"I shouldn't have taken the job. I could have got another which paid as well. I had no respect for the boss, either at the beginning or later. Yes, you know the story without my telling it. I cuckolded the guy, so to speak. That's the way I got my present business. I took it away from him. I wooed his clients and made them mine." Red took a gluttonous gulp of whiskey as if he wanted to play the sad, mad Russian before the evening ended and couldn't wait.

'That's the way the ball bounces," said Lance. "Incidentally, have you ever heard the one about the knight who wanted to go away on the crusades? He locked his wife in a chastity belt, but, as a precautionary measure, he gave a key to his best friend for use in case of an emergency. Then the knight rode off on his favorite stallion at a leisurely trot, elated at the prospect of performing feats of chivalry, valor, and high emprise. Before he had ridden far, his friend came galloping hell bent for election after him, shouting "Hey, you gave me the wrong key."

"Red, I reckon that when you said cuckoldry couldn't happen anymore, you meant that it couldn't happen any more than it does," Bernie bantered.

"Yeah," said Lance, "like the guy who doesn't drink any more—not anymore, but just as much."

"You know," Jim put in, "if you guys maneuvered this conversation along these lines in order to make me feel uneasy about being away from home, I don't think it's funny at all."

"You can bet on it, Jim, that that's not our idea of a joke at all. For myself, I thought when we began that we were talking academically about a lost art—I mean, about a silly theme for a romantic opera."

"Forget it, Jim," Lance said. "What that guy in Kansas City doesn't know won't hurt him. Let's take a final swig as a toast to Red's operatic hero: then set Jim down at his hotel in time for a little devilry; and after that, get ourselves back to the bosom of our families. Tomorrow is another day."

A Man in a Million

In a town the size of Sonora Springs, there's bound to be some characters—interesting ones, I mean, not police characters. It's not like Diz Brown says, that nowadays everybody's as like as two cars off the same assembly line. It's not entirely that way, I say. Jed Sparks chips in with Diz and says it's getting so the men are more like women, and the women like men, and both like machines. We have some real tough arguments, I tell you.

Now you take that there old Doc Gaylord. He's as loveable an old fraud as you could want to meet. I called him an old fraud, but he isn't the kind that goes around selling watered stocks to widows, orphans, and retired bankers. He isn't that kind at all. He's more sinned against than sinner, if you ask me. He owes me maybe $25 or $50 I'll never see again, but he didn't really borrow it from me. I lent it to him when he was out of ready cash.

That's one thing about old Doc Gaylord. He's hard up as often as not. That's a fact. There have been times, I know, when Doc's own kids had a bigger allowance than Doc kept for himself as spending money. Now, he's in his seventies; and been everywhere; done everything; and knows everybody. So he says, and I never have caught him giving the truth a downright drubbing.

Anyway, he wouldn't fib to me. And as far as knowing everybody, you just try him out sometime and ask him about anybody at all around town—about anybody that is anybody, I mean. He'll show you. He'll call the guy up, and the first thing you know they'll be talking and laughing about pranks that they played when they went to school together. It beats all.

Some folks say he isn't a doctor, and it's all nonsense to call him old Doc Gaylord, instead of plain old Gaylord. They may be right, but they do call him old Doc Gaylord just the same—and that's the true test about what he ought to be called, isn't it? I don't suppose he is a doctor, though once in a while I have heard him talk about trips to Hungary and Uruguay and far-off places to hunt for medicinal plants. Of course, now the wise guys that wear glasses and white coats make everything themselves out of coal tar and casein and don't need plants anymore.

Sure, Gaylord isn't his real name. I savvied that from the first. Roy Washington Gaylord. No boy ever had such a mouthful wished onto him by his parents. You can tell right away that a name like that had to push Jones, Smith, or McTavish out of the way first. Don't ask me why a McTavish isn't satisfied to remain that, or why his taste runs to Roy, French for king, to Washington for the Father of his Country, and to Gaylord for Lord of happiness and all. That's what makes a character a character: because they have peculiar knacks and likings. Anyway, old Doc Gaylord doesn't think he's Napoleon, and that's more than people could say for Bonaparte.

What's more he may have been a writer at one time or an actor. There's time to do a lot of things in seventy-odd years if you don't run along in one groove all your life in the monotonous way most of us have. Writers and actors often pick their own names, I guess. It's all right for them to do. Come to think of it, I seem to remember old Doc Gaylord telling me about having been the ace of feature writers once upon a time and about having covered the Japanese invasion of Manchuria for Reuters.

The first time I ever saw the man, he told me he just had finished writing a book. He expected that before long he'd be "filthy rich." I sympathized with him, because it isn't fair for a guy to be that rich, what with tax collectors waiting in ambush for you when you get home at night and peddlers of phony stocks coming at you from all directions. Old Doc Gaylord nodded. He'd thought of that. He would handle the taxmen and peddlers by giving everything he made to charity. If the book ever did come out, likely as not old Doc Gaylord used still a different name, not to fool the taxmen or his friends, but, you know, just to do it that way.

I don't know what the guy does for a living. I don't know. He doesn't scrounge. He's been in and out of uranium—in and out and all around: from around Riverton south to the Four Corners Area and on into New Mexico. You name it. He's been there. It wouldn't surprise me if he sold some of those claims to Pick that Pick sold to Odlum. There's no prying. No need to pry either, because Doc tells some pretty rare stories about his adventures. Not the financial end of things but about killing a nest of rattlesnakes or about rescuing a miner trapped in a shaft, tales like that. Who cares who took who when the mining claims were exchanged for stock? Except for being short of folding stuff now and then, Doc seems to get along OK, wherever the dough may come from.

Right now, my friend lives alone. He does have a family, though—a grown-up one. You might say he has two families. He's been married twice, and I gather that the first old gal is still living. The second wife is a bedridden invalid and stays with a married daughter somewhere in the East. It's rumored that the first wife nicked our friend for a goodly sum, but I can't make out whether that happened before or during the divorce. It's quite all right to do it with the help of the judge and no cause for hard feelings at all. The fact is that all I know about this I've heard from rumors and not from Doc himself, and I don't know which is the more reliable.

It isn't that old Doc Gaylord lies. He doesn't. The guy does have a terrific imagination, though, and sometimes the things he imagines are more real for him than the real. With some folks, that causes misunderstandings. When they hand out hokum, they do it intentionally. By their lights, this guy doesn't play the game fair. He lies. Well, no use arguing about differences like that. Things that are too matter-of-fact don't interest me at all. What's as plain as the nose on one's face is so unimportant that I don't care whether it's true or not. Aren't most people that way?

Old Doc Gaylord is a happy man, but there's one misfortune which I feel sure must haunt his dreams. It's about his son by his first marriage. It seems that when the two parents decided to have done with each other, way back when, the son remained with the mother. For years now, if not always, there have been no relations between father and son. I know the son, too—an eminently respectable man—but I would not dare to open the subject with him. May some odd stroke of fortune come along, in time, and grant to my old friend the strongest wish of his heart, a reunion with his son.

Meet Mr. Green

During the past winter, I happened to have a series of conversations with a young friend which I cannot forget. Johnny Green came to spend a weekend with me at a remote, old-fashioned cabin which had been in my family for years. Owing to an unusually fierce and grand snowstorm, my guest, a lawyer by profession, was forced to prolong his visit.

It was while we were thus magnificently snowbound that these talks occurred. We spoke of the half-forgotten past; of the kaleidoscopic, hurried, disordered present and even of the fearsome future; of cabbages and kings; dictators, deity, and destiny; of the human race, synthetics, and other things.

Ever since, I have been haunted by the experience, though not by the breadth of the subjects discussed, nor by the lightning flashes of interpretation of past or present experiences of myself or my friend. Rather, I find myself reflecting again and again on this guest whom I had met in high school, seen often since, but not really known. In particular, I cannot keep from rearranging his presence in my imagination, squinting down the dim corridor of time, peering at pages of his future diary, and even having, years hence, another heart-to-heart conversation.

In spite of myself, these images, these fireside reveries insist on materializing on paper. Difficult as it is to describe an actual acquaintance as he stands before me, I am compelled not merely to hold a mirror up to a conjured presence but to take a leap in time and to show you photographs taken in the candlelit darkness of the future.

Yesterday and Today

About a year ago, Johnny Green took an oath to the "ever-living God"—the expression is the Supreme Court's—and was admitted to the bar of the sovereign state of Colorado, or of New Jersey, or of Illinois, no matter. He sighed relief and looked around with a smile of pride and companionship at his brothers of the bar, on the bench and off.

In due season, Green sought for space in which to receive hoped-for clients and to ponder over their legal problems. He called upon one of the senior members of the bar who, it was rumored, had an extra office in his suite in the Palace Building. The eminent personage, Mr. Deal, would have the time to see Green, the secretary announced, a little surprised at this generosity on the part of her employer. The worthy Mr. Deal explained to Green briefly and with finality that he had no space available.

The matter of time but no space having been settled, Deal became jocular and even familiar. "Got an insurance company client? No? They are always nice to have, you know, when you're practicing law." Green smiled at his elder's undoubted cleverness.

Green took space on the fifth floor of the Constitution Building, an old but well-kept structure inhabited mainly by lawyers. Quite likely the occupants of the same floor took notice of Green's arrival, but they concealed their interest beneath an air of indifference. At times it seemed that his professional colleagues feared that some benighted stranger seeking a lawyer might by an odd chance enter Green's office rather than their own.

More often, Green just wondered about the behavior of these reserved and busy creatures about him. They reminded him of watches: they had faces, hands, kept regular time, and otherwise suggested intricate mechanisms enclosed in smooth and shining cases of nylon and Dacron. What was the reason for his neighbors' baffled expression when Green visited the adjoining offices? Were these people mystified that without a gold brick to sell he should bridge the distance between offices to make a friendly call, to acknowledge their existence and fix his own identity?

At a social gathering at a country club, Green recognized a girl he had known at college. She did not know he had gone to law school; Green did not know she had married. Sue introduced her husband, Ray, and the couple asked Green to sit at their table. "What are you doing now?" Sue wanted to know. When Green replied, there was an almost audible gasp of consternation. Sue exclaimed, "Why, that's what Ray is doing…" Her voice trailed off, but Green caught the unspoken words "and I so hoped you could be a client or a prospective one."

During an intermission at the theater, Green noticed Rusty, one of the well-known business men he had chanced to meet. The latter remembered Green. "So you decided not to go back—to Iowa, was it? Well, you'll like it here in the West. We're friendly people out here." Rusty put on his ready-made broad smile to prove his point. "Yes, sir, we make it our business to be friendly in these parts. I mean that's our way of doing things in this wide-open country." Green nodded, "Yeah, I know what you mean."

At a lecture course for the profession, Green took note of the others present, all young men like himself. They hurried in with a set purpose, grimly determined to learn the new tricks of their trade. The first speaker dealt with the grounds for divorce. With apparently unconscious humor, the speaker left the impression that all the various specific grounds dissolve into the one all-inclusive ground of marriage. The next speaker considered whether payments of alimony made periodically are periodical payments, mentioning chapter and verse of the Code. A fine point of law. The man at Green's side was taking notes, not missing a word. The others were giving rapt attention.

Green does not reflect much upon his experiences during his first year at the bar. At times, though, as he looks out the window of his office upon the people ceaselessly and swiftly crossing the street, milling and moiling, entering and leaving the Great Western Building, the Imperial, the Gold Key, and the Silver Lode, the people change to ants, the city to an ant hill, and the buildings turn themselves upside down to become hills in the ant hill. Whether he is in the office or out, however, his smile is ready, broad, and truly friendly, like Rusty's.

A Leaf from Green's Diary

February 2, 1970. Snowbound. This time all alone. Vaguely I remember a similar experience ten or fifteen years ago in the mountain cabin of some friend. A grand guy he was; funny, I can't remember his name right now.

If I have forgotten my host on that occasion, what of it? It seems to me I am getting acquainted with myself for the first time. Up here in the fastness of this white world, my own name, Johnny Green, means more. I scarcely knew Johnny Green before this day, though we were born on the same day in the same tiny village in Minnesota.

It seems to me, looking back, that I developed such powers of self-deception so early in life that the individual who gazed at me from the mirror each morning remained a stranger to me for more than thirty years. Always till this day, we strangers passed each other even within the narrow confines of my study or my office without looking—taking less note of each other than ships which pass in the night. Now, for the first time, I see myself face to face with a direct and level look.

That unknown self of mine was an imaginative, poetic, passionate fellow. It is a pity I did not know him—I mean myself—before this. Still, part of that passion was ugly anger, a deep-seated, moldering rage capable of a dangerous flame if it had erupted. That buried anger, hidden till now even from me, was like an underground fire in a peat bog. Perhaps that fierce passion originated in some simple equivalent of an unattended camp fire or discarded cigarette. Here and now, in this high, white, and silent solitude, the danger of a sudden flame seems illusory, non-existent.

I should like, after I leave this enforced retreat—this coming summer, not later—to revisit the scenes of my childhood. I will look once more on the fields of goldening grain and insist it is more than a crop which meets the eye. At my ease watching the redwings at play and over the meadow, I will maintain against all comers that flights of fancy are not for the birds alone. I was right as a child: a murmuring stream meandering through a pasture is more than a cheap drainage. I was right then and only half knew it. It is clear to me now, absolutely.

Before I make that trip this coming summer, I shall have to spend several months at the office. Perhaps the roads will be cleared tomorrow, and I can go back to town. I feel as though I have had a long vacation and can wrestle vigorously with the tax details of Wrangler's divorce.

An Evening with Mr. Green, 1985

In 1985, I read in the newspaper that my old schoolmate, Johnny Green, had been in an airplane accident. The accident was not fatal, but Mr. Green the pilot and sole occupant of the personal plane at the time, had suffered severe injuries and shock. I visited him several times at the hospital, renewed our old friendship, which had lapsed what with one thing and another, and offered as much help as I could under the circumstance.

My friend bore the misfortune bravely, but, even after the stage of his convalescence, he had the air of one who has difficulty in focusing his mind on immediate affairs and the material aspects of day-to-day living. As his health improved, Mr. Green's attitude changed imperceptibly from one of detachment and abstraction to a philosophic concern with age-old issues of religion, morality, and immorality.

I remember particularly a visit I had with Mr. Green one evening after he had returned from the hospital. We were alone; other visitors already had left, and Mrs. Green had retired early. Paradoxically, this venerable gentleman (even at his age then, he was venerable), who had always abjured the chains of professional habit, spoke as though in the numbered paragraphs of a lawyer's pleadings or briefs. On this occasion, too, he, who had more than once depreciated intelligence and the rules of logic in order to praise the institutions of imagination and feeling, expressed himself in the measured manner of a logician.

Our conversation had drifted to the consolations of religion. Then it was that my friend took over the subject and began to soliloquize. In a sense he began to complain of the religious orthodoxy which, in appearances at least, had clothed and supported him up to then. Yet, he voiced more than a complaint, for he always intimated the affirmation which seemed to him to be an alternative to the view or condition complained of. All this you can see for yourself in the following condensation of Mr. Green's remarks.

There is something important, something vital, lacking from the teaching that Divine Truth was revealed to men in ages past; that all efforts and good fortune of men now and in the future can only yield tiny particles of the low-grade ore known as scientific truth.

For me there is a forbidding sternness in the view that men are damned, unworthy, and lost unless they accept one of the packaged religious medicines offered in the temples. I prefer a faith which defies packaging and labeling, one which will be capable of expanding and appealing to the good sense and devotion of all the people, all over the globe, at whatever language or color.

To me, Nature is wonderful, as much so as any supernatural could be. The birth of a child, or of any creature, is sufficiently miraculous. The creation of the world by a gradual, evolutionary process impresses and satisfies me as much as would its creation by one fell stroke.

I know some people hold that men are prodigal sons of their Divine Father and are destined to wallow in a Serbonian bog of guilt and sin. It appeals to me more to consider the concept and feelings of sin as a fit subject of inquiry, like the origin and nature of typhoid fever.

In this same vein, my friend would have gone on, but I saw he was tiring. Despite my reluctance to interrupt, I thought it best to do so. As I took my leave, I saw that good old Johnny Green was quite ready for sleep and pleasant dreams. In a few months, I could see Mr. Green would be well enough to be back at his office.

My Father's Double

My father, who lost his life in the Korean War, was a great hero. Everyone is agreed on that. Besides, Mom has medals and citations to prove it. I wasn't far beyond kindergarten when it happened in Korea, but I knew about heroism and words and everything better then than now. That was before I had visits from Dad's double.

I can't remember Dad, as he really was, very well any more. I've heard so much about him that the gossip of neighbors and relatives has sort of pushed my own recollection of him into the background and over a steep cliff into the sea. Anyway, I was pretty young when Dad shipped overseas never to return. Of course, I've seen quite a few snapshots of the Old Man in uniform, and Mom keeps a great big photograph of the three of us on her dresser all the time. Still, that isn't the same as a lifelike memory of Dad's sight and sound and smell and feel.

Maybe that's why the double has come—to keep me company and to take the place of Dad and of a mental image of him. After all, a young fellow needs a personal souvenir. What Mom tells me isn't enough; and Mom isn't enough. A guy my age knows the stork is just talk, and he wants to know more and to connect more to his entire family back to Adam. I mean, a guy wants footing and rooting way back and deep down.

It is as hard for me to make sense of the descriptions Mom gives as to make the gobbledygook of those military citations fit Dad. The pictures and photographs don't even look real. All that seems clear to me now about Dad is that he always had a cap on—sometimes one of those stiff, leather billed deals but usually a soft, close-fitting overseas cap. But it takes more than a couple kinds of regulation headgear to add up to a memory of a man. No one needs to tell me that.

Dad's double never wears the least thing on his head, summer or winter. His hair is thick, dark, curly and rumpled. He's always out of uniform, as Dad himself must have been before the war. There isn't anything about the double, whom I call Grandpa, that smacks of gallantry in action or hints at duty—let alone conduct above and beyond the call of duty. Grandpa isn't terribly old; probably no more so than Dad was when he left home. I had to have a name for the newcomer so I called him Grandpa, seeing as both my granddaddies were gone before I was born. The name made the stranger one of the family.

I haven't told Mom or anyone else about Grandpa. What's the use? They wouldn't understand. Grandpa isn't at all heroic; and he gets drunk at times and is awfully impolite. Nothing could be more shocking to Mom than the way Grandpa acts up. She says Dad never even drank enough whiskey and such stuff to get high, let alone stinko the way Grandpa gets.

Speaking of stinko, there always is a strong odor about Grandpa. He gets all sweaty from doing something or other—bicycling, I suppose—before he comes to see me. You can see the little drops and roll of sweat and dirt in the creases of his sun-browned neck. Then, while we talk, he sits and smokes the vilest smelling, dark, stumpy cigars you can imagine. He never offers me a smoke, and I never ask for a stogey. One time after Grandpa left, I tried out a mild Coronal I came by somehow, and kee-ripes, did I suffer—sick to my stomach, light-headed and limp all over. A garbage-can celery stalk had nothing on me for being blooey. Boy, I had it. Cigars are strictly for Grandpa from now on.

When I was just a tiny tot, Mom used to get a laugh from the neighbors by telling how I went around with a gunny sack over my shoulders imitating the garbage collectors I'd seen come into the yard. Well, Grandpa's clothing is not a bit better than a garbage man's. I swear, he has no pride at all in such matters. I keep him out of Mom's bedroom where that photograph is. The contrast with Dad and his uniform would be too great. The plaster might drop on me from the ceiling—on me and Grandpa and the picture and Mom's bed. Maybe nothing at all would happen, but the risk is too great to take a chance.

When I go fishing or rock-climbing in the mountains, or exploring caves, or something like that with Larry or Dave or Steve, Grandpa doesn't come along. It isn't that he is jealous: he wants me to have fun with those of my own age, that's all. Grandpa isn't a model imitation of a modern major-general, but he has his own ideas of what is fitting and right.

I'm grateful for Grandpa's company, but I help him, too. It isn't one of those one-way affairs he and I have. When he's unsteady on his feet and wobbling—or just plain stinko, as I said—I run to help him get along. I'm big enough now so we can walk arm in arm without any trouble. It's pretty wonderful to be able to help; and

Grandpa can do with a little. He isn't one of those well-heeled, well-dressed, leather-laced, plaster saints that sets everybody rushing to the rescue. And Grandpa couldn't repay people for such services. He needs me.

One time last week as the two of us were going along like that, arm in arm with me steadying Grandpa, we had come within a block or two from home. Then, all the way ahead, there were people standing in front of their houses: neighbors. They should have known me, and I should have recognized them. Funny thing, though, we were strangers to each other. Folks who used to drool over Captain Dorcas' infant son now gazed at me blankly, and I could tell they didn't think much of either of us and of Grandpa least of all. He knew it, too. As we came up to one middle-aged couple, they stood right in the middle of the sidewalk so as to leave scarcely enough room for us to get by. Grandpa belched loudly: not so much to insult them as to give them notice of our presence, the way a motorist gives a little burp of his horn to warn an unwary pedestrian about to step off the curb.

That did it. They continued to stare at us, but they had been awakened half-ways. The rest of the idling, curious, gaping, householders made way for us as we approached. They were bewildered by the strange sight of the neat, brushed and combed boy proudly supporting his drunken, rag-patch father, but they offered no disrespect. Indeed, they stood aside, some at each edge of the walk, to let us pass between the rows. I couldn't have got more of a bang out of reviewing troops.

To tell the truth, I would he proud and happy to have Grandpa as mv father, but I guess you all know that by now.

New Maps for Old

Mary Tolliver was ready for romance with a capital R when she moved to Denver to take a job as a secretary, but mystery was something else altogether. For that she was unprepared. To her certain knowledge, a dozen girls had exchanged diplomas of the High Plains Business College at Colby, Kansas, for Denver marriage licenses; but it never even occurred to her that anything bizarre or unusual might happen in one of those modern rabbit warrens called a skyscraper. Well—to somebody else, it might; somebody in a newspaper, but not to her.

It might be gilding things a bit to call the Mountain States Building a skyscraper, but it was Denver's newest and tallest building. The Financial Security Center might have forty floors to thirty-nine for Mountain States, but the latter had a tower, and the one-legged weather-vane chicken perched on top of the ball on the dome was higher than anything else in town.

The plains people, like Mary, and the mountain people of the Western Slope agreed with old-time Denverites on the structure's rating as a skyscraper without a second thought, wholly unmindful of the winces this provincial consensus might bring to the faces of Manhattanites.

Mary worked on the seventeenth floor of the building for the regional branch of an eastern concern that manufactured snow-making equipment. Her boss, Homer (Doc) Aridite, was out of the office practically all the time trying to sell his curious, complex, cold-weather machines, with their whirling nozzles, to the operators of Rocky Mountain ski areas. It was a dry winter that year, but competition was terrific from the guy who claimed to have ways and means for bringing the flaky, powdery, downy moisture out of the clouds.

Across the hall from the Scalene Snow Machine Company was the Baronoff Oil Company. Here again, the boss, Phineas Baronoff, was away for months at a time. Mary had only seen the guy once. At five o'clock, as she was closing up her office one day, the oilman had his hand on the door knob of his own suite, just ready to enter. At the man's side at the time, crouching low was a large wolf-lean, black-shouldered dog on a short leash. She was so surprised at the unexpected encounter, and it was over so quickly, she couldn't remember afterwards quite how Mr. Baronoff looked. Just strange—that was her only recollection—that and the dog.

Paul Grierson, who worked for Mr. Baronoff, Mary saw frequently. It was a good thing she did, or, in view of the lightness of her office duties, time would have hung heavy on her hands, and she would have become extremely lonesome, maybe even homesick for Pa and Ma and the plains and her old home town. Paul called himself Mr. Baronoff's secretary, but actually, his main job was that of guarding his employer's office and, in particular, the oil maps kept there. Years before, when the company's office had been on the ground floor of a remodeled farmhouse in Oklahoma, Paul had fought off a couple of gunmen who had attempted to seize and carry away some of the maps in his charge. He still limped from a bullet wound received in that battle. It was a slight but genuine limp, not merely the odd, awkward walk that goes with those high-heeled, pointed-toe cowboy boots.

The two of them, Paul and Mary, managed, without getting beyond the sound of their respective telephones, to exchange visits across the hall and to have coffee together in the forenoon and tea or a soft drink in the afternoon. Paul was considerably older than Mary, but he was unmarried and good company in a reserved, silent moody fashion. Whenever she entered his office with coffee or simply to chat, he would turn away from a study of the maps on his desk. He would turn away from the maps, but oftentimes, he would listen in the preoccupied manner of one whose mind is still wrapped up in the geography and geology of oil fields, still imprisoned in the folds of the crisp, accordion-pleated, pastel-colored documents. She talked and he listened, and she was fairly content with it that way.

As she got to know Paul better, Mary began to wonder whether the charts that held Paul's mind captive really had to do with the location of oil wells and oil reserves. Besides, he seemed to have changed—grown, grown stronger and at once closer and more distant—since she first knew him. A time or two she had the idea that the map which Paul shoved to the far side of his desk at her approach might show, instead of valuable industry information, the general geography of the South Sea Islands. That suspicion increased when she noticed, on another occasion, one of the Pacifique Air Lines' folders describing Tahiti and its wonderfully relaxed, happy, carefree, colorfully clothed and unclothed natives: male, female, young and old.

Then, one morning, Paul went out to get coffee for both of them and did not come back. Mary went across the hall to Baronoff's. The office door stood open (customarily left that way so she could hear the phone in Paul's absence), but she could see that the door of the map vault was locked shut. On Paul's desk, in plain sight this time, was that pictorial circular and map of Tahiti. Beside the folder was a fresh, new but empty airline ticket envelope. At noon, when she felt sure that Paul wasn't coming back, Mary called the police and reported the affair to them. The unexplained, mysterious disappearance was too much for her to bear alone. It helped, though, to be as certain as she was that he was not fleeing from her.

New World Symphony

Once upon a time a great philosopher, after prolonged and profound meditation, reached the conviction that he was living in the best of all possible worlds. That was, oh, two centuries ago, at least, so you can see the guy was so far ahead of his time it is pitiful. His description is an apt one for our own environment today but scarcely can have fitted the situation when he wrote it, for think of the tremendous strides which have been made since then. The egg-headed German was mixed up, no doubt of it.

Time was when Mephisto, trying always to do evil, could do but good, which put him in a class by himself. Now an ordinary murderer is in practically the same boat. I heard a story the other day which illustrates, surpassingly well, how progress in moral principle has kept pace with the improvements in the material situation.

To all outward appearances, Konkel was a vicious, despicable, no-account, no-good desperado. He had been in and out of a half-dozen correctional institutions before he was old enough to vote. His passion for armed robbery continued unabated. The only thing corrected by those various sojourns at state expense was certain crudities in Konkel's technique. He would lie awake for hours during the long prison nights thinking up ways to improve upon the seemingly simple art of robbery.

Well, all that's past history, but I'm telling you the story as it was told to me.

Then one night, as Konkel was holding up a gasoline filling station in a western city, he pulled the trigger on his automatic pistol. No one knows whether the shooting was deliberate or whether the guy's finger slipped, and who cares? The result was the same: murder. And all for fifty bucks. He made his getaway to another state, but the escape was temporary. He was rounded up a few months later in Seattle; and, if he can't beat extradition, he's pretty sure to be a dead duck as soon as the last knot is tied in the legal formalities.

How does this prove that the millennium has, indeed, arrived? Well, wait a minute, Brother. I'm telling you the story as it was told to me.

The victim of this foul crime of Konkel's was Charlie Gutka, a man around forty, with a wife and three kids. Charlie was the steady sort: had been pumping gas at the same old stand between five and ten years; had seen to it that his wife was well dressed and that the kids were in school. Of course, it had been impossible for Charlie to do much more than keep up with his creditors. There were hardly any savings in the bank and no life insurance. He was an arrested case of TB, and that made him uninsurable.

The Magellan Oil Company had the reputation of acting fast. It had been one of the first of the drilling giants to do business on a world-wide scale. Immediately after the fatal stick-up, its officials issued a press release announcing that the receipts of the next weekend's business at the pillaged station would be turned over to the widow of the murdered man. In addition, a huge red banner carrying the inscription "Gutka Benefit Days June 26-27" in white letters was strung high and horizontally over the gasoline pumps several days in advance of the scheduled affair.

Ordinarily, this particular retail outlet of Magellan's had a daily take of a couple hundred dollars. Its corner location was on a main street in the city but not on a through highway. It was on the edge of the wholesale district. On Saturday, June 26, automobiles of all kinds converged on the intersection of Fifteenth and Bridger in such numbers that the services of five extra police officers were required to direct traffic. Receipts, as reported over the radio and TV and on page one of *The Daily Telegraph*, exceeded $2000. The next day, Sunday, was, of course, normally a quiet one in this vicinity, but, believe it or not, the sales volume came close to Saturday's record.

Most of the customers were fellow townsmen of the Gutkas, but the majority of them were not regular patrons of the station and had never seen Charlie. Many had gone out of their way to lend a helping hand. A number simply chanced to be going by, got caught in the tangle of vehicles, heard or guessed what was going on, and followed the flow of cars through Magellan's driveways.

Two farm implement salesmen on their way home after a "uranium vacation" in the high country had been exchanging war experiences with such concentration and enjoyment that they had missed a turn in the highway going south and, before realizing what had happened, found themselves and their Jeep inching toward Magellan's. They were in no hurry and entered fully into the spirit of the occasion.

"Don't you know," one said to the other, "that French soldier you told about who said he hated the Boches down to the soles of his boots and who couldn't understand how our GIs made war because it was their job, their business. He'd sure be stumped by this, wouldn't he?"

"He sure would," said the other. "For my money, the poor people of Paris overestimate the importance of love and hate and other feelings. It's the way of the backward goofs everywhere. I've always said 'business and principles come first,' and unless I miss my guess, this benefit is going to do a whale of a lot for the Gutkas, whoever they are. They've probably never had it so good."

"You're right, Joe. Principles above all."

This tale, just as I heard it, is a simple one, but it haunts me, the way a melody sometimes will. It's a sort of a New World Symphony in words. Can't you just hear it? Or maybe an opera with a rousing chorus: Principles first, forever and ever. Here and now the millennium, and for ages unending.

A Night to Forget

Fraser Schmidt thoroughly regretted the night before. He was by no means a drinking man; never had been, even in young manhood. His headache wasn't so serious—he hadn't drunk that much—but the evening's confusing conversation had left him terribly depressed. He had been on the receiving end of chatter which was better suited to the ears of a bartender than those of the editor of the *Colorado Cattleman*, confound it. Thanks goodness it was Saturday and there was no need to go to the office. Later on, he'd drive out to the ranch.

It had all started innocently enough. He had received a telephone call from Irv Greenslip in the late afternoon and had agreed to meet him for a quickie at the Captain's Choice, probably the most dignified and respectable tavern in Denver. Greenslip was a government tax lawyer who had been stationed in Denver before his transfer to Los Angeles. Fraser scarcely knew the guy, but Irv had been darn helpful in settling the dispute Fraser had had with Revenue a year or so ago over the income tax owing on the profits from his blooded, registered herd of Angus. It wouldn't hurt him at all to buy Irv a drink.

He had learned of Irv's habit of turning the most casual comment into tax channels, and he wasn't fond of that trick. Taxes bored the hell out of him and made him chafe inwardly at expenses, governments, and the damnable Russians who were responsible for most of the money being poured down a rat hole. Sure enough—Irv greeted him by asking whether he had acquired a new deduction since Irv's transfer. "How's that?" said Fraser. Irv laughed. "I mean, you married; got a wife; got income splitting?"

When Fraser replied that his marital status was unchanged, Irv good naturedly observed, "Costs money to be single. By the way, I got a new credit since I went to L. A.: a baby girl this time, just five months old, and cute as a bug."

It developed that Irv had come back from Los Angeles to try a couple of cases, and both of them had settled at the last minute, so he could catch a plane home in the morning. "Don't you know if anybody can drive a bargain, that Drinky Drotloff can," said Irv. "He was against me on both cases. I think the government did all right, but I swear he almost had me believing his story about his client having a cash hoard in a crock in the basement from before the income tax became law. What a load of baloney!"

"Drinky Drotloff?" said Fraser dubiously, taking a sip of his scotch and soda and making a futile attempt to place the fellow.

"Yeah. He's from South Dakota, but he gets a client down here now and then. He's a shrewd customer, that fox. Got a funny name, but it used to be worse. In college they started calling him Dirty Drotloff, as I understand it. He paid out good dough to have his cronies call him Drinky, and because he was pretty partial to fortified beverages anyway, the name stuck."

Fraser saw that a neighbor at the bar had taken quite an interest in Irv's remarks. He tried his hand at changing the subject. "Say, I heard a wonderful concert last night," he said. "The orchestra played from Bach to Bernstein." Irv laughed. "Ha ha. From Bach to Bernstein. That sounds like a letter from a lawyer to an accountant." He looked at the guy who had been listening in and invited him to share in the joke.

The latter did. "My name's Soule," he said. "And this is Walt Maurer and Swede Sundquist, old friends of mine from way back. I get such a kick in the pants and pain in the neck out of taxes, I couldn't help hearing what you were saying. I'm an investment man for the Second Bank here, and the other day we took a loss on a stock, wrote it off, and thought that was the end of it. Well, it was for us, maybe, but the fun was just beginning for the trustee in bankruptcy. Yes sir, he has gone to court, I hear, claiming the company's tax loss is an asset he should have. It's the funniest thing ever—the trustee and some operators pulling and tugging to see who gets that corporation's loss—two vultures, you might say, fighting for a dead jack rabbit. Like I was telling Swede and Walt, banking isn't what it used to be when losses were losses."

"No," said Swede. "Nothing is."

"No," said Walt, "I'm in the manufacturing business, and I don't mind sharing my salary and bonuses with the government. Who does? Anyway, I got into business through my wife's brother, which is a hell of a way to get into a business if you ask me—through your wife's brother." Here he fixed his gaze on Fraser, who nodded agreement and turned his eyes away and called for another round of drinks. Walt went on: "It's like your wife giving you your business. What the hell?" He gulped at his whiskey.

"Yeah, you got troubles, all right. You got a point there," said Swede. "But what about the title insurance business? That ain't altogether duck soup, you know, with the town sproutin' new subdivisions faster'n you can say Jack Robinson. How'd you like to be insurin' everybody with nobody insurin' you?"

"What's the picture there on your reserves?" asked Irv. "I mean what's the story on your reserves like life insurance?"

Swede had a baleful look in his eyes. "To hell it's like life insurance," he said. "Where'd you get that stuff?"

"He's from Los Angeles," Fraser put in.

"You know he's from Los Angeles," said Swede.

"I mean taxwise," said Irv.

"Yeah," said Walt. "A guy don't mind paying taxes on his damn business. Everybody does that. But what about paying taxes on every dime you take in on the market? I sold Gulf Oil, and I pocket the dough. Where's the government get at stuff—short-term gains? I'd move to Canada if I didn't have a wife and kids. You guys got troubles. Believe me, I got a wife and kids! It's a helluva a note, says I."

"You're not alone with a wife," said Soule. "I gotta wife, an' I tell you I saw her through the change of life, an' you think that ain't hell. And me an investment man with business marriages and mergers and messes poppin' all over the place, and I saw my wife through the change of life; bought her a place in the country; bought her horses to ride and jump and all; and me workin' twelve hours a day. And talk about diversification: I know one company's got a peanut farm in Georgia, a baseball park hell 'n' gone in the East, and makes furniture in Grand Rapids. All colonial designs, and you tell me about diversification, mister. Taxes don't have nothin' to do with it."

"You can go to Canada if you want, Walt," said Swede. "But for me it's back to the Service. There ain't never been a time like when I was a Commander in the Navy and just thirty years old. There was a girl in North Africa, I tell you, as black as I am blonde and not an African either. I know an African girl when I see one, and this one was just brunette, Sicilian blood, maybe pure Italian like she said. I wasn't bald-headed then, and that girl had everything—a bosom almost as big as that girl I told you about from Cannes—a real dark-skinned Venus in flesh and blood, perfection in every limb, too. And I'll let you guys in on a little secret insurance I have: the Admiral says he'll get me called up for duty whenever I say the word. You're a fool for Canada, Walt."

"And what about keeping up the reserves in your insurance business while you're sinking the Navy with your paunch?" asked Soule. "Let that go to hell while you look for a black girl that isn't black and isn't there anymore? By now she'd be a fat wench. You talk about girls, girls, women, women, and you want to look for them as far away as you can go. They're right here, fella, if you want what you say you want. Didn't I tell you how I stuck by my wife through thick and thin? And maybe you don't think that was something?" He wiped his lips with his sleeve. "You guys can eat if you wanta, but I'm leavin'. I got better things to do."

Soule lingered a minute with a compassionate arm on Walt's shoulder. "Better get home, friend," he said. As he turned to go, he took a final glance at Irv. "Taxes got nothin' to do with it," he said, and started for the door slowly, defiantly, alone. Fraser signaled for the tab.

The rest had dinner together in the main dining room of the King Cole Hotel, the swank Tabor Palace of bygone days. Fraser couldn't remember eating a thing. Irv, he recalled, had tried to pitch the table talk on a cheerful, lofty level: invented various new quips about Bach to Bernstein and harped on them and laughed in satisfaction with his cleverness; but Fraser had sat in a daze and, if he ate at all, had done so mechanically. It was all like a bad dream.

The cattleman sighed. Pretty soon he'd drive out and have a look at his good old pedigreed Angus. He was beginning to feel better.

Once upon a Farm

Somewhere along the road, I went astray. If ever a boy was destined to be an inspector of sunsets and cloud formations, it was I. Abundant evidence of my manifest destiny were strewn all over the place, but I ignored them all until it was too late to do anything about it—except to reminisce as I am doing. I became, instead, a well-fed, portly peddler of legal quibbles and quiddities: an earnest, respected, dignified, learned Sonora Springs lawyer.

At the start, I was a farm boy born and bred. The drought years of the early thirties lay ten years and more ahead. My brothers and I reveled in water. There were, of course, the swimming holes in the Clearwater River. One of our favorite spots was at the bend in the stream in the shade of the willow trees. We missed the sun there, and we had to wear an abbreviated pair of jeans as a swimming suit because we were visible from the farmhouse up the slope, but there was a special, compensatory delight in knowing that we shared this particular portion of the stream with shoals of the dark, red-eyed rock bass. At times, we preferred to sport, a la nature, in the sunny, clear, golden course of the river further up. Once, long ago, some gypsies had camped at this point, and, therefore, we always called it "the gypsy camp."

I must have been about kindergarten age when one of the valleys in our pasture flooded. The pond which formed was impressively deep; probably up to the level of my arm-pits at that time. The water was as clear as crystal in the summer sun. The green grass, slightly yellowed from immersion, was plainly visible at the bottom. Frogs leaped into the pond from the edges; mud turtles swam around in the middle at random; dragonflies buzzed busily over the surface; and dogs retrieved sticks for their whimsical, childish masters when the latter were not themselves lustily splashing and paddling dog-fashion in this democratic, heavily-populated, watery heaven.

The pond I've mentioned was a temporary phenomenon. There was another nearer the house which seldom if ever dried up, but the water was muddy from cattle tramping into it to drink and to brush persistent flies off their bellies. Now and then I would wade around the edges to pick a handful of the wild blue iris for Mother.

Mostly, however, I was satisfied merely to leave this spacious playground to our neighbor's ducks and geese and to the redwing blackbirds which used to fly and flock over it as they went to and from their choir perches in the black-haw bushes which bordered the pond.

In the summertime, my entrance into the shallower ponds, brooks and ditches was pretty direct for I avoided shoes like a plague. Only on special occasions could I be persuaded to put on shoes in warm weather. It was law that my feet should be washed before bedtime. I regarded it as a substantial compliance with the rigor of the law, however, to stroll across our lawn after the evening dew had fallen, provided I took the pains to drag my feet against the wet grass as I did so. In time my parents yielded to this liberal interpretation of my duty under parental law.

I was of high-school age before I acquiesced in the view that shoes were a daily necessity, or, rather, a necessary evil. Even so, I often succumbed to the temptation to feel the warm, soft earth beneath my feet and between my toes. And whether I fished from a boat or did so by wading into Lake Carolina from the shore, I took the precautions obviously required to keep my footgear dry!

After I had made the customary concession to civilization in the matter of shoes, it seemed to me that my favorite, yearly-recurring sprig of violet-colored wild sweet pea was less entrancing than it had been before. It was located at the edge of a field by a deeply rutted path. In my barefoot days I would be so engrossed by this charming wayside blossom that more often than not I would stub my toes against some of the rugged tree roots which protruded into the path. Perhaps these frequent pains enhanced the beauty of the flowers—if, indeed, it is possible to conceive of anything enhancing the loveliness of a wild sweet pea, whether it be violet or butter-white.

About this same time the lady slippers which for years had bloomed just over the fence on the neighbor's property gave up the ghost. They were the exquisite white and pink variety: the state flower. There had been a patch of the plainer, tougher, yellow kind, which we called moccasins, in one of our own meadows. This patch survived the other by only a few years. I'm sure it couldn't be that I ceased to notice these rare specimens. The more common morning-glories continued to be seen in their accustomed places; and so did the tiger lilies and the gentians. Those plants happened to be hardy enough to withstand any grief.

Generally speaking, wild flowers are not intended for picking. Most of the pleasure of beholding them is in seeing them in their native habitat. Similarly, the luscious clusters of rounded strawberries eaten straightaway in the meadow, or the single, sweet, pointed ones transferred directly to the connoisseur's mouth from their home on a wooded hill, were incomparably better than those taken home to be eaten later. It wasn't only that berries carried home in a straw hat become crushed. It was something else, but what I couldn't tell. The tastiest black currants I ever ate were those which year after year I picked and consumed on the edge of Lake Sunday. I am still puzzled by the fact that one batch that I took home in a pail was made into delicious jelly. An occurrence so contrary to experience and the usual order of nature is baffling!

It was elementary that one never even touched the tiny, speckled eggs of the ground sparrow in the nest at the base of a gooseberry bush in the pasture. It was enough to peep into the nest when it had been left unguarded. The same was true of the more colorful eggs deposited in the nests high above the ground; and, of course, nests never were so high or so precariously hung that they were out of reach of an agile youngster. I would see them and marvel, but I never laid a profane hand on either nest or egg.

The robin fledglings which fluttered and tried their wings beyond the granary were utterly safe when I was around, even from our prowling and predatory cats. After the passages of more than thirty years, however, I still reproach myself for once having taken home a young duckling which I captured on the shores of Crane

Lake. I'm sure I did my best to feed and nurture the unlucky creature, but I can't remember for the life of me what became of it. In a sense, my memory would serve me better if even the fact of the hapless young duck's captivity were permitted to slip into the abyss of the forgotten.

The attempted domestication of the duckling was not my only aberration. Another time when I was picking raspberries from a huge spread of bushes in a clearing near the Hog's Back River, I took it into my head that the gentle young skunks, which were ambling around on the overripe berries which had fallen to earth, would make good companions for the kittens in the barn. I seized two of them by the tail and quickly raised them into the air. When a skunk is so held, it is helpless. My young brother, who agreed to hold them for me until I had filled his pail with berries, discovered to his sorrow that quite the reverse is true if the unfortunate "wood pussy" has a chance to rest its hind legs on the stump of a felled tree. Even the cooling waters of the river were insufficient on that occasion to wash away the humiliation which my brother suffered on my account.

In those days the seasons were more than seasons. They were a glorious sequence of sensations. The early spring brought the delicate aroma of the dainty but hardy bloodroots which grew in scattered opulence along the brushy roadsides. It was permissible by my standards to pick tiny, household bouquets of these harbingers of spring and to feel the orange-red sap run onto the fingers and make them sticky and dirty. However, the blossoms in the orchards of plum, apple, and cherry trees were safe from possessory hands, no matter how profuse the blossoms might be. As the fruit trees were near the house, we could, and did, exult with them over the breezes which wafted their perfume beyond the confines of the orchard.

Later, during the spring plowing, I used to watch the white leghorn chickens as they flocked along the black furrow and plucked in great excitement at the earthworms which had been turned up by the plow. That is, I would watch the scene as long as I could, and then, giving up my ringside seat at the greatest attraction on earth, I would rush out to the field to tread in my father's footsteps and participate in causing all the animation, commotion and color behind us. The two horses which drew the plow seemed to realize that they, too, were important actors in this great adventure.

All the activity and idleness of summer were pervaded by warmth. The contrasting coolness of the raindrops splashing in the dust did but emphasize the warmth of the earth and the warmth of the air which had been and was to be. The croaking of the frogs in the pond in the cool of the evening was a reminder of the lingering warmth of the day. The haycocks in the meadow had a warm and pungent smell. The song of the cricket took on a drowsy warmness in the ear of the listener and contributed to the general atmosphere of intoxication and enchantment which gave a youngster the feeling of walking in a trance. No specific thing was seen in sharp, etched outline. Everything was sensed, vaguely, warmly.

Never in those days did I see or suspect I saw the elfin folk who like to inhabit the leafy glades along a stream, not even at the wonderful spring beside the Clearwater River, where I used to tarry after drinking from my cupped hands. Nor did I ever hear the reedy sound of Pan's pipes accompanying the liquid, trickling, rippling music of the river. Looking back, I'm sure that such things, and satyrs and nymphs to boot, must have been there to complete the setting if for nothing else, but I overlooked them in my childish preoccupation with the less hidden features of the landscape.

In the early fall the maples, birches, and sumac rivaled each other in a frenzied orgy of color. They resembled a bevy of runners making the final spurt of speed in a race. Later in the season, to prolong the wonder of it all yet awhile, I used to wallow in the holes left by trees which had been uprooted by the wind, raking the lavish leaves up around me with my hands. That way, I could feel as well as see the color. Or I would wade through the crisp, freshly fallen carpet of the woods, scuffling my feet to enjoy the rustling whispers evoked by the disturbance. The frightened squirrels, red and grey, would scurry to a place of hiding in the branches or flatten themselves against the opposite side of a tree trunk.

In the winter, the coat of my tawny collie would darken and so become conspicuous against the snow. The horses likewise took on a darker, silkier hue. With the weasel the process was just reversed; he exchanged his brown for white. Except for the black tip of his tail, which remained the same, he became invisible. Indeed, the wintry world was one of mystery and unseen presences, for there were tracks and runways everywhere to proclaim that life had not disappeared but merely retreated from sight. There were times, however, when the creaking, crunching sound of my boots in the snow would startle a cottontail into becoming a fleeting, grey-brown streak on the wide-stretching white surface.

The length of the winter in that northern region was a by-word among the inhabitants, even as it was a scandal elsewhere. Yet for us youngsters of the farm it was a land of milk and honey, literally. Chocolate milk was unheard of then. Whole milk, fresh from the cows and untouched by pasteurization, was our lot, and we were perfectly content with it. The honey combs we sampled tasted so good it never would have occurred to us that mere man could improve upon the work of the bees by any process whatsoever.

I have no wish to weep salt tears over my lost youth. Far from it! Rather would I shout with joy that I can relive it in memory as I do now. If there is any cause for lamentation, do we not all share it—that in easing and smoothing the drudgery and crudities of the country life of yesteryear we have taken from our own children and grandchildren so many of the delights and so much of the joyous flavor of the life which we once knew.

Parable of the Park

In my office during the day, I meet the finest people in the world. I depend on them for a living, and I wouldn't think for a minute of complaining. But they all have troubles—a world of troubles. Or they expect to have troubles as soon as they've shuffled off, unless I draw a will dividing their property between a baker's dozen of fifth cousins and specifically providing, mind you, that nothing whatever is to go to Uncle Sam. They've made ample provisions for Uncle in their lifetime what with income taxes and all. I understand that.

When I have heard more than the daily quota of woes, worth scarcely a variation on the theme, I like to start home, on foot, through the park between the Civic Center and the Capital Grounds. The walk is relaxing in itself. Besides that, the park is the favorite refuge not only of myself but of many others who tarry there to appreciate the scenery, to enjoy the late-afternoon sunshine, and maybe even to regain their faith in human nature. The plain, ordinary folks who comprise this tiny area's shifting, variable population always are a balm to my spirit, if for no other reason than that they appear serenely unconscious of the agonies of the income-tax bite, the insidious threat of creeping socialism, the horrifying dangers of galloping inflation, and the mockery of those grasping hands of the unknown fifth cousins at Ottumwa.

There may be some risks in casual, offhand conversations with strangers, as my wife is continually warning me. However, I am convinced, especially since yesterday, that the risks are worth taking. It is really because of what happened then that I'm telling all this, for the experiences related to me by my park-bench neighbor have made an impression I'm not likely to forget.

Here, as simply as it was given to me, and omitting only the preliminaries, is the story I heard from the lips of our mutual friend. I wish I could convey some into the man himself, but, alas, I cannot. The story is the man. There was a noticeable strangeness and sweetness in his manner, a solidity in his person, a wild, perhaps poetic frenzy in his eye, to be sure, but such vague impressions scarcely make a description. I fall back on what I have said: the story is the man.

Infancy begins for everyone at birth. Second childhood, however, is a more variable affair. In my case, it came when I was in my thirties. That may sound as if I am claiming to be unusually precocious, but nothing is further from my mind than vainglorious boasting. All I mean is that my first childhood was so unsatisfactory in some respects that I wanted more than anything else to repeat it under more favorable, happier circumstances, and, my fantastic wish came true.

It is not my intention to be more mystifying than necessary. Life is a mysterious, wonderful adventure. One has to take it as it comes; tell about it in his own fashion; and, on occasion, lend a willing, wondering ear to the mysteries of another's life, whether told with much or little art.

For years I had delighted in entertaining people with tales of my boyhood, while they listened with envy and exclaimed "How lucky you were." They were right. I had been showered with blessing. Still, that was but half of the story, for I had been unfortunate in ways which, being human, I had forgotten and didn't mention. But what was buried and forgotten was not dead. It was living and was as vital in a strange way, as the encoffined, temporarily entombed lady, Madeline, in Poe's *Fall of the House of Usher.*

The boyish activities which I recounted to my friends, as I have said, all shared the glistening magic of having taken place in the presence of the smiling face of Mother Nature: the beautiful bloodroots which, beneath the showers and breezes of April, heralded the retreat of winter and the coming of spring; summer's luscious wild strawberries on the hills; the exultant, melodious larks in the meadows; the whimsical flight of the gaily-colored butterflies; the smell of new-mown hay in the noonday sun; the drowsy, evening croaking of frogs in the pasture pond; autumn's bountiful, slow-ripening black currants at the edge of the lake; and winter's hushed wonderland of white.

If and when my intimates asked, I would tell them, as best I could, of my people, my parents; of my hustling, hurrying father, who died when I was nine years old; of Mother, who was so busy churning, washing, keeping house, making meals, mending clothes, tending chickens, weeding garden, and performing the multitude of other chores which fall to the lot of a farmer's wife (and widow) that she turned over to my oldest sister much, if not most, of the care of the brood of five children. Such recollections were matter-of-fact which I recited slowly, with pauses, being careful that I should get the history straight and do justice to the Fates and, most especially, to my parents, who, undoubtedly had done their best according to their lights and the traditions of the community.

There were, you see, reasons for wanting a second childhood. I can see it clearly now, too. The experience came, however, unannounced, and before I had any idea at all how much it meant and would mean to me. It was this way.

After my return from the European war, the doctors said I had a "nervous breakdown," an expression which was Greek to me at the time (and yet remains rather ambiguous). The staff of the hospital decided I should be given insulin shock treatments. Strange as it may seem, the hospitalization in general and the shock treatment in particular were my happier second childhood.

To awaken from a profound sleep and then to be given a sweet, refreshing, strengthening, reviving drink of fruit juice, followed by a hearty, tasty, nourishing breakfast in bed is close to the pinnacle of a child's wishes. The virtually unvarying patient, kind, sympathetic, helpful attitude of the attendants, nurses and doctors, though but dimly sensed and vaguely appreciated then, did make an impression and one which was as permanent as it was new. These things were the essence of my second childhood. There were other details, but these I have named were the heart and soul of my second childhood. My growing up again, complete with "growing pains," is a separate story entirely.

Someone with a keen wit once remarked playfully that youth is so precious that it is a pity it is wasted on children. However that may be, isn't one fortunate at having had his second childhood while he was young enough to enjoy it?

With a smile, the stranger rose to go.

So help me, I couldn't lift a hand to stay the guy's departure. I couldn't speak to thank him. I could only watch him ambling off to be lost in the current of humanity slowly pouring through the park in the dimming light.

As I was saying at the beginning, listening and dreaming are good enough for me. One isn't proud of being a provincial lawyer, I suppose; but he can be content with it, and the sweetly solemn satisfactions which come along now and then. Many who claim more settle for less, you can be sure.

The Pirate at the Party

There are times when a man just can't control himself. For example, when he comes into the living room to discover that his children have spilled black bean and tomato soup on the new carpet. "Didn't I explicitly tell you not to bring that stuff out of the kitchen? Are you deaf or just dumb?" Or when he comes home after a hard day at the office to discover that the misses has prepared chicken cacciatore for dinner. "Why would you ever think that I would like chicken cacciatore for dinner tonight? Didn't it ever occur to you to ask me first?" You know, things like that. But what are you goin' to do?

My friend Hadley Barksdale III, just called Hutch for short, was one of those known to have occasional breaches of less than perfect decorum, so to speak—at least more often than your average, otherwise well-tempered gentleman. Take that time when he rubbed his arm against the bosom of the department secretary as they passed going in and out of the supply closet at work. For him, the office work policy might as well have been "don't fraternize on company time with members of the opposite sex unless you just can't help yourself." When confronted by the unique temptations that only a winsome female can bestow, he had occasional episodes like that when self-control is as elusive as Bigfoot in summer.

It wasn't as if Hutch was maladjusted or unstable. He had a reasonable social life which he shared with his lady friend of twelve years. Chloe had immigrated from France to the United States as a young au pair girl many years ago. Now she worked as an agent in a large travel bureau specializing in European vacations. With her knowledge of French, she was known around town for arranging magnificent gastronomical adventures in France while riding barges up and down canals, viewing story-book castles, sipping the fine wines of the Loire region, and things like that. She and Hutch lived in the same apartment building one floor apart: he lived on the third floor, and she lived right below him on the second. Often, maybe four or five times a week, they would get together after work; he would buy the groceries, and she would fix him a fine dinner. Or, she would invite him in for a cup or two of caffè corretto after dinner at a nearby restaurant. Often he would just spend the night there rather than exerting himself climbing up the stairs to the third floor.

Most people would've assumed that they were married or destined to be so. But, to this point, they enjoyed the pleasures of connubial bliss without tying the knot. Either Hutch hadn't popped the question, or Chloe hadn't answered in the affirmative. For some folks, this arrangement amounted to living in sin, but I says it matters to me about as much as the number of spots on a butterfly's wing.

This routine went on with few disruptions. Oh, maybe Hutch had to work late or, as in the case I'm going to relate, Chloe had friends over for a dinner party. Yes, on that fateful evening, she had a group of lady friends from work for a French dinner of crab casserole with steamed leeks on the side, and a cheese soufflé made from genuine Gruyère cheese imported from France. For dessert, she planned on individual servings of cherries jubilee topped with freshly whipped cream and shavings of Swiss chocolate accompanied by flutes of sparkling wine, genuine French champagne. Such a grand dessert she wanted to share with Hutch, who, she knew, really appreciated such splendid cuisine.

As Hutch wrote in a letter to me later that evening, despite the fine dessert, all did not go well at the soiree, for no reason other than he had one of those episodes when he just couldn't control himself. But this episode must have been particularly upsetting—different from his usual romantic indiscretion—because Hutch writes letters about as often as birds fly upside down. So this must've been something special that he had to get off his chest.

"I have just returned from Chloe's party. Present were her colleagues from work: Mrs. Green, Margaret M., Mrs. McGillicuddy, and Mrs. McMillan. I was high strung. I took the bit in my mouth and ran wild. I scarcely permitted anyone to get a word in edgewise. I returned tense, whereas I went down calm.

"I spoke toward the end of my boyhood: of the talks in the barbershops, at the garage, etc.; of the sauerkraut festivals, old settlers picnic; of the various colonies. Perhaps this made me nervous. Perhaps I was repudiating my old neighborhood.

"Chloe had urged me to come down. I surmise that she regrets it. It may have seemed that I was repudiating, puking up, vomiting the whole company; everybody, everywhere. I can't imagine that my visit was relaxing, enjoyable, or inspirational. I certainly did not enjoy the company. In a sense, I spit in their faces. I insulted them and Chloe as well—without even intending to.

"The theme of the latter part of my monologue was the difference between me and my environment. I painted the environment as peculiar, spotted by nationality groups and surfeited with malicious gossip. I passed judgment on it all. I left it. I couldn't stomach it. I never went to a sauerkraut festival.

"There was no basis whatsoever for a sensible conversation. I have nothing in common with this group which itself has little in common except for their place of employment. I at least did show that I had roots in a rural community. I showed as well that I have vigorous, hardy offspring. It was apparent, too, no doubt, that I am a vigorous, robust, hardy man. Earthy or inclined to reject the earth? Which? I referred to the messages written on the public toilets. High strung. Talkative. Set in my ways.

"Chloe apologized for the dessert. I said it was okay as a second dessert. I said the coffee was good, and it was all I wanted. This sounded harsh, abrupt, and so forth. The truth is that I didn't care about either coffee or dessert. She had entreated me to come down. I went to please her, but I was scarcely in a mood to palaver with a bunch of females.

"In a sense, I refused to stand still. I scurried around, verbally beating them over the head. I sensed that I was to be backed into a stall and saddled. I backed into the open and rushed at them to whip them and drive them toward a stall. I usurped the floor, did the talking, let them listen, and when I was tired of talking and the company, I left before they could counter attack.

"I ignored all the individuals toward the end. None had any individuality. None had a distinguishable personality. Here was a group—a monstrous entity of vicious propensities—diabolical tendencies, intentions, and purposes. I lashed at the wolf pack with a whip in a terrible frenzy.

"Mrs. Green had intended to draw me into a seemingly innocuous chit-chat about Legion personalities. I passed that by. I let the mention of "Will" and "Father" go by. Chloe seemed unable to suggest a harmless subject. I made no attempt to find one. I couldn't conceive of myself sitting and playing verbal tennis with these people.

"It is not too much to say that I associated these people with the gabbing, gossiping men of my hometown. I almost stated that these men were old women and the company of women were gabby men, and I had little time for either set. This much is sure: it wasn't a love feast.

"The women who had attended the rodeo the other evening mentioned how quickly Casey Tibbs (the reigning rodeo champion) had been thrown. Who was the bronco and who was the bronco buster? I felt as though they had expected to saddle me and halter me. Their plans went awry.

"What I did, I did with ferocity and abandon; with frenzied hostility. Seldom have I worked myself into such a frenzy. I didn't work myself into it. The situation triggered all the long-pent animosity in my system. The flood gates opened.

"There was nothing in my conduct tonight suggestive of the kindness, the calm strength, and the patience so characteristic of me. I was just about the reverse of my usual self. I horse whipped these people. I bucked them off. I kicked my heels at them. I was a bucking bronco. I would set the pace—a fast, hectic, feverish, whirling dance of death. A hymn of hate.

"Chloe had given me a picture of the eldest woman as a bossy, efficient strangler. I shut her up. I backed her into a mud bath. This was a war of movement with many swift changes in topics: deadly dives, baths, mud baths, medicinal treatments, the Crestmore Hotel spa and swimming pool, etc. I mentioned the terrible dive into the shallow end of the pool. I told of the woman in the Dallas bathhouse whose offer of help I declined as superfluous.

"'Pools, swimming pools, may be death traps—or, at least, dives maybe visited with serious injury,' someone mentioned in connection with the mud baths. I said 'Nearby there's a salt lick.' I am not fooled by traps. I do not choose to wallow in mud like an animal. I don't need help with a bath when the help is questionable.

"The biddies probably preferred being pushed around, held at bay, whipped, bucked off, etc. to being met with a complacent smile which matched theirs, an amicable acquiescence in the social classifications and dispositions.

"I lashed at them with my sword, gave them a whipping, finished them off, and then left them. That's what they wanted, and that's what they got.

"As for Chloe's part, I declared war on her colleagues in her presence. It is, of course, more important to her that she get along with them than that she get along with me. At least her office associates will not care for me, which is quite okay with me. I don't covet their company. The question is whether in making war upon Chloe's esteemed associates I also made war upon her."

After reading this letter, I was disturbed. I got nothin' against having a little fun at a party, jokes and tall tales, but in this case, my friend had gone off the deep end! Like a crazed pirate, he lashed at Chloe's female guests with his sword, and like a pirate, he stole the pleasure from her party, insulting her colleagues from work.

I surmise that Chloe was disturbed by his behavior that fateful evening as well. I suspect that afterwards he was as welcome at her place as a burr under a horse's tail. In fact, about two weeks later, she moved to a new apartment located several blocks away from her old apartment and Hutch's apartment. A while later, Hutch mentioned her move to another apartment, suggesting that the rationale for the move was to save a few bucks in rent. Money may have been the primary rationale for the move, but, I wouldn't be surprised if most people thought that Chloe wanted to put protective distance between her and this man who, through their eyes, had just shown troubling signs of mental instability—that his behavior at the party was the advanced agent of general disaster. But then again, I see it real differently. Like I says, sometimes a fellow just can't control himself. What are you goin' to do?

Poetry and Revolution

Harold and I were sauntering down Cactus Lane in the Western metropolis, Sonora City, which we called our interim pad—just enjoying the sunny, spring weather. We already had passed the Yucca Club when Harold turned to me in excitement. "Did you notice anything special, different, about the Yucca Club this morning?"

"No," I said. "I didn't."

"There were only two guys sitting in the window this morning, looking out. Fatso and Skinny were there but not Baldy. Do you know what they were saying?"

"I can guess."

"No, you can't. You never can. Fatso was saying to Skinny, 'The doctor's ordered Baldy to a complete rest. He can't look out the window anymore.'"

I don't know what had come over me. Harold had always called the tune up to then. When I say always, I mean the entire month or so that we'd been in Sonora City where we met. This time, though, I said, "I think they were talking about Revolution."

"You think. Which revolution, for crying in the beer?"

"The Cuban." It was the first one that came to my mind--because it's the nearest, I guess.

"Phooey, you don't know what they were saying."

"But I do. Fatso was telling how the Revolution hadn't changed things there."

"But it has."

"I'm telling you what Fatso said. It hadn't changed a thing, he said. Only little things. The more things change, the more they remain the same."

Harold was listening. I went on with Fatso, for Fatso. "When I was in Cuba, it was ruled by Batista, the greatest Cuban ever born. I can remember it like yesterday. I was at Sloppy Sam's. It was about three o'clock."

"In the morning?" Harold wanted to know.

"Of course. I'd taken the wife to the hotel around midnight. She was sick of Sloppy Joe's and its white-shirted bums, she said. A middle aged woman, a pimp, came up to me as I was leaving the bar. She pinned a red rose in my lapel and walked with me. I thought she was selling them and gave her a buck. She was selling them, but just as a cover-up.

"'Wanna girl?' she asked with a pretty terrible accent—pretty but terrible. "'Sixteen?'

"'No.'

"'Fifteen?'

"'No.'

"'Fourteen?'

"'No.'

"'Thirteen?'

"'No. That's robbin' the cradle.'

"'Oh, no; the younger the better.'

"'Now, if it was you, I might be interested.'

"'Me?'

"'Standing up by this tree,' I said "'or lying in its shadow.'

"'I thought you Yankees were all business—had no romance in your soul.'

"'This is business.'

"'Oh no, it isn't. I'd never think of charging for my own services.'"

Harold cut in. "What'd Skinny say?"

"He said, 'You remind me of the first time a guy offered me a job; said he'd pay me what I was worth. I said, Oh no, you don't. I can't live on that kinda money.'"

Harold was amazed and angering. "Next thing you'll say is that Baldy really was there at the Yucca Club."

"Yes. He's just coming up and apologizing for being late. He says 'I'm sorry, Gentlemen. I'm sorry for bein' late, but I just been readin' Santayana, and I read the most extraordinary statement. It set me thinkin'. He wrote Poetry is emotion recollected in tranquility. If I'd read that in my youth, it would have changed my life. I mighta been the Hobo King, instead of the Bulldozer King, the way I am.'"

Harold was eyeing me with utter disapproval. "Yes, and you're the bullshit king," he said coldly, not like a friend at all. It was as if a gal had come between us buddies—or as if a gal, with a sudden, scissor-like movement cut in two the pink ribbon of our eternal, month-old friendship. As I said, it was springtime. That'll do things to a guy sometimes, any guy.

The Rebel Chieftain

We thought we knew all about Chris Maddux before he actually arrived and took his place amongst us. We did have a lot of details about his past career; and so, while we gabbed about him and his coming, we really wondered what a man with such a record as his would think about us and about Ladner-Perkins Company.

It is hard to say whether we employees were more uncertain of ourselves or of our employer. When one of the vice presidents had been summarily dismissed by Pa Perkins, the head of the business, we joked about holding a farewell party for the departing guest in a telephone booth. Actually, no farewells were spoken at all. It would have been the same if any other official had been cashiered. That was the kind of a company it was; and, that being so, we weren't in the least sure it was possible for one of us employees to have any pride in himself.

Chris wasn't taken in from the outside and put in a managerial spot above us (though there was ample precedent for such a course in the company's history). He was to be simply a staff-assistant like the rest of us; that is, like the rest of us who weren't clerks and maintenance personnel. Ladner-Perkins called itself "Publisher to the Professions," but the label was more than a little misleading. It had no editors (as such), and its salesmen called on the members of three professions only, the Ministry, Law, and Accountancy. Besides that, the wares in the salesmen's station wagons were not limited to books but included, among other things, religious calendars, decorative desk pads, astrological almanacs, and super special loose-leaf services for lawyers and accountants which never got out of date.

If Chris realized he was as junior as junior could be in our organization, he didn't show it. He never sought to redeem himself from the supposed lowliness of his position by reminding us of his past accomplishments and acquaintanceships. We watched for him to do it, ready to pounce on him with innuendoes about has-beens and quips on the theme "how hath the mighty fallen." At times, we would get into heated disputes about the revolutionary ferment in Africa and make a generous display of our ignorance just to provoke him into a lordly settlement of all the issues on the basis of his years at the mission in Togwanda. He didn't rise to the bait. He remained on our level.

He managed somehow to preserve his self-esteem without realizing it was in danger. There was nothing in the power of Ladner-Perkins to give that he would go out of his way to get. His salary, surely a pittance, he earned in the fullest measure. To give his labor was not to give himself entirely, it seemed. The time-serving staff supervisor, Willie, who had made a career out of disparaging Pa Perkins, tried to impress Chris with the idea that he was at the mercy of a cruel fate at Ladner-Perkins, subject to the will of a tyrannical taskmaster. Chris took on the assignment, whatever it might be, as if he were the master, and the particularly miserable chore was of his own choosing and by no means an indignity inflicted by Willie.

My guess is that Chris's opinion of Ladner-Perkins and its lack of leadership differed little from our own, but I never heard him hold forth to that effect. He did get a laugh out of it when one of his colleagues said something like, "Leadership? Why, I wouldn't follow that guy across the street to a free lunch." He was amused, too, whenever someone referred to the colossal, the ponderous tome known as *Ladner's Annual Tax Bible* as Willie's Commentaries on Lincoln's Gettysburg Address. It is quite possible, as some of the fellows claim, that the first time he heard the remark he asked, "Which volume of the Commentaries?" Chris wasn't fooled; he saw Ladner-Perkins for what it was. I'm sure of it. He knew it wasn't necessarily typical; he had his reasons for staying with it, and he gained his subsistence without putting his self-respect on the auction block. In the meantime, he was enjoying our town's sunshine, high altitude, crisp air, serene mountains.

If not the obvious target for as many poisoned arrows as certain of his colleagues, neither was Chris out of range. For example, when one of the staff assistants seated near Chris caught sight of the purchasing agent passing in front of his desk and called the latter's attention to the scuffed and scarred condition of his antediluvian chair, the agent responded with, "Well, I tell you, Brother, it's a lot easier to get office help than it is chairs." Such shafts, ordinarily capable of wounding all within earshot, fell at Chris's feet as if he were possessed of a secret armor. Indeed, in his presence, they seemed more like boomerangs. It was the debaser who was debased.

In every large business concern, there probably are various small cliques of employees deserving the title of mutual insult societies. It was so in Ladner-Perkins, but worse. When Chris first joined the firm, the twenty-four staff assistants, all men, were seldom far away, in word or deed, from cutting every individual in the department down, "taking him down a notch," emphasizing each error, its importance and possibly dire consequences, referring to the minimal salaries paid and the difficulties of providing for future emergencies, retirement and all that. Chris held himself sternly aloof from this depreciatory sport, these disquieting verbal antics— not, it seemed, on principle but merely because that was not his way. It occurred to me, as an old-timer at Ladner's and a veteran of a stint in Korea, that the peculiar esprit de corps of our department, our company, was that of an army furiously bent on making war on its own soldiery; but I doubt that Chris ever bothered with comparisons of that sort.

It had been the policy of the company to promote this internal warfare of its staff assistants. Willie and especially those over him, for Willie counted for nothing in his own right, considered it desirable to stimulate competition between team members. They relied on jealousy, strife, and competition between and among the workers to speed up production, to improve the quality of the miscellaneous products, and to bring about single-minded devotion to the company's prosperity. Chris knew this. He didn't drag his feet in order to make his colleagues look better, but then, he didn't need to. His fellows resisted their employer's technique by the simple expedient of not vying with Chris (who was unbeatable in any case). In some mysterious way, Chris was more than a tacit collaborator in this resistance movement. He was the actual rebel chieftain. As for Willie, he never learned. Each new failure for his method convinced him of the splendor of competition.

Without being obsequious, Chris avoided any indication of a challenge to Willie's authority and to that of the omnipresent but seldom seen Pa Perkins. Willie, of course, would have welcomed any overt sign that his key importance in the company was questioned, for he, more intensely than the others, believed in cutting people down to size, his own size. Chris, however, made no more claim to present status in the hierarchy than to past achievement, and this very humility, if that is what it was, conspired to give him authority and, in our eyes, to set him over us and even over Pa Perkins and Willie. It was curious: an authority without authority. It was as if a private first class were blowing smoke in the face of a general without lifting a cigar to his lips.

Chris surely wasn't playing a part. That would have been unplayable. As it was, his natural role was virtually impossible. All the iconoclasms which the corps of staff assistants had developed on their own since Ladner-Perkins began to publish and purvey its products throughout the Mountain West fifty years earlier, began to come out of hiding, like wild horses out of the hills, to trample over official versions and fables agreed upon as if those were but so many small animals scurrying for safety. There was nothing of the evil genius, of the conspirator or of the secret, sinister, shyster manipulator about Chris. Yet he seemed to breathe respectability into the most irreverent folk wisdom, as in ancient legend the Earth imparted strength to Anteus. Though he was not the natural father of these suddenly green-growing, harum-scarum ideas, Chris was being recognized as the adoptive parent, a sort of sponsor of war-orphaned waifs.

Originally, Ladner-Perkins had served the Ministry only. In the advertising of the company there never had been any quotation marks around the word "served," but in the gossip of the office the scope of the company's operations was synonymous with areas of exploitation, historic hunting grounds, legitimate prey. Chris didn't cause the gossip nor increase its currency. He didn't stamp it as his own view. He stood apart from it, but more as one who is saddened by the truth than as one who disapproves.

When, after World War II, Ladner-Perkins expanded its business to include the legal and accounting professions, it didn't cease to be a religious publishing house, according to those who labored with hand and pen to put out the products. It merely took on law, the religion of regulated hatred, and accountancy, the sacred lore of the nicely calculated less and more, and added those to the ritual of fine pretenses. I doubt that Chris stopped to ponder these evaluations evolved out of the pains and burdens and disappointments of his colleagues and predecessors. He certainly expressed no impatience with them. He understood them and simply by doing so made them as constitutional as could a decision of the Supreme Court.

His capacity to understand human frailty was equaled by his indifference to the grand systems and grandiose theories which spawned from that frailty. Chris unquestionably knew of the rival isms locked in mortal combat like two giant octopuses struggling on the ocean floor. That so called Cold War, that confrontation of ideologies, was one of the recurrent themes of the babble by which we staff assistants relieved the tedium of our daily work. On this vital issue, however, Chris was silent as he was, say, about the latest hammer murder in Denver. He didn't call for a plague on both houses. He wasn't that interested. He completely distrusted both patent medicine routes to the welfare of the human race. That was clear to us all.

We studied Chris ceaselessly, fitting every remark, response, and action into the jig-saw pattern we had formed from past observation. He took on solidity with every passing day as a point of land does as it is approached by sail from the sea. He was as steadfast as a star, as strong and permanent as the Rock of Gibraltar. Durability was the word for Chris. So it was, even though we knew—at least I knew—a change was as inevitable as those seasonal hurricanes that come howling out of the Caribbean, hurl themselves northward along the Atlantic Coast, and finally blow themselves out.

One day, it was the Wednesday before Thanksgiving, Willie stopped at Chris's desk and murmured in low voice, yet with a harsh undertone of belligerence, "Will you come back to my office?" He turned and went back. Chris followed him between the rows of desks. It lacked five minutes of closing time. From past experience we knew the portents were ominous. We looked at each other apprehensively.

Sandy Saunders, whose desk was crowded up toward Willie's office, leaned back in his chair until his head touched the thinly-paneled wall. He appeared to be lazily watching the minute hand of the clock on the opposite wall as it crept toward five o'clock. We knew that position of Sandy's well. He was listening. We were quiet. It was, in all likelihood, the first time in company history when everyone in the department, without exception, silently waited in place until two minutes past closing time. Then Sandy signaled the interview was over, and we all rushed to go. I saw Chris emerging from Willie's sanctum to head for his desk. He looked as usual, unperturbed. No one waited for him. It wasn't the time for it, for commiseration, for indignation, for anything.

By telephone that evening the message spread like wildfire. I no sooner got home than Sandy was on the line giving me the word and asking me to relay it to Ray and Gordon. This was it, all right. Willie did all the talking. “We have a request," he said, "from the Purdon Press that we can’t turn down. You think they're a competitor of ours, maybe, since the Government got that antitrust decree. Well, we aren't; we aren't married any more since that anti-trust fandango. But, put it this way: we're still sleeping together, actually closer than before. It all comes down to this, Chris. We can't use you anymore. Brisbane Cheadle himself, of Purdon Press, called Mr. Perkins about a bill of yours. You paid for the book you ordered from them, but, whether you know it or not, you agreed to pay for annual supplementary updates for it as an extra. And now, three months after the first supplement was sent to you, that bill hasn’t been paid. I'm sure you have a good excuse, yes, a good defense even, but you see how it is. We can't turn down Purdon's. It's the Old Man’s own order.”

The next morning at the office there was a vacant chair and desk. Willie went hustling around with news that Chris had been fired because he didn't pay his bills. "Think of it," he said, spitting his words into the vacuum of silence, "a Minister of the Gospel, a chaplain in the army, a missionary in Africa, and he should come to this. I knew there was something wrong with him all the time: a fundamental fault; no commercial virtue; no sense of the day-by-day values.”

We were bending our heads over our desks. Willie might be pronouncing the verdict of history, but his words were flailing our shoulders rather than finding entrance to our ears. So far as we were concerned, all the Perkinses and the Willies since the beginning of time couldn't hold a candle to Chris Maddux.

The Red and the Blue

I wish I could learn from experience the way I'm supposed to, the way some folks do. With me, it doesn't go that way at all. When I got out of Hayward Business College two years ago, there was a pretty good-sized world of information at my beck and call. And what has actual experience in business done for me? Knocked everything into a cocked hat, that's what it has done. Take, for example, the latest thing that happened. I mean the proxy contest.

I never thought when I went to work for the Western Jig and Die Company that I'd ever have anything personally to do with a proxy contest. That was the furthest thing from my mind—like something one reads about in the papers. It was natural for me to sign up with Western Jig and Die Company, right after business college, because my brother had gone to school with the president of the company, Conrad (Kip) Bartle. If I thought anything in particular about the company, when I started with it, it was what a funny name for a manufacturer of a line of steel products.

I'm assistant to the president of the company, Kip. He's just twenty-nine years old. It isn't that he's one of those child prodigies that's ceased to be a prodigy. Kip really clicks. Of course, his old man was president before him—you know, the Wilhelm Kaplowitz Bartle that everybody used to talk about. When the old man died, Kip took over. He kind of inherited the job, you might say—just one of those lucky things.

The way that proxy war got started was like nothing at all. I mean as smooth as sailing on Moonlight Bay. We just eased into it. One day soon after the first of the year, I got a long distance call from a guy by the name of Koontz. He wanted to talk to the president himself, not me, he said. I explained that Kip was a mighty busy man. The guy came back with "He's not too busy to talk with one of the company's biggest stockholders, is he?" Then I knew right away who it was. I mean I remembered hearing Kip say "That guy Donald Koontz has bought another five hundred shares. I wonder if he's up to anything."

We set up a conference for the coming weekend. In the meantime, we learned a bit about Don Koontz. He used to be a lawyer in the East. I mean in Chicago; for Sonora Springs people, Chicago's back East. He was disbarred twice. The first time it was because he made it a point to get to automobile victims first with the most cash. The dough was a sort of gift to help the unlucky fellow with his hospital bills, but a part of the arrangement was to make Koontz the guy's attorney in the accident case. Koontz was given another license, and, the second time, he paid a witness to forget what he saw at the scene of the collision, but the witness regretted being on the short end of the bargain and reported the deal to the judge.

Koontz had a gall that was beyond curing with an elephant's dose of those little liver pills. After a few half-hearted pleasantries on both sides, Mr. Koontz got down to brass tacks. "I like the company," he said. "I've bought stock because of its great profit potential. Of course, it's an unrealized potential, but nothing that a few major reforms wouldn't take care of. I want to buy more stock. We—Kris Dorcas, Smythe Lashley, and myself—would like your cooperation in getting more stock." Kris and Smythe just sat there without saying anything, just giving Koontz their silent backing.

"How much at what price?" Kip asked.

"That we can't say till we're sure of your cooperation," Koontz said.

"You already have about one tenth of the stock. I can't speak for the board, but I think we might cooperate to the extent of allowing you to name one member. That's roughly proportionate to your holdings." Here Koontz looked at his associates with a smile of disbelief, amazed at Kip's simple-minded reply. "If representation on the board was all we wanted," he said, "we wouldn't be here. We could buy a little more stock, and with cumulative voting we could vote ourselves that. What we want is control, period."

"I see," said Kip.

"We had hoped to avoid a proxy contest," said Koontz. "We came here to ask for your cooperation and to invite you to join with us in naming a slate of directors."

"We'll cooperate, all right. You want a fight, and we'll give it to you. So that we start on even terms, we'll give you a list of the stockholders, without your going to court for it; but I'll tell you this: I'll never sit on a board of directors elected by the votes you round up."

I had sat in on the confab to make notes of what went on. Since Kip had no idea what Koontz was going to spring, none of the directors except himself had been on hand. Kip now assembled a meeting of the full board for a council of war on Tuesday. He told me beforehand what his plans were. "This character thinks that the cumulative voting we have in our corporation is a great advantage for him. The first thing we'll do is show him how slight that advantage can be. As it is, with a board of nine, a ninth of the shares voted in his favor gives him one man on the board. So, we'll cut the board to three; we'll get resignations from six members, effective immediately, and we'll propose only three nominees at the annual meeting in March. Then we'll have to have the proxies of a third of the shares to name a single director, and it'll take two-thirds of the votes to give him clean control."

"Whew," I said, "pretty clever."

"Yeah," Kip said. "And if one of our candidates doesn't make the grade, we'll take another quick tug at the rug Mr. Koontz is standing on. We'll up the board to four. That way the management will always be pretty sure that it has the support of a majority at any board meeting."

"Is it all legal?" I asked.

"You bet it is. I checked with Hallinan and Hogan, and they say the program is perfectly consistent with the law and the prophets, the by-laws and corporate charter; as much so as cumulative voting itself."

Through Snodgrass and Stebbins in Chicago, Koontz and his cronies made an offer to buy all the stock of Western Jig and Die that was tendered at $70 per share, which was a little above what the bid-and-asked quotations had been just before that in over-the-counter trading. The brokerage firm gave the offer wide publicity. Another piece of news was given less, but adequate circulation: there was a little bonus of 75 cents a share for every broker, anywhere, originating a stockholder's tender.

A week or so later, Koontz mailed to every stockholder a six-page circular renewing his offer to buy and asking for proxies. The circular was on a reddish paper, and at the top of the first page it carried the bold headline: "Remember, Red Means Reform!" The proxy accompanying the circular also was cherry-colored. The main feature of the program of reform spelled out in the rosy literature was greater dividends. These apparently were possible, whether or not earnings were increased and whether or not plant improvements were made. The gimmick was to elect the roster of directors put in nomination by Koontz (and his so-called Stockholders' Protective Committee): men with diversified experience. For example, Kris Dorcas was plainly qualified as a director because he owned a chain of ladies ready-to-wear shops in Tennessee. Smythe Lashley would be able to work wonders in the jig and die business with the tricks learned in his consumer finance companies in Kansas.

Kip sized up the battle of bulletins and circulars as sand cast into the wind. It would blow back on those who threw it. Still it was a necessary tactic. Koontz would have to be answered. The aim would be to say as little as possible in the maximum number of words. The pamphlet of the Western Jig and Die Company was printed on blue stock, as was the proxy. The keynote on which the management pitched its campaign was: "For a True Blue Administration, Sign and Send the Blue Management Proxy."

Kip was much more worried about Koontz' offer to buy shares at 70 than about the bulletins. "Money talks" he told me, and I know he told his fellow directors the same. It cost them all a lot of soul searching, but they decided that the company would have to match Koontz's offer to buy at $70 a share or admit defeat before the battle had fairly begun. The company made the offer but gave it limited publicity. The difficulty was that the shares probably weren't worth the price.

Koontz reacted immediately by boosting his offer to $75. Kip convinced his associates they had no alternative but to increase their offer by the same amount, but it took a couple of days of wordy argument to do it. There was grumbling, too, as I know, that at such a figure the company might win the battle and lose the war. Kip himself didn't like to be merely following Koontz's lead, to let Koontz call the turn and keep the initiative. So far as bids were concerned, what could he do?

The next blue circular put out referred to Donald Koontz as a Johnny-come-lately who had begun buying stock in Western less than a year ago; as a raider, a plunger, and a shaggy and shabby financial wolf. It took a few other cracks at Koontz that were just as vague but more personal. After the guy's first disbarment and before the second, he had become for a relatively short time the fifth husband in succession of a much-married heiress of a department store fortune. The blue leaflet didn't brief its readers on this phase of Koontz's private life, but the more sophisticated and knowing shareholders were treated to this sly dig: "That Donald Koontz has made a success of the practice of law and of matrimony is no sign he can perform miracles in our company's specific situation." The comment was unlike Kip; it didn't originate with him; but the public-relations man sold it to him, and Kip bought it.

Koontz raised his offering price to $80 per share. Then he got out a high-pitched falsetto blast against Kip, appropriately printed on red paper. It went into Kip's ancestry, literally, and pretended to describe how Kip's father, the venerated Wilhelm Kaplowitz Bartle, had resorted to trickery to foist Conrad (Kip) Bartle onto the stockholders as president of Western Jig and Die in the first place. And Kip: hadn't he been guilty of selling fifty shares of Western Jig and Die during the past year? As for the other two candidates on the management slate, one of them couldn't have much faith in the organization, because he held only 500 shares of the company's stock.

Kip said to me: "Ernie, I'm not going to answer that. Those who can be persuaded to vote for us already have a blue proxy to use. We're not going to go up to $80 either. There's no use kidding ourselves. The shares aren't worth $70, much less $80. There are three big shareholders that Koontz may not be able to bag. Maybe we can't either, but I'd like to have you talk to them. One's in Omaha, one's in St. Paul, and the other is in Koontz's home-town of Chicago.

"Mrs. Bahnstock in Omaha is the widow of a doctor who was one of the original investors in Western Jig and Die. Dr. Horace, as my father used to call him, was killed in an auto accident six years ago. His widow never has voted at a shareholders meeting before, but the management has never been fighting with its back to the wall before, either. Maybe you can corral her votes.

"Paul Ferguson in St. Paul is a retired broker. He knows values, and he can practically smell shenanigans. He bought his shares at a figure closer to ten than eighty. Maybe he'll hold onto his shares to avoid a tax on his capital gain, and maybe he'll vote the blue ticket. There's no telling. As for Rapelli in Chicago, he probably knows too much about Koontz to vote for him; but he is erratic, an old-fashioned eccentric. See what you can do."

The gal in Omaha was a case. She had an unlisted phone, so I couldn't call and tell her in advance what my business was. I had to call on her cold. She answered the doorbell but left the door on the chain, and as soon as she saw me she began to weep and get incoherent. I couldn't make any headway at all. I went over to a neighbor's to get the lowdown on how to make a proper sales approach. The housewife next door explained that Mrs. Bahnstock had been driving the car at the time of the accident in which her husband, Dr. Horace, was fatally injured. She met a giant, oversized vehicle on a narrow bridge and lost her nerve. That was the way the accident happened.

Mrs. Bahnstock doesn't realize her husband is dead, but she expects notice that he is any minute. That's why she has an unlisted phone—so the line will be open when the feared and expected news comes. She thinks any visitor who comes to the door is a bearer of the sad tidings. That's why she wept when I called on her, according to my informant, the lady just down the block.

At St. Paul I suffered another setback. Ferguson had sold his shares to Koontz. He hadn't "sold out" to Koontz, but he had sold; same difference. I said I understood how tempting the price of $80 per share must have been. Ferguson squinted at me as he said: "I sold at $75, before you guys upped your offer from $70." As I looked at him in amazement, he added: "I'm an ass. I know it; but what can I do about it?" I said "Well, anyway, your income tax will be less." Ferguson snorted.

I was in low spirits on my way to Chicago. I had a saleable product in my sample case, so to speak, but up to now, had had no luck in my stars. To say that Rapelli was a character would be the understatement of the year. I couldn't make out whether he was a fool or a philosopher. He stayed at one of those apartment-hotels where a girl at a switchboard announces guests, but Rapelli's phone was busy at the time of my arrival, so the receptionist told me to go ahead, that the line would be free in a minute, and she'd announce me. "He sees everybody, anyway," she said.

When I got to Rapelli's apartment, he apparently had received no word of my coming. He was, however, expecting a messenger boy from a bank or brokerage house and persisted in fitting me into that role without giving me an opportunity to explain my mission. Finally, I got my point across: that I was the Assistant to the President of Western Jig and Die Company, manufacturers of jigs and dies in Sonora Springs. This led him to laugh at his mistake and from that to launch into a lengthy meditation on youth. "It's the fashion of the times to put a premium on youth," he declared. "I can remember when it was just the other way around, as it is in the Orient today. Styles in thought change less rapidly there than here," he said.

I nodded my agreement. "It's useless to batter one's head against the currents of the time," I said, mixing my metaphors eggbeater fashion.

"How right you are," Rapelli exclaimed, beaming at me with good humor.

"Kip Bartle is only 29," I brought out.

“'Who's he, now?”

"The President of Western Jig and Die."

"So?" he said. "But you're here on business for Western, aren't you?"

"It's about the proxy contest," I told him. Before I could get further, he had grabbed the reins of the conversation and was galloping furiously in the wrong direction. "Now you take Donald Koontz," he said.

"There's a man for you. He's been disbarred twice. I like a fellow who does things in a big way. It's the curse of our times to do things by halves. I've heard it said that genius is just the habit of excess, and there's a lot in that, in my opinion."

"Yeah, Koontz is an all-right guy," I said. "Trouble with him is he's swimming against the wave of the present. You wouldn't vote for a guy like that, would you?"

"I'd never vote for a genius," he said, "but I don't have any scruples about selling to one. When money talks for a genius, it says the same thing as for anyone else."

I could see I was getting nowhere fast, so I said, "It's been wonderful talking to you, Mr. Rapelli. I've spoken to many about the advantages of a true-blue administration, but it's been more fun talking to you than anyone else. And you've illuminated many dim pages of philosophy for me. I'll be forever indebted to you for that."

"Pshaw, don't mention it, Kid," he said, as we shook hands. "It wasn't anything at all."

I don't mind telling you that when I walked into Kip's office the next day, I did so with my tail between my legs, figuratively speaking. I was a beaten man. Kip had trusted me with a mission, and I had let him down.

Kip looked up at me with a broad smile. "Ernie, you're a wonder," he said. "How did you do it? I figured there was a less than even chance you could sign up Bahnstock and Ferguson and none whatever that you could get Rapelli on the dotted line. How'd you do it?"

"Do what?" I asked.

"How in the world did you get to Rapelli? His blue proxy came in this morning, air mail, special delivery."

"It did?" I said, sinking into a chair.

"And that guy has more shares than the other two together," said Kip. "It's the only really good news we've had since you left."

"Well, I'll be darned," I said, and I told Kip about the trip and the interviews.

"The picture doesn't look at all bright," Kip said.

I didn't go over to see the final tallying of the proxies. The First Bank was in charge of that. Kip went, of course, and he told me about it when he came back. "Three out of every four votes for Koontz were for stock he bought," Kip said, "but, just the same, he topped us by 20,000 votes. It's all over now but cleaning out our desks."

That's the way with Kip. If he's tagged out sliding home, he knows it and doesn't forget it. Not Ernie Gainsborough! Here I've been telling you all about this proxy mess as if I were still Assistant to the President of Western Jig and Die. As I was saying at the beginning, learning from experience is the hardest thing I do.

Romance of Lousy Hall

Joe Knecht hadn't been with the firm quite a year when they fired him. Only they didn't use the word "fired." Mr. Ed Stevens, the managing partner, definitely ruled out that word when Joe, in simulated surprise, exclaimed in a high-pitched voice, "You mean you're firing me?"

"I didn't say that, and I didn't mean it, Joe. We're just letting you go. It's more like a Mexican divorce, for incompatibility of temperament, you know. Mr. Ed, as he was called, made no reference to the incident which had been the last straw, which was kind of him. Anyway, it was wholly unnecessary. Joe knew well enough.

Locksley, Hall, Barkdull, O'Hara and Pastoza had been warned in advance that Joe was temperamental, but they didn't believe it. They had had no experience with a young lawyer of that sort, and they had been taking on at least one new man from each crop of graduates since the memory of man runneth not to the contrary. Besides, the dean of the law school coupled his warning with the recommendation of Joe as "the most promising young man in the history of our School."

Right from the first, everyone but Mr. Ed had been slightly dismayed at the way Joe carried on. Mr. Ed had pacified the complainants. "He's just off the North Dakota prairies. Give him a chance. He'll smooth, he'll polish. Wait and see. He's young, you see, and naturally bumptious."

The firm was generally known by the shorthand expression of Locksley Hall, and Joe was by no means the first of the annual newcomers to experiment, in moments of disappointment and disillusionment, with the nickname Lousy Hall. The partnership's engraved letterhead gave the dates 1878-1958 after Hugh Locksley's name in the listing on the upper left to show that the founder of the firm was gone but not forgotten. Hall was the senior partner now, and no one, repeat no one, in this modern law factory got a raise in salary without his approval. Mr. Ed might have the final say about getting ten new desks but not about a five-dollar raise for a file clerk.

When others had kidded about Lousy Hall, the senior partner had been pleased and flattered rather than righteously angered. He enjoyed being a distant, gigantic ogre who could generate fear, frustration, and obedience in underlings by postponing an increase in what he called the "emoluments of office." Joe, however, put less of vehemence and complaint into his use of Lousy Hall. In his conversation, there was nothing personal or vindictive in the nickname. There was no embittered writing down of the assets of G. Wesley Hall, and the dispassionate, scientific descriptiveness of the words as Joe used them seemed to extend beyond the loop law firm: to embrace not only the erstwhile City of the Big Shoulders, but, in some certain but incomprehensible fashion to reach around and shake the entire legalistic world in which G. Wesley played such a prominent part.

That was G. Wesley's impression, but he wasn't accustomed to acting on impressions, however nettling. If his reaction to impulse was to wait until it passed over, his handling of impressions was to give them a chance to fix and fasten upon some concrete event; better yet, to seize upon a whole series or complete pattern of incidents and episodes. Mr. Ed, of course, saw eye to eye with G. Wesley in this respect. What both of them overlooked was that this prepossession of theirs, like the wearing of dark glasses, cast a shadow over everything their junior did: not that they weren't justified in throwing the book at the fledgling finally.

The way Joe asked questions was disconcerting. It implied that if the senior bothered to state his problem exactly, he wouldn't need to ask someone else to find an answer in the law books. Those high in the office hierarchy were by no means the only ones to notice this trait of Joe's. Stan Marko and Waldo Kent, middle-aged "comers" with whom Joe most often worked, had felt hot flushes or anger on this account more than once. One time when Stan was himself baffled by the client's request, he passed it on to Joe, saying "the Midwest-World Finance wants a draft of a bill for a state legislature which will draw the line between speculation and investment," and Joe came back with "Drawing the line for what purpose—taxes or what?" Stan kept his temper, but he couldn't refrain from caustic comments to others behind Joe's back.

When Stan and Waldo had been alone together, before Joe came, they had liked to take respite from the daily grind by batting the breeze or playing tennis with the various crises on page one of the *Morning Tribune*. Mr. Ed had found it necessary on occasion to come in and break up these gab fests in what he called the "interests of production." He overrode their protests and their apology that they were only taking momentary refuge from routine by saying "I'm sorry, but your refuge is becoming too routine."

With Joe, the problem was different. He kept his conversation to a minimum. He might neglect his tasks to listen to his colleagues and overlords, but that was something between Mr. Ed and Stan and Waldo. Who could help but listen when Stan started sounding off? He had a hoarse, whispery voice, but with it he was as well off as if he had a built-in public address system. Moreover, he was always as excited about the latest crisis or proposed solution for it as Hitler ever got about the demilitarization of the Rhineland or the Treaty of Versailles. Waldo, too, has a way of catching the ear with his what-can-be-done-about-it ranting at the stupidity of whichever party at the time happened to be in power in Washington or City Hall.

Just the same, Mr. Ed preferred the palaver of Stan and Waldo to Joe's sticking to business. He wasn't alone in this. As a rule, Joe did a bang-up job, far exceeding anything Stan and Waldo had been able to turn in at a comparable stage of apprenticeship. His memos were models of concision, clarity, and analysis and fitted into the firm's briefs like jewels into a setting. In the course of his research, however, Joe would look up now and then from his stack of opened books and make a straight-faced remark which was enough, one way or another, to keep his colleagues on edge for the rest of the day. He might only say "Here's a prosecution for larceny of false teeth." If required, he would fill in the details by reading from the reported case: how the thief crammed the stolen goods into his own mouth and ran. If not requested to go on, Joe would duck back into the books, but only after leaving an image of those false teeth suspended in air laughing to high heaven at the white-collared, tweedy, bespectacled John-Harvard drudges at their desks.

Or, Joe might say: "Listen to this. They tried to execute this guy in the electric chair, but the wiring didn't carry enough current. So the warden wanted to have another go at it at a later date. The Court said 'Sure. The Executioner is entitled to a second try, same as in the old law a horse's first kick or a dog's first bite didn't count against the owner.'" Such remarks rubbed Stan and Waldo the wrong way. For them, law reports were to be read with reverence, not relish. It would be useless to argue with Joe. They couldn't get specific with Mr. Ed, but they could and did pass broad hints to the latter that in their estimation the eternal conflict between Plaintiff and Defendant had nothing at all in common (as Joe seemed to suppose) with such entertainments as a chimp doing a jig in the street for the organ grinder's vagrant audience of passersby.

There was, though, pretty general agreement on one thing. Joe was talented enough to give Locksley Hall an edge over other firms if, as Mr. Ed put it, "he could only be humanized." By a similar consensus, that meant giving Joe a healthy push toward the hot pursuit of a single female. Opinions varied, however, on the way to start the ball rolling. Mr. Ed, for his part, surmised that the guy, being a relative stranger in town, was simply spinning his romantic wheels temporarily till he got acquainted, and, like a motorist on packed snow, needed no more than a slight shove to set him going at full speed ahead. Stan and Waldo were not inclined to place any bets on romance in any situation whatsoever. Knowing Joe to be willfully blind to the income-tax advantage of joint returns and to the cash premium which the firm itself put upon the nettled status of respectability, they both were quite defeatist about the whole affair. Anyway, if the guy didn't get starry eyed and lapse into a lisp over such fine phrases as "due care under the circumstances" and "due process of law," was he likely ever to fall in love with a dame?

The girls in the office had their own slant. They were of all ages and mostly married, but they followed the lead of the most knowing few of their sex, and those few cleaved faithfully and firmly to the line that Joe was dawdling with too many too young and needed nothing but persistent exposure to the fleshly temptation of the mature. That temptation they all did their best to provide, within the limits of propriety reasonably construed.

There was, however, one secretary in the firm who was unmarried. Moreover, she had many appealing, attractive qualities. First and foremost was a decidedly prominent bust ("magnificent mammillary equipment," according to Stan). Besides that, she had a ready, if erratic, sense of humor. She would giggle on the slightest provocation. It is true, her face was plain, and the expression of her eyes was somewhere between sad and scowling. She was thirty-five, more or less, but not yet really old maidish, and she liked to be with and to work for the younger attorneys. Finally, she was a thoroughly competent secretary.

Mr. Ed, with the finesse of a diplomat, promoted Stan's present secretary, Mrs. Glebe, to the new "paper" post of Assistant Librarian. Then he transferred Miss Emily Ensor, for that was the name of the dame in question, to the vacancy that had been created. So far as appeared, the moves were merely in the interest of production. Few knew better, and they weren't talking. And Joe most certainly was not one of those in the know.

Nor was Emily Ensor, although of course, this lucky lady could scarcely be unaware of the manifest opportunity that was hers as the unmarried secretary of the firm's only bachelor.

Under the watchful eyes of the entire staff, a romance began to bud. It was early spring. Joe was attentive to Emily and evidently appreciative of her fine physique, efficient typing, and excellent character. Emily's eyes lost some of their sadness, and that latent, lurking scowl disappeared from around her mouth. It was known Joe had taken his "girl Friday" to dinner a time or two when their work required overtime. Emily didn't deny other dates with Joe when, at coffee break, some of her friends became inquisitive.

Nevertheless, early spring telescoped into early summer with no conclusive proof that Joe had been completely and finally humanized. Whenever Stan and Waldo decided that there had been an improvement in Joe's attitude toward Lousy Hall at the center and everything on the periphery, the guy shows traces of his old form, which would make them suspect the jig was up, and Mr. Ed's diplomacy a fiasco. One time, for instance, he said, "Here's a case of a fellow convicted of homicide because of his reckless hit-and-run driving, and then while the judge is waiting for the pre-sentence report, the real culprit turns himself in to the zealous prosecutor and confesses." Stan and Waldo knew that the word "zealous" wasn't in the court's opinion; that Joe had supplied it; but as for taking Joe to task and claiming the adjective didn't belong, their hands were as good as tied.

If Emily's effect on Joe's approach to his work was doubtful, his influence over Emily was certain. To begin with, Emily aimed to please all her bosses and especially

Joe, but there was more to it than that. What the schemers apparently hadn't taken into account was that Joe might please Emily, and with incalculable consequences. He put the "old Indian sign" on her, as some said. Indeed, Emily went overboard for Joe so wholeheartedly as to give an assist to the very Fates who were conspiring to bring about his downfall.

It was this way. One Friday, Emily received an inter-office memo from Mr. G. Wesley Hall that she forgot to deliver to Stan until Joe had left the office for the weekend and couldn't be reached. It said: "Sorry to have to ask you and Mr. Waldo Kent to stand by this weekend, but I will need that memo on the Odin-Atlas merger on my desk Monday morning as President Weeks of Odin will be in then to confer with me. No doubt Mr. Joe Knecht and your girl, Miss Ensor, can do all the work for you and have it in good shape so you and Waldo can handle your end with but little time lost from your respective homes and families during this splendid June weather. Remember, Mr. Weeks is in the 90 percent bracket."

Because Emily happened to fumble the message until Joe was beyond recall, Stan and Waldo fell heir to the urgent business intended for their assistant. Because of it, too, Emily's friend was fired. That is, he was let go. Poor Emily. She was doing her best, as she saw it and so far as anyone could tell; and she remained on with Locksley Hall. She's presently secretary to the newest man, Gil Cooper, but he's as regular as a robot and doesn't need her to humanize him. Now and then, though, during gaps in the daily flow of dictation, she remembers that guy Joe Knecht who was forever confusing her name with another's and calling her Rosy Kinsella.

A Talk on the Terrace

I guess the thing I like most about my home town of Sonora Springs is its unconscious humor. If its citizens or city fathers should get pretentious, as will happen you know, in the best of regulated families, they have no idea they're doing any such thing. And in that case is there any pretense?

I could give an unlimited number of examples of what I mean, but my wife is due to meet me here any minute for dinner and a movie. But take that park right in front of City Hall, for instance. There's a Greek Theatre on the south side that in the summer is used mainly for Sunday-evening religious services and during the week for square-dancing. Facing it at the opposite end of the park is a classical entrance colonnade no doubt modeled after some glory of Athenian creation five hundred years B.C. In between are bronze, equestrian statues of a cowboy with a rope and of an Indian brave with a spear. A royal flush in a serio-comic game? Ah, but wait!

This very hotel is another illustration. So far as I know, it is the only one in town that has anything approaching a sidewalk cafe. Do they call it the Cafe of the Two Magpies or something like that? No. Is it the rendezvous of a motley crowd of bibulous loafers? Seldom, if ever. Those characters head straight for the bar inside. As you can see, this narrow, rectangular patio is raised a little above street level, surrounded by shrubbery like a porch and protected against sun and rain by a canvas canopy or awning. It's called simply "The Terrace."

The title of the hotel itself, The Heather, will evoke, in the imaginative, visions of a Scotch or English countryside and, perhaps, a golf course with sheep grazing on one of its distant hills. Actually, The Heather is situated on Farragut Avenue close to downtown Sonora Springs. The boulevard, of course, gets its name from the civil-war admiral who had nearly completed his climb to fame before this city was born on the banks of Custer Creek.

Ah, let the world travellers revel at the Cafe de la Paix in Paris, and let the sophisticates rave about the good old days and the refreshing stimulation of those cool Tom Collinses quaffed on the Shoreham Terrace and put down on the expense account in Washington, D.C. For the long haul, at least, I'll take Sonora Springs. It's a bit like a small town—not much happens, but what you hear makes up for it.

There is maybe just time enough before my wife shows up to tell you about the conversation I overheard on this terrace a week or so ago. The waitress had just brought me my first bottle of beer when a guy in a sport shirt with a cap on his head extricated himself from the MG he had parked at the curb and made his way to a table. He had the evening paper folded tightly in his hand and evidently was anxious to settle down to reading it. I judged there was something special in it which attracted his fancy as inexorably as a light draws millers.

It was a beautiful summer evening. A gentle, pine-scented breeze from the nearby mountains fluttered the shrubbery immediately behind me. I sat at a corner table against the brick wall of the hotel. The newcomer took a place across the center aisle and along the low, wrought-iron railing just inside the shrubbery on the street-entrance side of the terrace. It was about five-thirty or six o'clock, and the sun had sunk so low by this time that its rays entered beneath the awning and brightened the pages of newsprint which the late arrival spread out on the table.

While I sat on this terrace drinking in the soft sunlight, the evening zephyrs, the general atmosphere of ease and contentment, as well as absent-minded draughts of a local brew, the newspaper reader gulped in the contents of his journal. The waitresses were leisurely in the attention paid to their customers, and this pleased me. A number of youngish, well-dressed, eye-appealing couples had, by this time, come in and seated themselves at the far end of the terrace. Another man alone, more of a gentleman than a sportsman, had sat down to a long, tall, frosty drink at the table next to the newspaper reader. We three were in a sort of bachelor's corner. None of us spoke, but a buzz of voices drifted our direction from the animated patrons down the line.

The sun was beginning to be intercepted by the western hills, and the daylight had dimmed slightly before the reader put aside his paper and poured generously from his untouched bottle into the empty glass in front of him. He was thirtyish but prematurely bald, and the top of his head was as red as his thick, fat face. I surmised that at times he rode in his uncovered sports car without a cap. It was obvious, now, that the guy was through reading and wanted to talk. He addressed himself to the gentleman at the nearest table.

“Quite a story in tonight's paper. Did you read it? About the murder of the druggist.”

"No, I haven't seen it. Just got back in town from a little business trip to Topeka. The wife is going to stay with friends there for a few days, but I had to get back."

"I've been home from my vacation a week, but it seems like a month. I have bachelor's quarters in the residential wing here. The police claim they've solved the case and they’ve made an arrest. They’ve got a confession, but it doesn't ring true to me. There’s more to the murder than what the suspect says. I think he's covering up for somebody—the triggerman or maybe the druggist's wife."

"What's the dope on the guy who confessed?"

"His name is Hoag. What a name, H-O-A-G. He’s got a prison record. He isn't a lily-white character, that’s for sure, but that's why his story could be phony."

"Was the druggist shot in a holdup? Is that what happened?"

"No. He was shot from ambush. After he locked up the store for the night and was going to his car to drive home, he was shot from his own car. That's Hoag's story. He emptied the pistol into Hindry's body. He aimed the empty gun at a chance passer-by and pulled the trigger, but, of course, that fellow escaped. He witnessed the shooting and reported it to the police as soon as he could get to a phone, but. he says he couldn't identify anyone. It was too dark, and he was too excited.”

"Why would any guy do a trick like that? Did Hoag know Hindry?"

"Well, yes. He says he knew Hindry's wife. Says he'd been dating Hindry's wife and that Hindry objected, and that made him mad. Here are the pictures. Look at 'em. Doesn't Hindry look more like a bad actor than Hoag? Look at those, thin, pinched lips. I would be afraid of that guy. The wife is pretty good-looking, much younger looking than her husband; not a day over 40, I'd say. That's a picture of her weeping at her husband's funeral. Do you think she did it?"

"I don't know. If she had been dating Hoag, I suppose she had a part in it all."

"Do you think she might have done it—the actual shooting, I mean? I mean, I find it awfully hard to believe Hoag did it."

"He has a prison record, you say?"

"Yes, I know. He could have done it. I'll admit that, but I don't think we have the whole story yet."

"Maybe not. He isn't convicted yet, just accused. But there's the confession."

"Hoag pried into Hindry's car with the teeth or jaws of a pair of pliers. I'll bet the wife at least gave him those and maybe the pistol—if he did it at all. The pistol and the pliers haven't been found yet. He says he threw them into Sloan's Lake. I can't get over the notion that Hoag had a confederate who did the trigger pulling or, if Hoag really did kill his love rival, that he was put up to the job by the wife, or maybe was ordered to kill by the head of some crime ring or narcotics syndicate or something."

"Is this Hoag a young man?"

"He looks like it. There's his picture. He looks young enough to be Hindry's son, sure enough. Of course, he doesn't look like Hindry's son. He doesn't have that thin, sharp face Hindry has. Huh, Hindry and Hoag—sounds like the name of a partnership, doesn't it?"

"Pictures are interesting, aren't they? One can read a lot into them."

"Yeah. I can get a lot out of pictures, all right. I guess I put more store in my father's photograph than anything else I own. You see, Father died suddenly from a heart attack when I was just a lad in my early teens. Mother gave me the picture as a keepsake. To this day she has as thick a head of black hair as Mrs. Hindry has in that picture in the paper."

At this, the younger man folded his paper briskly and said, "Well, I gotta go. My name's Joe Blough—not Joe Blow, as some jokers make it, but Joe Blough. Care for the paper? I'm finished."

"Thank you," the gentleman replied, taking the proffered gift. "I'm Dr. Pinza of the Freud Mental Clinic in the Park Hill District." Then he added with a chuckle, "Not Dr. Pizza of the De Muth Dental Group. I specialize in anti-paternal impulses, guilt repulses, and mother-fixations, not toothache and bleeding gums."

"Well, cheerio Doc," said Joe, taking off in the direction of his MG.

"Good luck to you, Joe," said the doctor, and he turned to signal the waitress for his bill.

Ah, here comes the little woman now. Thank goodness she was late. You know she got a great kick out of the chat I've just recited the first time she heard it: guessed right away that all the big words used by the doctor at the end only added up to the Greek for Oedipus.

But as I was saying at the beginning, there's no place like home, and for me that's Sonora Springs.

A Texan Confesses

I see by the papers that a bunch of preachers is kicking up a fuss over a governor's appointment of a military man to fill the vacancy left by the death of the late Senator Wesley B. Jackson of Sonora Springs. Well, I knew Colonel Emory well during World War II, and in my opinion, he'll make an excellent representative in the nation's capital for the state of Colorado.

Don't get me wrong. Colonel Emory served overseas in both world wars, and I don't say he came out untouched by what the pastors call the "dirty business" of war. And I don't say he'll add any luster to the intellectual capacity of the United States Senate, and maybe it would be nice if he could. The fact remains, however, that my old comrade is second to none in love of country, and he has a lot more horse sense than a horse.

Sure, this is all preliminary to a little confession I'd like to make. Why would I want to do any confessing and do it under a pen name beats me, and I'm from Texas. To my way of thinking, figuring out such stuff is more up the clergyman's alley than picking out the right man for the United States Senate. In any case, I'm not apologizing or asking anybody's forgiveness. What I did was beyond me, as much as if Fate itself took matters out of my hands for once—out of all human hands, including those of the gentlemen of the cloth who are now finding fault with Colonel Emory. You might say I'm not doing any confessing at all, not bragging either, just telling a story and wondering out loud.

If I violated a couple of articles of war in the course of this strange affair and maybe a few dozen army regulations, all I can say is that it was a long time ago, in another country, and who cares? Colonel Emory wasn't mixed up in it at all. I remember he was with me at the beginning, but, gad, it started as innocently as a guy could imagine, and no one can possibly blame Colonel Emory for not foreseeing what kind of a deal, so to speak, I was going to make. I had no idea myself at the outset, and later I never mentioned the incident to my friend. He doesn't know of it to this day.

We both were in the headquarters of a Signal Corps outfit. It was after VE day, but not long after. Our unit was making its home in an old castle south of Munich a ways. Corps Headquarters was located, say, twenty miles from there at a small town near a lake everybody called Tegernsee. Maybe the "no fraternization policy" hadn't been called off yet, but that didn't cut any ice. Those who wanted to talk to Germans did, and those who didn't want to didn't. Up to then, I had no more to do with those folk than necessary.

Colonel Emory was about as old then as I am now, which is to say that he was young enough to have an eye for a cute number. He could take women of leave 'em. He wasn't a chaser. Same for me. He had a family, and I had been married for a few years before our outfit shipped overseas.

We had been to Corps on some business or other, and afterward we drove past Tegernsee and stopped to have a look. It was a beautiful lake, as nice as anything in

Colorado according to the colonel; and I'll have to admit I had never seen the likes of it in Texas: a broad expanse of rippling, glistening blue in a setting of mottled green hills and forest. We got out of the Jeep and walked out on a dock. A well-built blonde woman in a bathing suit made a picture-dive into the water as we approached. We watched her swim.

In a little while she came back to the dock and pulled herself out of the lake. Like I said, she was well put together, a woman of about forty. She smiled. Colonel Emory spoke. She had lived in England once, and we got along okay talking. She invited us to her house for tea. We accepted. She slipped into a beach rope, and we walked her home along a dirt road.

Her name was Frau Henkel, but I've never called her that. She was Hannah to me, almost from the word go. She got into a dress in no time at all, a blue one. It wasn't pale, and it wasn't navy. Women would have a name for it. I'd call it a medium blue. For me, the dress worked no great change in things. It looked good on her, but that was all.

In the house and dressed, maybe she was more of a lady. Anyway, I could see that Colonel Emory was a lot cooler to the lady than to the nymph. Some men are that way, you know. She offered us rum with our tea. We both took it, though neither of us cared for either beverage. It must have irked the colonel to see Hannah, the German, sitting there in comfort and luxury serving tea with rum and ginger and cookies. He was in no mood to tarry, was absent-minded, and now quite indifferent to Hannah.

She didn't excite me either, but I wasn't looking for thrills. It was the set-up which appealed to me. It would be wonderful to get away from military uniform at times, into a home, and close to a woman. An intimate mix-up with Hannah was not part of my plans at all. She had a husband and lived with him. She was ten years or so older than I. Besides, she was a lady. In view of what happened later, you may think I am an ass to insist that Hannah was a lady. Well, in spite of all, I do insist. The disgrace of our escapade never left a smudge on her: maybe none on me, but surely none on her. That's the way of it.

I paid a couple of platonic calls on Hannah, once with Colonel Emory and once without. They were polite to each other, but it was plain that they didn't hit it off very well. We met Otto, her husband, a dark, stocky, unfriendly man. He had been a German pilot in the first war and sort of a civilian official in the one just ended. To me, Otto's hostility was as understandable as Hannah's hospitality, if not more so. I also met Otto's unmarried, younger sister, Alma, who had taken up with Captain Sievers from Corps Headquarters.

One day Captain Sievers telephoned and said that Hannah had a memorandum she'd like to have me put in the hands of the right official. It concerned a factory property the Henkels had at Klingen in another part of Germany—I don't remember where, maybe the French Zone or even the Russian Zone. This property was something Hannah never mentioned to me. I had the typed transcript in my hands later, but I didn't bother to read the text of it. Such things were out of my line. At the time of the telephone call, I told Sievers to tell Hannah I'd come out in a week or so and talk to her about it. Colonel Emory knew nothing whatever about the matter of the memorandum.

I had occasion to go to Corps Headquarters every once in a while. On the next trip there, I went to see

Hannah. This time she was different. It was plain she had been aching to see me. She was mine for the taking and without asking, I could tell. Had I then just reached out, so to speak, and plucked the forbidden fruit—the easy and obvious thing to do—the whole affair quite likely would have settled into a dim and dusty niche in the catacombs of my recollection, and I wouldn't be writing this.

But no, no, no. I wasn't entirely a prey to yearning or desire or lust, call it what you will. I must have been partly in the grip of another, stranger passion; I wasn't rational, but I can't say what it was: a sort of an aboriginal, subtle malice, if it is possible for any emotion so darkly primitive to be subtle. In brief, I told Hannah I would convey the memorandum if she would sleep with me. She consented right off, with a gasping laugh, ignoring the fact that I was only going to deliver the paper, not recommend anything or use my influence, if any. She didn't even listen.

This affair with Hannah lasted but several months, and then I was ordered back to the States. Short as the time was, we saw a lot of each other. Otto seemed forever, and fortunately, away. The woman grew on me, because she wanted to, I guess. What had begun as a base bargain flowered into something quite different and, yes, wonderful. Believe it or not, I secretly treasure the memory of the months with Hannah.

Just the same, my relation with Hannah always was spilling over with mystery, the unknown, and the unaccountable. You can say, if you want to, that she brought out the essential cad hidden deep within me. I don't care a damn about that; but what I mean is: here she was, just another moderately good-looking woman such as you pass on the street every day. But once you get to know her, she walked veiled in puzzles and riddles, and you didn't know her. For example, just before I left for home I learned positively from an officer in the higher headquarters that the Henkels had no factory property, and there was no such place as Klingen.

You figure it out. Women are out of my line. But, as I was saying at the beginning, Colonel Emory will make a darn good Senator. No doubt about it at all.

Thanksgiving Day

The year 1959 has not yet been buried beneath an avalanche of leaves from the calendar, but it is not too soon to say that it is my most memorable year. There was the first Christmas which my family and I spent in a Jewish home; there was the conversion of one of my best friends to Catholicism; there was, finally, that Thanksgiving Day guest whom I shall never forget. His name is Dick Nussknacker.

Dick was almost a stranger to me. He had come over to Sonora Springs from Utah in order to be a witness in the patent infringement suit which I was engaged in trying in the local federal court. The case had been going along more slowly than expected, and Dick's testimony on direct examination had not been more than half-finished when the judge declared a recess for the holiday. The guy would be due to go back on the stand on Friday; there was no way out of it. I knew that hard times had been knocking on the door of the Nussknacker household in recent years and that Dick was not flush enough to fly home for the holiday, five hundred miles, and then fly right back. I invited him to have dinner with me.

My younger son, Peter, had the presence of mind to be born on Thanksgiving Day thirteen years ago. In 1959, the last Thursday in November again fell on the twenty-sixth of the month, so as to make the date doubly special once more. Consequently, the little woman and I invited several guests besides Dick. There were our nextdoor neighbors, Mr. and Mrs. Vrooman. They were building a new house in a swank suburb and would cease to be so close by before long. In addition, Pete's favorite teacher, Mr. Medoc, was coming with his wife and their three-year old daughter.

Had the celebration been on a less grand scale (a grand one for us), I should have been tempted to veto turkey. Not because I have a special fondness for the big birds. I don't. On the contrary, I'm inclined to spare the bare-necked buzzards by reason of a childhood prejudice against them. While I was growing up on a farm in Minnesota, one of my chores was that of tending the turkeys. It was the most disagreeable and thankless task I had. The gentlest spring rain would decimate the ranks of the young ones; the slightest early summer cold would carry them off like a plague. Then, in the fall, the flighty critters were harder to round up than cattle on the open ranges of the West. Even snow wouldn't drive them to cover. Under the circumstances, however, I had agreed with the little woman that nothing but turkey would do for this particular Thanksgiving dinner.

Dick had a nice way about him. He wore no grievances, no chip on his shoulder, no envy on account of his inability to be with his family. His wife and numerous progeny—the oldest being a year or two younger than Pete—would be all right at the great family get-together at the home of his parents. "Anyway," he said with a laugh, "every day is a sort of thanksgiving day with my folks." Pete said afterward, "That Mr. Nussknacker's a good guy. I like him." But that was afterward.

Dick passed up the drinks I offered before dinner. Not so Mr. Medoc. Not so the Vroomans. In fact, Pete wondered out loud if his newly-acquired status as a teenager did not carry with it the privilege of drinking a highball. "No sirree, Pete," his mother let him know, "not even coffee." The little woman hurried away without bothering to argue. There were important things to see to in the kitchen. Mr. Medoc diverted the conversation by remarking that though named after wine, he had grown to prefer whiskey as a before-dinner beverage.

"Does Medoc mean wine?" Pete asked, and then having gained the piece of perfectly useless information his question called, he promptly forgot it and was ready to listen to, and indeed hope for, new twists in the conversation of the grownups.

The dinner was one of those typical extravaganzas so dear to the heart of the spiritual descendants of the Pilgrim Fathers: turkey galore, dressing, sweet potatoes, hot biscuits, fruit salad, and pumpkin pie with whipped cream; lots of mumbled and jumbled words and gasps and sighs of laughter. And no one even asked if it was safe to eat the cranberries. The wife was ready with the answer: they were from last year's crop, from Wisconsin to boot, but nobody appeared in the least concerned. So Minnie told them, regardless, to prevent the slightest shadow of necessity for anyone's suffering in silence.

To Pete had gone the honor of saying grace. His words, though few, were adequate; but, they by no means added up to a keynote speech. It was not till toward the end of the meal that the table talk casually drifted toward a counting of blessings. Mr. Medoc said he was grateful that he had been able to turn that fall from teaching mathematics to ninth graders to coaching athletics at Blair Junior. "There's a lot more satisfaction," he said, "in training bodies than in training minds. I never could escape the awful feeling that there are more things in heaven and earth than are dreamt of in the various closed systems which we teachers are duty-bound to sell to the children. Mathematics, to be sure, is no worse than science, history, and the rest, but I prefer coaching. It's more like helping than teaching. It's fun. I like doing it."

Paul, now in high school, had been listening as intently as his brother Pete. The two exchanged glances but said nothing. Paul thought the world of Mr. Medoc as a mathematics teacher.

"I say amen to that," said Mr. Vrooman, as his wife looked startled. She was, however, seated too far from her husband to give him a kick of admonition under the table, and he went on. "I say amen to that, and Allah be praised. I've had my share of good luck this year, too. Of course I haven't been selling automobiles all these years without learning something, but I don't claim all the credit. I've been lucky, too. I've been favored more than a lot of my competitors, and God knows I've got competitors.

"Outside the low-priced three, new cars haven't been so easy to peddle lately. It isn't like after World War II. Not by a long shot. Even the dealers handling the low-priced three have noticed a difference. So what do I do? I make a business out of repairs—and a real profit, too. I put up a big sign over the service entrance: 'Through these portals pass the best people in the world, my customers.' That isn't just so much guff, either. But nobody, I mean nobody, drives through the exit without leaving a nice slice of his cash behind. It takes some doing, but I'm here to tell you I've made it pay." The glance at his wife said "Now there."

"I've had some hard times lately," said Dick. "As you know," he added, looking at me. All I knew, as a matter of fact, were the vague reports I had heard, but I made no comment. "It's common property," he said, "that my business isn't what it used to be. Even the kids at school throw it at my kids. My oldest boy, Hiram, was about ten when he said to me one day 'Dad, you're good at everything but making a living, aren't you?' I knew that he'd heard that on the school playground and that he didn't have any idea what it meant. Still it rankled. The gossip was so true, apparently. I was having a red-ink bath during a period of general prosperity, while everyone else was swimming in gravy. And things were getting worse rather than better in my business."

He could see everyone at the table was hanging on his words. He gave a nervous little laugh and continued. "Last night I didn't sleep at all well. I kept dozing and waking, drowsing and rousing. I'm not used to hotels and hotel rooms. I'd been on the witness stand all afternoon and got all keyed up. The sight of the opposing lawyer watching me like a coyote had bothered me. My testimony was hurting him, and I knew he could hardly wait to tear into me on cross-examination. As I said, I felt keyed up and waiting to be fired on, so to speak, by a sharpshooting enemy sniper like in the war.

"Then one time I was awakened by my own voice. It wasn't a scream or a shout. It was, rather, low, throaty, hoarse, explosive. What I heard myself saying was: "So what, if I'm good at everything but making a living? I wouldn't trade places with all those guys who are good for nothing except making a living." Dick looked as harried as though he were reliving that portion of his restless night.

"Boy, Dick, a lot of us don't come up with such good sense when we're awake," I said, "not to mention when we're asleep." Then affecting nonchalance, I asked "Shall we adjourn to the living room?"

That was about all Dick Nussknacker had to say about giving thanks and being well off, which was more, at that, than the rest of us could digest at the moment. But Dick is a guy who will linger in my memory a long, long while. To tell the truth, he would be enough, if there weren't more, to make 1959 a thoroughly memorable year for me.

The Thinker

I got to thinking about things real hard lately. It's not like I don't always think about something or other: things like my favorite Beethoven symphony or van Gogh painting, even silly things like the number of flamingos in Africa or the love songs of trans-Atlantic whales. No, this time it was really something different, something existential: disturbing thoughts. I got to thinking that I have a double.

That's right. Starting several months ago, I began to think that I had a double. It wasn't a physical twin, a *Doppelgänger*. In fact, the double was just the opposite; it was an individual representing an alternative aspect of myself. My double and I had opposing viewpoints of society, opposing relationships with people, opposing standards of behavior. Before you decide that I'm crazy or something like that, let me explain.

Maybe I got the idea from reading Stevenson's *Dr. Jekyll and Mr. Hyde.* That guy Stevenson is a master storyteller I tell you. I suspect that the story came straight from his subconscious with the greatest of ease. I would go further and say that Dr. Jekyll is the Stevenson which we would observe and Mr. Hyde the Stevenson which the world did not see. The story opens with Mr. Hyde trampling over a girl. Later, he murders a man, an

MP. I began to wonder if everyone carries within him a Mr. Hyde, a self which would trample over a girl or would club a man to death. That is to say: beneath the surface of us all is there a being capable of hatred, as capable of hatred as the surface man is capable of politeness and courtly etiquette?

After reading that masterful story, I had strange dreams, the kind you don't forget so easily. For starters, I dreamt that I was at the VA hospital and was to be operated on for the removal of a certain duality of organs. Maybe one of two livers or something like that. You can see where I'm headed, can't you?

Even stranger, much stranger, I dreamt that I was walking along the highway to my childhood home with two army nurses. Just before I reached the bridge, two men called out and asked me if that is what I called a "chef." I looked and saw a muskrat. His head was all that stuck out of the water. I said yes and intended to watch him and his mates at work. Thereupon the furry fellow came out of the water and set upon me. He made a slight abrasion of the skin before I got my hands over his jaws and prevented him from further biting me. This was not a frantic struggle. The animal was fairly tractable, seemed to resemble a turtle face. I held him. I asked the two men present to come out and help me. I had in mind putting the animal painlessly to death or to sleep, perhaps by sticking a needle into the brain. They were coming. I wished they would hurry but wasn't frantic. Then we would go to a doctor and test whether the animal was rabid, whether I needed the Pasteur treatment. I awakened with the word and tune "Blow the man down" running through my mind.

But what does this have to do with my double, you may ask. Plenty, I tell you, but it took some hard thinking, some serious reasoning to figure that out.

You see, the muskrat is a mysterious animal. He is a house builder. He has fur which is warm enough to protect him against the frigid waters of winter. Part of his house is below the surface and part above. He uses reeds, as nature used seaweed to create life which moves. The animal, immersed in the actuality of life, in the swim, so to speak, spies the dangers of the pedestrian biped on shore. He senses the current of life around him and sees with his eyes the motion and commotion of the animals who bestride the earth. The animal is in touch with the subconscious and the conscious, of himself and of others.

As I thought about all this, I came across an extra facet hitherto unnoticed. Note that the subconscious is likened to an animal which is not vocal. The muskrat is a "chef" because he stands guard and silently warns his mates of danger. He has no voice; does not slap with his tail like a beaver; appears always to be busy in his work. He expresses itself, presumably, in action, merely descending beneath the water surface, communicating with his mates without words.

My thoughts about this creature in the dream were running amok. Where was all this headed? Slowly I began to see the way. The muskrat attacked me because he didn't want to be watched. Eureka! My thoughts converged to a conclusion: there are two me's, you see. The muskrat, my double, does not want to be spied upon. Who can blame him? He is my double instead of me, precisely because he does not like publicity. He wants to be left alone. Right there, that's the key: I must have a double. Maybe not a muskrat as in the dream. In fact that would be silly. But surely some earthly person somewhere.

Before you dismiss these thoughts as products of a deranged mind, I must relate what happened yesterday. I saw proof of my human double when Lucy and I were at Spangler's repair shop. Spangler is a man in his late fifties. He had junk all over the place, in cluttered, jumbled disorder. He had told Lucy: "We have more work than we can handle, if you want to go elsewhere." One or two of the lamps had been old gas or kerosene lamps of the kind used in the country. I was not in the least attracted to the place. This man's ability to repair, of which Lucy had made much, did not impress me especially.

Lucy probably made a deal for the repair of her lamp when a young man came in with his hands jammed down in his overcoat pockets. I was convinced that he was concealing a weapon and intended to rob the place and all of those in the store. Lucy was roaming around, pretending to have an interest in Spangler's junk. Spangler was at the cash register on the counter. As the young man hesitated, I reflected that I did have money and could evade a personal hold-up by stepping outside before the young man acted. He didn't act, and I then saw he was a pretty good-looking, red-haired, well-dressed young man.

It seemed to me that I was not too seriously involved if the young man were to rob the shop and those in it. I almost counted my money and said yes, I have quite a bit, but I could slip out before the young man acts. I scarcely had seen the guy—only had noticed the hand shoved stiffly, tensely into the overcoat pocket. I sensed hostility. I wished it to be expressed.

Spangler, to return to him, fixes lamps. He is a specialist in artificial illumination. He had told Lucy it would be necessary to rewire her lamp. He symbolized, as it were, the champion of artificial illumination, false illumination, and, at the same time, he was agreeing to serve Lucy, to fix her connection, to accept a subordinate status. Junk, lamps, lamp repair, plethora of work. All this served to make the young silent, tense man appear as an avenging angel, an ominous figure of Force bent on the destruction of falsehood and hypocrisy.

In a sense, the young man with clenched fists jammed in his pockets was me. His supposed rebellion at the strength of cluttered junk was mine. His rebellion at masculinity, supposedly incident to the menial repair of women's damaged properties was mine. His determination to rob the shop, the situation, of its phony strength, its false pretention, was my wish to strip falsehood of its cunning camouflage. The young man was but a soldier in my war against falsehood and hypocrisy.

So, you now see, at the lamp-repair shop I met my double. He was silent and sinister, with his fist clenched in anger. He was possessed of an ominous, concealed, destructive weapon. Why did my double show himself there? Because the shop was a junk shop, because the owner-operator had been given a buildup by Lucy at my expense; because there were in this clutter junk lamps such as we used, prized, and cherished in the farm house in which my tender years were passed; because the repairman had spoken of threading new wire through the hollow stem of the lamp, and the symbolism of the remark was easily evident to me; because lamps symbolize artificial illumination.

My thoughts began to consume me, to dominate my rationality. I saw a terrifying conflict and competition at the lamp shop where none existed. It was a conflict of youth and age, of artifice and maturity, of society and individual, of truth and falsehood, of matter and spirit. Previously, as in *The Sorcerer's Apprentice,* I had seen such a conflict in abstraction. Here I saw it in the concrete, but as I thought longer about it, I realized that I saw it where it did not exist.

How can I say it did not exist? It did exist. I was there. It existed within me. Given all the extraneous factors, they triggered, they kindled what was in me. I was illuminated as a force to oppose artificial, mechanical illumination. My double did not know he was my double. I did a little manipulating, a little string-pulling on my own.

Why did I attribute my own angry feeling, my own competitive rancor, my own destructive spirit to another? Because I did not wish to acknowledge that such anti-social, disapproved qualities were part of me? But society approves competition and hostility more than it does cooperation, altruism, and friendship. Because I wanted to do a little manipulating in approved fashion, while at the same time, I disapproved manipulation? Was it a way to get around my own disapproval? No. I don't know why I created my own double.

This much I do know. My double was bent on robbery. He was not mocking me; he was not accusing me; he was not persecuting me. I was a minor factor in his intended actions. He was going to take actions directed towards others. He was perhaps accusing and judging others and was about to destroy others in the sense of robbing them of their false front, their mess of pottage.

I thought endlessly about that encounter with my double. I couldn't help thinking about it, reliving every minute, analyzing every detail. It possessed my rational spirit, depriving me of any rest, of any meaningless reverie.

Exhausted by the events of the day, that night I fell into a deep slumber. But, my double twisted his way into my subconscious being in a different form, a different manifestation. I dreamt that I entered a new, big house, which had just been built. The surrounding lot had not yet been leveled and seeded. After walking from front to back, I returned. There was a younger, better-looking version of the nincompoop I used to see in early days when I worked in the Treasury Department, the guy who had married a girl from Duluth. It seems that this guy and his wife had built the house, and now the wife didn't like it. The guy was acceding shamefully to the wishes of his wife. The salesman indicated they could sell the house to another but perhaps not without loss. The young man put his head down and ran his hands through his hair and mused "Will they have me committed?" The guy was good looking, not like the Treasury twerp in appearance.

The Treasury twerp thought he had a "political job," and he was forever sounding out people to see what they thought and thus what he should think. The picture of the handsome youth suggests that my brother Kenny was also in the dream. And, of course, I am. The twerp is my double and my brother. I created a double after the image of my brother. If he rated greater acceptance by reason of his compliance with mother's wishes, others' wishes, why shouldn't I follow his example? Kenny had this apparent advantage over me. He could conform with enthusiasm. The guy at the Treasury seemed to be but the shell of a man, incapable of enthusiasm, in need of constant indoctrination.

In the dream, my double is going to succumb to the pressure to sell. It is for me, the dominant me, to put a stop to that and to dictate to my double. When I, rather than the herd, dictate to my double, he ceases to be a double.

Now, here is a strange fact which occurred to me after I had awoken as my thoughts wandered frantically through this dream like ants scurrying from place to place after a well-placed footstep disturbs their hill. I was trying to extinguish, exterminate, cast off my double. Why must I have a double? Am I not all right just as I am? One who is so worthless that he needs a double surely is incapable of the creativity to produce a double of any value. I have despised my double, fought with him, labored to rid myself of him.

If my double is all people care about, I might as well commit suicide. My double is a rival. Yes, yes! I must cast off my double. My own creation became a Frankenstein. He dominated me and was, in turn, dominated by others because, of course, he had been created to please others. That was his sole excuse for being. I plan now to dominate my double and not to be dominated by others. "Somebody else has stolen my place. Somebody else now shares your embrace," Ah, but it is not I who has lost place. It is my accursed double. He promised me the world, this Mephisto, and he gave me but matter. Contentment, satisfaction, happiness were not at his disposal.

Indeed, had nature wished me to have a double, I would have had one. My creativity is not to be wasted in building and manipulating a double. But even as I objected, I built one and pulled the strings on him. The double and I were not one. I entered a double in the social, conventional rat race reluctantly. The more cleverly the double performed, the more I despised him and his admirers. And, at the same time, the more dependent I was on him.

My thinking had become fervent, burning my soul, depriving me of peaceful musing. I couldn't extinguish it. It took me back to reverse the old decree. Now I wish to scuttle the double and take my chances with society and the world. Instead of employing a double to go out and round up business, to court society and win its approval and good will, I stay soberly in my office and say "You court my good will. You follow me. You seek me out. You ask my aid and approval. I have fired my advertising man, my advance agent, my scout."

I have now to count on my own merit, talents, and superiority. I expect my brother lawyers, whether they read forums like *Morningstar*, slave for employers, or have simple practices to take notice of me, to seek me out. I will be available, like papa, to whosoever wishes my help, advice, advocacy.

Now you see, I've been thinking, thinking beyond the boundaries of rationality. Relentlessly, these thoughts whirl beyond control in my mind, like a wild Dervish, twisting, bobbing, leaping up and down and from side to side, confusing the rhythms of my brain, depriving me of solace, inducing me to near madness. All of this thinking must come to an end if I am ever to have peace.

Writing this narrative, sharing my turmoil with you, gentle reader, brought relief, but it was only temporary. The demons within my troubled mind were tamed but for a short time; I now feel them beginning to stir again. I have no recourse but to visit Dr. Walton at the next opportunity. As in the past, he will listen to me without rushing to judgment of my sanity. Surely someday he can help me reconcile these thoughts about a double. After all, that's what I pay him so handsomely for—peace of mind. That's all I want.

A Time for Greatness

Dear Charlie,

It's been a long time no-see, but I been awfully busy, and now I got a four day stretch of time off from the job—Saturday, Sunday, Monday, and Washington's Birthday—and I'll make up for lost time. Boy, I've got some great news for you. It's the lecture I went to hear, and I ain't going to tell you about anything else. What I mean, it was tremendous.

I could go on and carry on about the way my girl left me a week ago, but I'm not going to. Yeah, after I been buying her beer for eight years, Bunny just up and threw me over for another guy—a jerk of the first water, a truly colossal ass, a good-for-nothing Goddam pharmacist second-class, and I'll maul the living daylights out of him if he ever gets within range. But that's just my personal, private misfortune, and I'll keep it to myself. Besides, she'll soon learn that there isn't such a helluva difference in men, and she'll be back. I want to see to it that this letter is intellectutyule. (I know how to spell it, but it's my typewriter, and I ain't got no eraser handy.)

You know I've been telling you how things have been looking up in Denver since you pulled stakes for Florida? Denver won't play second fiddle to no place no time nohow. That's good enough to be Chamber of Commerce stuff, isn't it? Yes, you bet we've got a

Chamber on the job here. Don't think you Floridians got a corner on such things even if you did think up that one about where the sunshine spends the winter.

We got any number, I mean two or three, excellent management bureaus, and Cadwalader and Hayes is one of the best of them. They've got a wonderful lecture series, and I've got tickets to the whole string. The first two were good, but they couldn't hold a candle to Dr. Elmer Bickford, who was on last night. I mean they were about what's happening in India and laughter's the best medicine. Oh, the second guy got off a couple of pretty good ones. He said an apple a day is enough apples, but it takes more laughter than that. He didn't go for that guff that "it only hurts when I laugh." That's the second lecturer who said that, not Dr. Bickford.

No, Dr. Bickford really has a curve on the ball, Boy. The circular said he was equally at home on Wall Street, Madison Avenue, Hollywood Boulevard, or the Champs Ulysses, which is enough to show you what a well-traveled, rounded character he is. And speak—Man, that fellow knew every word in the dictionary. By the way, I forgot to tell you that Cadwalader and Hayes begins where Chautauqua left off. They got a little square space in the Yellow Pages that says that, under Management Bureaus. And they're the people that brought him to Denver, I mean.

And you should have heard what Dr. Bickford had to say about your old home town before he lit into the subject of the lecture. He said "Everything's up to date in Kansas City in song and story, but everything's strictly up to date in Denver in reality." Isn't that pretty good? Made me swell up like a balloon, and I don't mind admitting it.

Dr. Bickford said a lot of things that made me perk up. I was feeling kind of blue, you know, about Bunny leaving me and all that—but I swore I wasn't going to bore you with the lurid details this time, didn't I? Maybe some other time. Anyway, I was barely scraping along, low as a snake's track, and it did a world of good to hear a genuine optimist. Believe me, they're an extinct species, like the dodo, and it sure does sound sweet to hear one for a change, especially when he has the facts and figures to prove it.

And Dr. Bickford had them, and I don't mean maybe. Best of all was his delivery. He says, "I don't hold with those who say this is a time for greatness." He says: "That sounds like we gotta stretch up and stand tall; and I insist that we already possess greatness, see it everywhere around us, here and now." That's the way he began; only it sounds better spoken out loud and spoken as only he can do it. That was just the beginning, and, of course, I can't give you his whole oration. All I can do is hit the high spots. Be sure and hear him if Dr. Bickford chances to get in the South. He has message, Man. What I mean: straight from the heart to the head, as he himself says. If you like educational TV, as you say, you'll like him.

He said there are no ordinary times. I said to myself, "Brother, you can say that again," but I had no idea what was coming next. I've told you, I think, what the title of the lecture was. It was "A Time for Greatness." Well, he said, "You'll remember the Lincoln-Douglas debates. I don't mean personally but from history. Lincoln won the debates and lost the election. We did it differently in 1960, and that wasn't so long ago was it? The winner of the debates also squeaked out a victory at the polls, which is the way it should be.

"But notice this. Those weren't just Kennedy-Nixon or Nixon-Kennedy debates. By the consensus of journalists, newscasters, and thoughtful people generally, they were great debates, about Cuba, Laos, and all that. And great debates are almost always the very hallmark of the age we live in. Remember, and I can see you're old enough to remember, those stirring days in the late thirties and in 1940 and 1941 when the bark of a mad dog was disturbing the sleep of Europe? We had a great debate on how and when we should leap into the fray and put an end to the war Hitler started."

Dr. Bickford went on and pointed out that even if the issue of war and peace wasn't decided for us by the great debate, but by a wholly unexpected, sneaky surprise attack at Pearl Harbor, still we did have a debate in keeping with the greatness of the times. We covered ourselves with glory by heaping high the wisdom of eternity, and of our revolutionary forefathers, on both sides of the question. He said the word revolutionary itself, or I wouldn't think of whispering it. The evidence is mountain high, the doctor said, that we are heirs to greatness: not just we Americans, but all peoples the world over. That's our destiny, he said, the wave of the future. Forget the wave of the present, and the destiny is greatness, whether we will it or not.

I recall him saying, as clearly as if he were repeating it right now, "Some people are born great; others achieve greatness; and still others have greatness thrust upon them. The last is the case with us: every man, woman, and child alive today, regardless of nationality, color, creed, of previous condition of servitude. Let us carry the burden nobly and keep our chins held high..." Maybe I'm getting ahead of myself, ahead of Dr. Bickford.

Maybe that was toward the end that he said that. But say it he did, and it was thrilling to hear.

Somewhere in there he said: "Historians like to distinguish between big wars and little wars, and they have every right to do so. All the important distinctions civilization knows are but differences of degree. This is the verdict of the sages and of the wise men who most surely deserve our praise. But note this: in our particular division of time, the twentieth century of the Christian era, we have had two great wars. We have had two world wars, and can anyone seriously claim that world wars aren't great wars? No, we didn't piddle with the picayune. It's beneath us.

"The great transformation has taken place before our eyes—perhaps so gradually that some of us haven't noticed it, but if so, it only remains for the fact to be documented, and that's what I'm here for. A few rustics, a handful of men at the most, may cling to the simple, backward credo of plain living, but they are just the exceptions that prove the rule. The rule is greatness, because nine out of ten people living today—at least nine out of ten—are adherents of one or the other of the world's great religions. And so be it from here to hereafter."

Dr. Bickford is no preacher, I guess, just a professional optimist, but so help me he has the power to move men. It wasn't a sermon he gave, not at all. He called it a "testament of faith."

He said: "There isn't enough littleness left on Earth now for what the military men call a 'mopping-up operation.' That's why the Great Powers are so busily engaged in space exploration. It is too early yet to say which nation will be the first to put a man on the moon successfully, but before long every nation, if there are nations left, will have representatives in the heavens spreading the gospel of greatness. Don't think this nothing but an old man's fantasy of the millennium. Nay, not so. Again and again and again, as often as several times a month, the newspapers herald great new breakthroughs in science, and do you suppose all of them get into the newspapers?

"Rejoice. Suffer no craven fear of greatness to hold you down. Shoulder your cross of greatness and walk confidently and bravely into the sunset with your little woman at your side..."

Charlie, I don't mind telling you that the last part about your little woman at your side got me as much as anything. It sent me, Man. But I hope to have more news about that and about Bunny the next time I write.

Your old pal,
Ell

A Visit to the Governor

I remember when Mrs. Roosevelt used to say she'd never been to South Dakota. Even then she'd been everywhere else, and I knew perfectly well she ought to go to South Dakota. I hadn't been there, either, in those days, but it never occurred to me to mention the fact. If there were any guilt involved in the omission, let her who had confessed the sin carry the burden. That's what I would have said if I'd felt any pricking of conscience whatsoever, which I didn't.

I might explain, though, this had nothing at all to do with my decision to go from Sonora Springs through the Black Hills on my vacation trip to Minnesota or that I am the youngest of three children. When I say I am, I mean I was, because, alas, my childhood is definitely a thing of the past. My older brother and sister were born in the Coyote State, and, yes, Father and Mother were married there. I came long later, after they'd all moved to Minnesota, which, I guess, makes me a genuine gopher.

Well, the easiest way to go to Minneapolis from here is to head out over the plains, the Eastern Plains, as we call them, for Nebraska. To tell the truth, there's good train service that way and no need to drive at all. However, my war-time comrade-at-arms, Timothy Maloney, had become Governor of South Dakota, so I'd heard, and being as I'd never seen him since the good old days—I mean since those rugged, muddy-soup and snow-cold months in France, Luxembourg, and Germany—I thought it would be fun to go a bit out of my way and look in on Tim at the state capital. As every schoolboy knows, that's Pierre. Incidentally, the local inhabitants don't pronounce it like they're talking about a dehydrated Frenchman.

Unless you got enough dough to go by plane, there's only one way to go to Pierre from here. That's to drive. The Black Hills weren't so terribly far off a bee line for Minnesota. Pierre, now that's another thing. Big Stone and Milbank, they're quite a way off the direct route, too. That's where the Governor lived, Big Stone City, when my brother and sister were born. I mean my father, not Tim Maloney. I don't know where Tim lived then, if at all.

I swear that Tim was the funniest guy I ever knew overseas, a real character. He wasn't funny ha-ha, but he brought quite a smile to one's mind (if not the lips) as if you were seeing yourself as a little boy in rolled-up blue jeans and in some slightly ridiculous position, say standing on your head. He was short, and instead of tucking his pants into those dirty, rough-finished combat boots like the rest of us, he wore shiny parachute boots. His hair was about the color of his footgear, reddish brown. He was a young lieutenant with a full face, a broad, though not a fat, belly and a pair of blue eyes that had trouble coming to focus on us guys, us soldiers and sergeants, or anything near. At times, he seemed to be seeing things in the air or to be looking around corners. That occasional far-off manner made a guy think of Napoleon.

I didn't know Tim had been elected governor till I saw his picture in the paper that time he and a bunch of other governors toured Japan—or maybe it was South America. Anyway, I saw his name and picture in the *Post*. But how a guy named Tim Maloney ever won a victory at the polls in South Dakota beats me. Sigstad Olson, Anders Nelson, Trygve Anderson, yes. But how Tim ever wowed those voters to put him in high office, I can't even guess. I'll say this: I lived in Minnesota till I was twenty-five years old and moved west, and it couldn't happen there. Not in Minnesota; at least, not in Minneapolis.

It was knee-deep in July when I hit the highway northward-bound. The winter wheat had already been harvested, but I could smell it. The odor of it still lingered. It permeated the air. When I got further north, where they grow spring wheat, No.1 Dark Northern, there might be some of those immense fields of standing grain I knew as a boy. Good heavens, what would I do then? The dusty, nose-filling aroma of ripe and ripening wheat might be overwhelming, overpowering, all pervasive. I worried. I was afraid of that scent; well, if not afraid exactly, leery.

The odor grew stronger as I went along. The Black Hills were behind me. It wasn't an unpleasant sensation. I liked the smell, the invisible pungency, except that it was unsettling, exciting, intoxicating, on the order of a stimulating drug or that unearthly poppy-weed. I don't know why. I was born in July, in the middle of the harvest-season. My father, who died when I was ten years old, was a farmer. My fondest recollections of him were those harvest-scenes when he held an old-fashioned three-tined pitchfork in his hands. He was short and solid and blue-eyed, much as I am now. When he came into the house from the fields, he was as aromatic as a straw stack or a granary, redolent of the creased, nutty kernels he'd let run through his hard, sun-browned, sweaty hands.

I decided to skip Pierre and Tom Baloney, the friend of my bitter days. I roared onward to Milbank and Big Stone, but, once there, I was too impatient to make inquiries and locate the farm my father used to call the Home Place. Some other day, I would go back and inspect the ground-in path made by the sharp, hard, cloven hooves of that blind ox he used to drive to the water's edge to drink. That was Big Stone Lake.

Delirious with the sight and smell of the rich, dark, ruddy-red grain, I set my course eastward across the Grain Belt to the city of lakes and Swedes and shopkeepers. I didn't even stop to fix myself and my gaze momentarily upon father's monument or, farther on, my own birthplace. All, all this land, his land, was my land. Not just two specks of it. All was mine to swim in. He, my father, was in this very air which tickled my nose, filled my lungs, and unaccountably brought tears to my eyes.

As I approached the flour-milling metropolis which had been Mother's home almost from that cold day of Father's demise long ago, my fever subsided. It is a good thing, too, for there's no place for wildness in the traffic of a big city. That is a crime the time-set, red, green, amber, signal-control lights could never understand, much less forgive. Something there is, too, in a metropolis that doesn't like the serene sweetness of alfalfa or the heady fragrance of grain. Funny thing, I didn't know so much about that thought-saturating smell of grain, myself, till I began that trip to visit the Governor and Mrs. Roosevelt. I mean—oh, you know what I mean—who I mean!

A Visiting Celebrity

Times change. Or maybe it's just me. What I mean is that in the old days my imagination and that of my playmates was fired by the annual appearance of the circus as by nothing else. Now what is there to excite a guy's curiosity? Nothing at all in my home town of Sonora Springs except the visit once in a while of a bigwig from the East.

Maybe the difference is in me, but Brother, the change is tremendous. Things aren't the same at all. Of course, no one expects a celebrity, even one from the East, to be as big as a circus elephant, but—well, I'll give you an example.

Not long ago, a VIP breezed into town to give a talk. His picture was on page one of the papers, and there was a story all about it. The guy was a commissioner of something or another in Washington, something pretty special, and he would have a lot to say for people smart enough to listen. That smart enough stuff made me kinda leery, but I had nothing to lose by trying, only some time. So I went.

According to the papers, the Commissioner once had been a partner in a couple of plushy New York law firms. Of course, I've heard a lot about New York and its cold cash canyons and its Great White Way and the rest of it, but that didn't send me much. It was the names of the firms that sent me wondering: acted on me a little like bait to a fish; gave me the old come-on. Even in a town the size of Sonora Springs the lawyers always play around behind a lot of panky names like Gorgeous, Gauleiter, Hokum, Huffsmith, and Anonymous or Schweinhaupt, Obolosky, Olson, Gaumnitz, and We the People. So help me, this guy—pardon me, the Commissioner—had been with Smith and Jones and before that with Johnson and Brown. Mind you, I wasn't suspicious, just wondering a bit the way a fellow will.

Lord knows what super-duper plans there were for welcoming the Commissioner to town. As it turned out, he came on the day of the Big Snow, and everything got so fouled up in the storm that Mr. Commissioner wasn't welcomed by much except the swirling white flakes. Hardly anybody showed up at the auditorium to hear the talk, and so yours truly ended up with a first-rate seat for the ceremonies.

The chairman of the meeting said the affair was under the auspices of the Citizens Committee for Adult Education. That wasn't enough to drive me out, though. I hadn't come through all that wind, snow, and cold for nothing. Of course, improving the mind wasn't on my agenda. What good would it do to learn a book full about banking and finance and such stuff and me with only so much dough as goes into the hole of a doughnut? You might say I came to learn about people, but I reckon the high-brows on the Committee wouldn't count the blinkety human race as a fit subject of interest. High finance, the overpopulation of India, and more of the same are their meat. Just the same, I stayed for the proceedings. Like I said, I was set on getting good and warm before I started to go home again; that much at least.

The Commissioner opened up with a couple of jokes. They were funny, all right, and I'd sure like to pass them on, but this isn't the place for that. Anyway, they've plumb slipped my mind. Oh, I do remember this much. Instead of building his audience up by his lead-off story as I've notice most celebrities do, the Commissioner wrote everybody down. With the second joke, he wrote himself down. The speaker wanted a real low starting point, I guess.

Mr. Helmuth Singer, or should one say Mr. Commissioner, was wearing a dark suit, worsted maybe or flannel, with light stripes up and down. He wasn't a tall man, and he had put on as much weight as a "feeder" from the Texas Panhandle since he got the suit. You might say he filled it to the brim and ran over a bit. The effect was that of a fellow pretty pudgy and rumpled. Then he had on a vest, which left an extra button at the bottom and made the singer, I mean the Commissioner, look awfully squeegee from the waist clear up to the shirt collar.

His talk was more interesting than I had expected, but nobody could say it was exciting. There was a little bit of the circus about it, and that helped some. The Commissioner wanted to seem as casual as he could about it all (the way the rubes are in the "provinces"), and he kinda went back and forth and sideways on the stage like a juggler. So far as I could tell, he wasn't juggling nothing but words: the Dow Jones average, gilt-edge securities, convertible debentures, fifteen billion dollars, forty billion dollars, fifty billion, the option of the holder, first mortgage trust indenture. If phrases were balls, he kept plenty of them in the air; and gestured faintly with fingers and hands to boot; and wrinkled his forehead on top of all that. The show was better than I had expected, but it wasn't like the old days, not by a long shot.

For one thing, the juggling wasn't the whole picture, just the best part. He was only putting himself into the performance halfway, wasn't pretending to deserve top billing. It seemed like he didn't believe much in the goings on. His low voice went through the nose and came out flat. He was short of breath. His upper lip was motionless, as though unwilling to take part in a two-bit farce. The lower one moved up and down with the jaw, but that was all. During all the speechifying, it didn't do anything on its own. You've heard the expression "clickin' the teeth." Well, it was like that. Yakity yak. For my money, there wasn't enough of the guy, the Commissioner, in the act.

One of the words Singer favored was new to me. He kept saying how he had to take a "hard-nose" position on this or that. Come to find out, "hard-nose" doesn't mean a thing. Now and then the guy has to take a plain old position on something, and he doesn't like to do that, the way some fellows around here draw back at making decisions. You know.

It could be that Singer's brain cells were operating on all six or eight cylinders. I wouldn't know. But anyway, it takes more than that to suit me. I like genuine red-blooded action, and who'd call the invisible motion of the gray matter action? Give me activity I can see. According to my old-fashioned notions, a great brain is only part of a person.

Of course, I wanta give the devil his due. The visitor sure made me feel more contented with Sonora Springs and my lot and this wobbly old whirligig of ours. And as I was saying at the beginning, maybe as a fella gets older he has to trade excitement for contentment. That's okay, but Brother, I sure wouldn't trade places with a celebrity, not even to be called a Royal High Commissioner and travel on an expense account.

What a Salesman

When I was a young man about town, I always wanted to do something pretty special and be famous overnight. Trouble was I never could make up my mind exactly what I wanted to do. Every kind of talent was mine, I guess, except making decisions. I sure was short-suited there.

The advertisements in the magazines all agreed that being a postal inspector, or anything at all, would be duck soup for a guy as gifted as me. Just the same, all those things sounded so good that I was stymied on dead center. That's gone on for a long while, and chances are you've never heard of me till now. But, Brother, this instant I'm right behind the eight-ball if I don't "click" real quick.

You see it's this way. I just saw a salesman who made everything absolutely clear. He said "Just leave the decisions to me." Well, that took a load off my chest, and everything seemed better right away. This fellow has known me for years; name's Dave Hart. Neighborly is not the word for it; Dave is a prince if there ever was one. "At your age," says Dave, "it's too late to set the world on fire by doing anything. That's old-fashioned anyway."

Come to find out, that is kid stuff. Dave was selling something as new as tomorrow. It beats all what people won't think of and sell to the lucky ones. Dave has been around a lot, and he knows. He's pretty lucky, too. It's only because he's tried out about every kind of trade and job that he's fit to be a career counselor. Otherwise, he wouldn't know the ropes in every specialty the way he does. And if Dave wasn't a career counselor, the company wouldn't have hired him to sell the sure-fire course and equipment he does.

I signed on the dotted line without losing any time. The course will make a new man of me in no time, Dave says, and if I'm ever going to make a mark for myself by what I do, I'd better do it before I start with the "conditioning." Just what the "conditioning" is, Dave didn't say. It will make the old-style personality training, like Dale Carnegie gives, look sick and tired, Dave says. And that new sleep conditioning of the subconscious is no match for it at all. I'm getting a bargain price because the results in my case are bound to be such wonderful advertising for the course. I'll be living proof of what science can do.

Yes, sir. Already I can see the difference in myself, just as Dave said. Just to show you: remember way back when you could get a lot of dough for just telling your most embarrassing moment? Well, I had so many embarrassments, it was impossible to count 'em, and every one was equal to the other. I simply didn't know where to begin. Then I always wanted to write a story in the newspaper contest for most interesting experiences. You'd think that would be easy for a man that ain't done too much that is out of the ordinary. But you have no idea how many exciting accidents happened to me. To put one before another was harder'n choosing between good potatoes and bad ones. Again, I never was able to get going on the most unforgettable character I've ever met because Sonora Springs is my home town, and it is brimming with that kind of people. That's the way it would go.

Dave says now I'm bound to have a powerful personality and to be a big shot without turning a finger. I guess I'll have to turn a switch on whatever machine is that goes with the course, but that'll be about all. He says I can be a big name in business, movies, government, or whatever I want, and that's all there'll be to it. Hey…I knew there was a catch somewhere. How'm I going to decide what I want to be a big name in?

I knew there was a catch somewhere. What a salesman that guy Dave Hart is. If he wasn't one of my best friends, I'd be mad at him for pulling a trick like that on me.

www.ingramcontent.com/pod-product-compliance
Lightning Source LLC
Chambersburg PA
CBHW031619100726
47898CB00006B/1868
9781736453421